"Daddy, give me a kiss goodbye."

Jake's smile was genuine and breathtaking. "Julia, you're only going into the living room."

"I need a kiss."

Julia clearly wasn't going to change her mind. So Jake leaned forward, and Julia reached up on tiptoe to plant a noisy kiss on his cheek. Before she moved away, Jake cradled her head in his big work-roughened hand and touched his lips to her forehead.

"You're scratchy, Daddy. You need to shave." Julia laughed in delight as she left the kitchen.

Allison could only marvel at the change in the little girl who not so long ago had been sulky and intractable. "She's like a different child."

"Julia's three. She's as changeable as the weather. But she has been getting a little out of hand."

"Maybe she needs to be around children her own age more often."

Allison knew by Jake's frown that she'd overstepped the boundaries of their relationship.

"That may be. But keeping Julia here with me is my way of keeping Beth's dreams alive." His voice was rough with anger and grief. "Sending Julia to day care would be one more piece of Beth that I'd have to lose. And I'm not going to do it. I'm damn well going to hold on to this one as long as I can."

ABOUT THE AUTHOR

Carol Wagner and Marian Scharf—the award-winning writing team of Marisa Carroll—are sisters living in a small Ohio town, where they are surrounded by lifelong friends and five generations of family. *Before Thanksgiving Comes*, a story of friends and family in a town not so different from the one they live in, is the duo's twenty-eighth book.

Books by Marisa Carroll

Don't miss any of our special offers. Write to us at the following address for information on our newest releases.

Harlequin Reader Service
U.S.: 3010 Walden Ave., P.O. Box 1325, Buffalo, NY 14269
Canadian: P.O. Box 609, Fort Erie, Ont. L2A 5X3

BEFORE THANKSGIVING COMES
Marisa Carroll

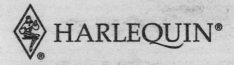

TORONTO • NEW YORK • LONDON
AMSTERDAM • PARIS • SYDNEY • HAMBURG
STOCKHOLM • ATHENS • TOKYO • MILAN • MADRID
PRAGUE • WARSAW • BUDAPEST • AUCKLAND

ISBN 0-373-70811-4

BEFORE THANKSGIVING COMES

Copyright © 1998 by Carol I. Wagner and Marian F. Scharf.

For the little ones:
Erika, Jennifer, Sarah, Allicyn and Matthew

CHAPTER ONE

IT WAS A PERFECT NIGHT for trick or treat, Allison Martin thought as she looked out the kitchen window of her grandmother's small white frame farmhouse. The sun was down, the late October twilight fading away into the long purple shadows of evening, although it wasn't yet six o'clock. Later the moon would be high and bright and there would be frost on the grass. She had come to love the view of the fields and woodlands that stretched to the horizon beyond her windows. She would miss the spectacular sunsets and the simple, uncomplicated life she'd been living when she returned to Chicago.

By the time Thanksgiving arrived, her leave of absence would be over and she would be back to her twelve-hours-a-day, six-days-a-week career as an assistant trust fund manager for Tanner, Marsh and Fairchild. There would be no more watching sunsets as she washed supper dishes, no more lazy summer evenings on the porch swing, no more dressing up to pass out Halloween treats. She looked down at the costume she'd sewn on her grandmother's temperamental old Singer and smiled. "You make a great witch," she said aloud, and felt her smile turn into a frown. Spending the past few months in this house near the small Ohio farming community of Riley Creek had changed her outlook on a lot of things, but talking to herself wasn't one of them. It smacked of eccentricity and loneliness and was a behavior she couldn't indulge.

Allison reached for the crockery bowl full of popcorn balls she'd made from a recipe she'd found in an old cookbook of her grandmother's. She'd been very domestic ever since coming to live here. She'd made new curtains for the kitchen and bathroom, worked to reclaim the garden and flower beds and learned to cook more than just the basics of salads and pasta and chicken that had been all she'd had the time or energy to prepare in her other life. She'd kept herself busy from morning until night with all those things because she knew what would happen if she stopped for just a moment. She'd want a drink.

It was a longing that was always with her. And one she fought hard to ignore.

Bowl in hand, she headed for the front porch. The old-fashioned screen door slammed shut behind her with the satisfying slap of wood against wood. The sound always triggered long-ago memories of the summer vacations she'd spent with her grandmother before her warring parents had left Ohio and taken her off to California, in what proved to be their last attempt at saving their foundering marriage.

She hadn't seen much of her grandmother in the years after that, even though she and her mother had moved from California to Chicago after the divorce.

Her mother and grandmother had both been strong-willed, independent women who seldom saw eye to eye on any subject. A long-distance relationship seemed the only way they could get along, although it deprived Allison of the special closeness of grandmother and granddaughter. Still, when Allison had married Brandon Martin, an ambitious and fast-rising account executive at Tanner, Marsh and Fairchild, she'd hoped her grandmother would attend her wedding, but the old lady had died just weeks before the ceremony, her mother two years later. Her marriage hadn't survived many months beyond that.

The sound of running footsteps and childish laughter drew Allison's attention to the trio of costumed trick-or-treaters coming her way. Michael, 10, Libby, 8, and Julia, 3½, were the children of Jake Walthers, her widowed neighbor from across the blacktopped county highway. They were accompanied by their young aunt, Jake's sister, Jenny. Allison watched them with a wistful hunger. She'd always planned to have children of her own. Until her marriage had failed and her drinking had taken control of her life. Now she wasn't certain she could ever trust herself to be a mother. Especially since she couldn't trust herself not to take another drink.

Once more her thoughts had taken an unacceptable turn. She lifted her hand to straighten her pointy black witch's hat and found her smile again. She was determined not to let her longing for a drink gather enough strength to pull her back into the nightmare of alcoholism. She had resisted every hour for the past seven months. God willing, she would keep on resisting. Tonight the only ghosts and goblins inhabiting her world would be the children coming to her door to beg for treats.

"What have we here?" she asked the children in her best imitation of the Wicked Witch of the West. "Three plump little pretties to invite into my castle?"

"Hey, I'm not a little pretty," Michael said with a ferocious scowl. "I'm Hammerhead. Can't you tell?" Hammerhead was a monstrous comic book villain with bulging eyes and a thirst for human blood, who lived in the sewer system of a mythical American city. Or so Michael had told her. He'd even brought her one or two precious copies of the comic to read. Hammerhead had a cadre of giant rats who followed him on his nefarious travels through the city's bowels, and Michael had affixed a number of realistic plastic rodents to his shoulders and the front of his grotesquely bloodstained shirt to mimic the gruesome character.

"All children are pretties to me," she informed him, and cackled loudly, rubbing her hands together as if in anticipation.

"You look really great, Allison," Libby said with a timid smile. "Just like the witch in the *Wizard of Oz.*"

"Thank you." Allison gave another evil laugh, pleased the children had noticed the costume it had taken her three days to sew. "You had no idea of *my* secret identity, did you, my pretty?"

Libby giggled and shook her head.

Allison had watched the comings and goings of the Walther children all summer. They had been shy at first, but by the end of July they were regular visitors to her front porch, more often than not bringing gifts of the fresh fruits and berries Walnut Hill Farm was noted for. And Allison would reciprocate with the cookies and brownies she'd gotten into the habit of baking almost every day. Libby would sit beside her on the porch swing, decorously drinking lemonade and nibbling cookies like a great lady at high tea, while Michael lounged in the grass beside his bicycle and Julia danced up and down the wooden porch steps like a pigtailed perpetual-motion machine. They talked about their new beagle puppy and the kittens in the barn, about swimming in the pond at the bottom of the gentle rise on which their huge farmhouse sat, and later of going back to school. But their visits had dwindled as the summer waned and Allison had missed their chatter and squabbling more than she cared to admit.

"Aren't my rats cool? Dad got them for me."

"They are handsome beasts," Allison agreed, still using her witch's voice. "I would like to have some of them for my own." She cackled again, then came down the steps to stroke the rodent perched on Michael's shoulder. It reared up as though it had suddenly come to life. Allison jerked her hand back with a startled squeak and Michael burst out laughing.

"Gotcha! Got you good! It looks real, doesn't it?" His brown eyes were shining inside their ghoulish rings of black and red.

"Yes." Allison clapped her hand over her racing heart. "It certainly does. How did you manage that little trick?" She knew that was the question Michael wanted her to ask. Michael was an inventor. It's what he wanted to be when he grew up. You could be an inventor and a farmer at the same time, he'd told her earnestly one hot August afternoon. Farmers invented things all the time to keep their machinery working.

"It's easy, really." He turned his palm upward to reveal a small rubber bulb attached to plastic tubing that disappeared under the cuff of his shirt. "You just pump air into it like this." He squeezed the apparatus, and the rat jumped. "I found this old frog toy of Julia's that hopped and took it apart and cut a hole in my rat's belly—"

"My Froggy!" Julia shrieked, clearly making the connection between her brother's moving rat and a missing toy. Julia threw herself into her young aunt's arms. The little girl was small and sturdy with a gossamer-fine mop of straight, sun-streaked blond hair, although tonight her hair was concealed by the hood of her costume. Julia was dressed as a cow, complete with a pink plastic udder and a tail with a tuft of black yarn on the end that hung down and threatened to trip her with each step she took. "Make him give it back!"

"Be quiet, brat," Michael snarled with typical big-brother heartlessness. "Dad will be here in a minute to take us into town and if he hears you crying like that he'll make you go back home and go to bed. I told you to take a nap when I got home from school."

"Libby!" Julia turned a snub-nosed, tear-streaked face in her older sister's direction. "Look what he did to Froggy."

"I'll tell Dad on him for you," Libby said magnanimously. She was dressed like a fairy princess in pink ruffles and lace, complete with jeweled golden crown and a magic wand. She was tall for her age, all arms and legs, with sparkling blue eyes the same shade as Julia's and Jenny's, and a gap in her smile from a missing front tooth. Her hair was paler than her sister's, the same color as the day-old chicks she'd brought for Allison to see on the trio's very first visit.

"I want my frog fixed." Julia stuck out her lower lip and glared at Michael.

Allison suspected the toy was beyond help. "Have a popcorn ball instead," she coaxed. "I made them myself." An experiment she wouldn't repeat. She still had a pan lacquered with hardened sugar syrup soaking in the sink.

"A popcorn ball?" Julia, Allison had learned over the summer, could be instantly diverted from tears by the offer of food. "What's a popcorn ball?"

"It's popcorn all stuck together with candy," Libby informed her sister in a world-weary voice. "Mama used to make them when I was little. Before she died."

"My momma's dead," Julia said. "She went to heaven when I was born."

"I know, honey." Julia had spoken of her mother's death once or twice before to Allison, reciting the words the way three-year-olds repeated things they didn't understand but accepted as the truth.

Jenny was frowning now, like a mother hen whose chicks were getting out of hand. The teenager never talked about her late sister-in-law. The older children seldom talked of her, either. It was as though the loss was still too raw to be mentioned in front of strangers. And for all their little visits over the summer months, Allison was a stranger. What she knew about Beth Walthers's unexpected and tragic death from complications of childbirth she'd learned from Stella LaRue, the manager of the Walnut Hill Farm Market, which Jake Walthers owned and operated in the century-old barn directly across the road from Allison's house.

"Come on, kids," Jenny appealed, her patience wearing thin. "Trick-or-treat time only lasts until seven. We have to get going if we're going to stop at the Reimunds' and the Christmans' before we head into town." The two families Jenny had named were "next-door" neighbors on either side of the Walthers farm, although their houses were over half a mile away in each direction.

Allison took that as her cue to drop a popcorn ball into each of their jack-o'-lantern containers, and as she did so, Allison remembered a compliment she wanted to pay Jenny. "I've been meaning to tell you, you've got some great jack-o'-lanterns at your place," she said. "Did you carve them?" The scenes and faces were varied and detailed, ranging from a cemetery with ghosts and headstones to a teddy bear with a honey pot.

"Nah. I can't draw a straight line. We used patterns that come in a book. They really help sell pumpkins, though. Which is great because Jake had a bumper crop."

"I wish I'd known," Allison said, giving her own very traditional, gap-toothed jack-o'-lantern a little nudge with the toe of her shoe as it sat grinning feebly on the top step. "I just assumed you were extremely talented and there was no use trying to compete."

"I'm not very talented at anything."

"Let's go. I'm outta here." Before Allison could respond to Jenny's disparaging remark about herself, Michael spun around, dislodging one of his rats. The toy dropped to the grass. Michael made a lunge for it just as a dark, silent shape pounced from the trees. Libby screamed. So did Michael. Julia burst into frightened tears as Jenny pulled her into her arms.

"What is it?" Jenny's eyes were as wide and frightened as Julia's.

Allison wasn't certain what had happened. "I don't know."

Michael dropped into a crouch, hands over his head. "Is it a bat? I hate bats."

"A bat!" Libby screamed again and pulled the cape of her princess costume over her head. "It'll get in my hair."

Whatever had swooped down at the rat lay on the grass, unmoving. "Michael, come here. Get away from that thing," Jenny ordered.

Michael had already gotten over his initial fright and was examining the form on the ground. "It's not a bat,'' he said, excitement rising in his voice. ''It's an owl.''

''An owl?'' Allison set the bowl of popcorn balls on the railing and joined Michael. She had never seen an owl, although she'd heard them calling occasionally in the trees outside her bedroom window.

''I think it's hurt.'' He was whispering now. ''It's not moving.''

''Don't pick it up,'' Jenny commanded. ''It might have rabies or something.''

''I don't think owls get rabies. Do they, Allison?''

''I haven't the slightest idea,'' Allison said truthfully. ''But if it's hurt, Jenny's right. You shouldn't touch it.''

Michael ignored her. He squatted down and picked up the small bird. ''It's not dead. It's just a baby.''

''A baby? Isn't it awfully late in the year?'' Allison was a city girl. She had no knowledge whatsoever of the breeding habits of owls.

''Maybe it's a tagalong,'' Jenny said with a wry smile, her face just visible in the glow of the porch light. ''Like me. I was a huge surprise to the rest of the family.''

''I want to see,'' Julia said from the safety of Jenny's arms. ''I want to see the baby owl.''

Michael turned toward her, cupping the bird in his hands. ''It hardly weighs anything. That's because its bones are hollow.''

''Let me see.'' Libby was whispering now. ''I've never seen an owl up close.''

''Put that dirty thing down,'' Jenny demanded, apparently deciding to assert her authority. "If it's not hurt, it'll fly back up in the tree on its own."

"We don't know it's not hurt." Michael tipped the little owl this way and that, assessing its condition. The small bird, feathers puffed out, followed his every movement with eyes that were as round and bright and shining as the little boy's. "I don't know if it can fly."

"Then leave it on the ground."

"No!" Michael and Libby chorused. "One of the cats will get it."

"Okay," Jenny said impatiently. "Put it back up in a tree."

"The branches are all too high." Michael swiveled his head from side to side, much the way the little owl in his hands had.

It was true. All the trees in Allison's yard were very old and very large.

"We need a ladder," Libby said.

Allison thought a moment. Where had she seen a ladder? The memory clicked into place. There was an old painter's ladder, at least ten feet long, lying against the side of the house, behind the daisies that had bloomed in profusion all summer long. She hadn't even noticed it until the first hard frost had bowed the last of the flower heads. "Wait a moment. I just remembered something." She hurried around the side of the house. "Jenny, please come help me carry this thing."

Jenny glanced over her shoulder. "Okay, but hurry. I'm meeting a friend...friends."

The ladder was heavy, still wet from the autumn thunderstorm that had overflowed the gutters two days before. They set it against the trunk of the big maple beside the porch. "This should do." Allison was panting by the time they'd wrestled the heavy ladder into place. "I've heard owls calling off and on all summer, but I've never been able to tell where they were."

"Sounds echo good around here," Michael said. "And owls are real quiet and they mostly come out at night. That's why you hardly ever see them. I'll put him up."

"No." Allison spoke more harshly than she'd intended. But she wasn't going to let a child put himself at risk while he was even nominally in her care. *Never again.* "I'll do it. The ladder's old and rickety."

Michael looked mutinous. "I can—"

"I'm the adult." She smiled, taking the sting from her words. "And I'm taller. Let's do this my way, okay?"

JAKE WALTHERS WONDERED what was keeping his children. They'd been at the Martin woman's house for over ten minutes. Even if they did like visiting their reclusive neighbor, they would never spend ten precious minutes of trick-or-treat time making chit-chat when they could cross the road to her house whenever they wanted. He backed the van out of the garage and headed down the driveway, catching sight of his children and sister and a witch—complete with pointy hat and flowing black robes—grouped around a ladder propped against a big maple tree. "What the devil's going on over there?" he muttered aloud.

Jake clamped his mouth shut. He'd caught himself talking to himself more often than he liked lately. He was only thirty-four, way too young to be getting senile. Maybe it was because most days, outside of Stella LaRue, he didn't get much chance to speak to another adult. Hadn't really wanted to since Beth had died. The reason didn't matter; it was a habit he intended to break. Just like he'd quit smoking cold turkey when he realized his kids only had one parent and he owed it to them to take care of himself.

Maybe when his parents got back from Florida where his dad was recuperating from heart surgery, he'd start going for coffee with the old geezers and the few other full-time farmers who gathered at the Country Kitchen restaurant every day. That would give him something to do, someone to talk to.

He pulled into the driveway of the Bremer place and punched the button that lowered the driver's-side window of the minivan. "Hey, kids," he called, his voice a little gruff with a residue of anger and loss that almost four years' passing hadn't eased. "Time to be heading into town or you'll miss trick or treat."

"Dad! Come here," Michael hollered back excitedly. "An owl tried to get one of my rats. It was awesome. I told you they looked real."

"It's hurt, Daddy." Jake turned off the ignition and stepped out of the van as his youngest child waddled toward him, her costume hood askew so that one pink-lined cow ear flopped over her eye. He gathered her up, holding her tight for a moment as he always did, a silent plea for forgiveness and understanding for the long, terrible days after her birth when he couldn't hold her, or touch her, or look at her because he'd been so angry after Beth had died.

Thank God that darkest of times hadn't lasted past the sight of his twelve-year-old sister struggling to change the tiny infant's diaper. Stiff-legged and raw with pain, he'd made himself go to Jenny's aid the morning after Beth's funeral. And then Julia, red-faced and wailing with an infant's single-minded intensity, had stopped crying as soon as she'd felt his reluctant touch. She'd opened her blue, blue eyes— Beth's eyes—and smiled at him. Never mind that everyone said a four-day-old couldn't smile. She had. And his broken heart had been lost to her, as it had been lost to each of his other children, and Jenny, too, after his mother had let him hold his baby sister for the first time.

"What's up, kitten?" he asked, tipping Julia back in his arms to see her face.

"An owl! A baby owl. It hurt itself. Allison's going to put it back." She pushed her little round face closer to his. "That's not a real witch," she said, nodding wisely. "It's Allison."

"I think we'd better check this out." He shifted the little girl into the crook of his elbow and took her pumpkin in his other hand.

"Allison's gonna climb up the ladder."

"Damn," Jake muttered. "That thing's a relic.

She'll be lucky if she doesn't fall and break her neck.''

"Daddy, that's a bad word."

"Sorry, kitten. I'll be more careful." He had seen to the mowing and upkeep of Rufina Bremer's property since she'd died. He'd known the old wooden ladder was leaning against the side of the house behind the daisies. He'd just never figured anyone else had. "Hey! Wait," he called as Allison put her foot on the first rung. "I'll help you."

"That's all right. I can manage." Allison was reaching down for the owl. A little saw-whet, he noticed, although they weren't usually around at this time of year. Not a baby, but probably not a very experienced hunter, which accounted for the unsuccessful attack on Mike's rat. He set Julia on the ground and walked toward the tree.

"Hang on a minute. I'll steady the ladder."

She was already halfway up with the owl. "It's okay." Her voice was a bit breathless, but her tone was steady. Too steady. She looked to Jake like a woman who didn't relish being several feet up a rickety ladder but was up there anyway. He didn't blame her all that much. He wasn't overly fond of heights himself. But there was no excuse for trying this stunt in that ridiculous witch's outfit with its long, flowing skirt and cockamamy hat.

He didn't know Allison Martin well. Truth to tell, he'd barely exchanged a dozen words with her all summer. He couldn't order her down off the ladder the way he would Jenny or the kids. "Look, why don't you let me do that.'' She had hiked the skirt up at the waist. He spared a glance at her legs. They were good. Very good.

She shook her head, the hat slipping a little, but she ignored it. ''Just one more rung and I can get him to that nice wide branch—'' The word ended with a squeak as the ladder began to separate at the bottom and slowly lurch sideways.

''Daddy! The ladder...'' Libby's shriek was high and shrill and skittered along his nerve endings like sandpaper.

''Move your butt!'' Diplomacy forgotten, Jake grabbed at the ladder to steady it. Allison glanced down, her eyes wide and her mouth opened in a frightened O. Her pointy hat and the black wig she wore under it went flying. Red-gold hair tumbled around her shoulders. She shifted her weight, not to jump but to set the owl on the branch she'd chosen. Then the ladder came apart in Jake's hands, throwing Allison backward as the owl hopped to safety.

''Catch her!'' Libby screamed.

Automatically, Jake reached out. For a moment, a fraction of a second, he was aware of the warmth and softness of a woman's body in his arms again. And then he felt the strain of her weight. He took a step back, twisting to avoid being brained by the falling ladder, tripped over one of the big, upraised roots and fell, hard, with Allison Martin still wrapped in his embrace.

CHAPTER TWO

PAIN STABBED through his chest. He could hear Julia crying hysterically somewhere nearby, but he couldn't see her, couldn't open his eyes because the world spun madly in front of them. Mike was calling him, Libby begging him to get up off the ground. How had he gotten flat on his back on the wet grass? Then he remembered the owl fluttering safely onto its perch, the ladder breaking and Allison Martin tumbling into his arms.

Jake groaned and tried to sit up, but something held him down. The weight shifted, eased, but still he couldn't draw a breath. He felt as though he was drowning, or suffocating, and didn't know which was worse. He struggled to sit up.

"Lie still. Is anything broken?" A firm hand pressed on his shoulder.

"My ribs." He forced open one eye to see Allison Martin kneeling beside him, a nasty scrape along her cheekbone, her auburn hair catching glints of moonlight in its depth. "Are you okay?"

"I'm fine." Her tone was level with only a hint of a quiver. "I'm sorry. I had no idea the ladder—"

"Your cheek."

She lifted a hand as though she hadn't noticed. "It's nothing."

"I need to sit up."

"You shouldn't, not until we know how badly you're hurt."

He ignored her words of caution. His kids were scared and they weren't going to be reassured as long as he was lying helplessly on the ground. "Help me." He must have managed to put more command in his voice than he thought. She did as he asked, reaching out a hand. Jake dragged himself upright against the tree trunk, his left arm cradled against his chest. The kids were still crying. "It's okay, guys. I'm okay."

"You're not okay." Libby launched herself at him. Jake flinched, anticipating more pain, but Allison Martin caught his daughter's arm just in time, holding her back gently.

"Wait, honey. Let your daddy catch his breath."

At the moment, he wasn't certain he'd ever breathe normally again. "I'm fine, Bug." Bug was his pet name for Libby. The first time he'd seen her he'd told Beth she was cute as a bug, and the nickname had stuck.

"You're not okay." Libby sobbed harder. "Are you going to die like Mama?"

"I'm not going to die."

"I'll call 911," Allison said.

"No." The word came out like a rifle shot. "No ambulance." The children had been at his parents' house in town when his father had had his heart attack that spring. The experience had frightened them. Hospitals frightened them, Libby especially, since one of her most vivid memories was of her mother never coming home after going there to have Julia. "I'll be fine," he said stubbornly. He didn't much like hospitals himself.

"You need to be seen by a doctor."

She was right and he knew it. He stared into her gray eyes for a moment. She stared back. Cool, composed, in charge. He imagined this must be how she acted directing the buying and selling of millions of dollars of stocks and bonds every day. He hurt too bad to put up much of an argument. "Okay. Will you drive me into town? Jenny, take the kids back home. I'm sorry about trick or treat, guys." The four short sentences nearly exhausted him.

The little girls started crying harder. "No!" Mike bellowed. "We're going with you."

Allison Martin quelled the threatened uprising before it started. "We'll all go. Jenny, get the kids in the van. I'll help your brother."

She crouched down, and he put his arm around her shoulders, feeling her tense to take his weight as he stood. She staggered a little as he leaned against her. "Sorry," he mumbled, then focused all his concentration on putting one foot in front of the other. Stepping up into the passenger seat of the van wrenched a groan from his lips.

"Are you going to faint?" Allison Martin asked in a low voice so the kids couldn't hear.

"I'm not going to faint." He rolled his head toward

her. "But I'm not all that sure I'm not going to pass out."

"Hang on." She moved around to the driver's seat, made sure the kids were buckled in and put the car in gear. She drove quickly, but the five-minute trip to the small brick-and-stone hospital that was Riley Creek's pride and joy was agonizingly long.

ALLISON PARKED THE VAN under the portico that sheltered the automatic doors to the emergency entrance. "Stay here," she said. "I'll get someone to help your dad." She went inside and looked around. A small plump woman wearing pink scrubs and a matching pink lab coat came out from behind a glass partition and greeted her with a friendly smile.

"If you want to get your children's Halloween candy x-rayed, it's straight down the hall, third door on the left. Just follow the green line on the floor."

Allison had forgotten what she was wearing. She glanced down at her ruined but recognizable costume. "No. I..." Her heart was pounding so high in her throat it was hard to speak. She swallowed and started over. "There's been an accident. A man's been hurt."

The nurse's smile disappeared. She moved back behind the partition to press an intercom button. "Mary," she said, "this is Lynn Babcock in ER. Page Dr. Bostleman, will you? We have another patient and Dr. Whitney is busy in cubicle two." The nurse took a wheelchair from near the entrance doors and followed Allison outside. She pushed the wheelchair up to the door of the van and opened it. "Jake!" There was genuine concern in her voice.

"Hi, Lynn." By now, Allison was no longer surprised that everyone in Riley Creek seemed to know everyone else. It was a very small town after all, only a few thousand people. A heartland version of Mayberry.

"What happened?" the nurse asked as she helped Jake into the wheelchair.

Allison answered the question. "I fell off a ladder and landed on top of him."

"Broke a rib or two," Jake gasped. His color was ghastly.

"We'll let Dr. Bostleman decide that," Lynn said.

The children and Jenny tumbled out of the van. "Where're you taking him?" Mike demanded.

"Inside to see the doctor."

"We're not staying out here. We're coming inside, too."

"Of course you are." She stopped just inside the automatic doors. "The waiting room's there on your left." She turned the wheelchair to the right, toward another set of doors marked Patients and Staff Only, the children close on her heels. "Sorry, kids," she said gently, "you have to stay out here."

"I want my daddy." Jenny picked Julia up and hugged her, but it didn't stop the little girl's sobs.

"You can see your dad just as soon as Dr. Bostleman says it's okay."

Jake reached out and brushed a tear from Libby's

cheek. He looked at Allison. "Look after them, will you, please?"

Allison forced words around the sudden knot of foreboding that tightened her chest. "Yes, of course," she said. "I'll be right here." Then the nurse wheeled Jake through the doors and disappeared into a treatment room. Allison turned Libby around and guided her toward the small waiting room. "How about a soda?" she asked, then remembered she'd come away without her purse, her driver's license or even any money.

"I've got a couple of dollars," Jenny said, figuring out the problem. She fished in the pockets of her skin-tight jeans. "Here." She held out the singles.

"Thanks, Jenny. I'll pay you back as soon as I can."

"Don't worry about it. They're my family, not yours."

Allison ignored the rude remark. Jenny was as frightened as the other children, and not all that much older. Allison bought the soft drinks from a machine in an alcove at the back of the waiting room while Jenny settled the kids in the uncomfortable plastic chairs that lined the walls. Mike and Libby had finally stopped crying and Julia's wails had given way to an occasional sob. They drank their sodas and pretended to watch a cartoon on the TV in the corner. But every time Allison lifted her eyes from the magazine she, too, was pretending to read, she caught them staring across the lobby to the place they'd last seen their father.

Almost half an hour passed. Julia was growing restless and tears threatened again. The nurse had brought some small toys and a couple of picture books to help pass the time, but they'd only kept the children occupied for a few minutes. Dr. Bostleman was with Jake, Lynn had said. It shouldn't be long now. But it seemed like ages. Allison was almost as nervous as the children. What was going on in the treatment room beyond those big wooden doors? Had Jake been more seriously injured than they'd thought? Was he unconscious, in surgery? Or worse... What would she do with the children if he died?

The automatic doors to the parking lot whooshed open, an eddy of cold air and the sharp scent of burning leaves momentarily overpowering the smell of disinfectant in the waiting room. A policeman, red-faced and solidly built, with a distinctive beak of a nose, entered and went directly to the nurses' station behind the glass partition. A few minutes later, he returned, followed by a young woman in a dark business suit holding two disheveled-looking, sad-eyed children by the hand, a boy of eight or nine and a little girl who looked not much older than Julia.

"That's Will Parsons and his baby sister." Libby had come to sit by Allison a few minutes before, leaning her head against her shoulder for comfort. Allison had hesitated only a moment before putting her arm around the little girl and drawing her close, savoring the warmth of her slight body. Her face was streaked by dried tears, and her crown had slipped sideways over her ear at a rakish angle. Her blue eyes were big with apprehension when she turned to Allison and whispered, ''He's in my grade. Why are they here? Who's that lady with them? That's not their mom. I know what she looks like.''

''She's taking them to kid jail, I bet,'' Mike said. ''That's what they do if something happens to your mom and dad and there's no one else to take care of you. They come and take you to kid jail.'' His brown eyes were swimming with fresh tears. He blinked hard. ''I saw it on TV.''

''Mike's right,'' Jenny said, coming forward with Julia in her arms. ''I mean, she's probably a social worker. Randy Parsons knocks his wife around sometimes. The kids've had to go to foster homes before.''

''How do you know that?'' Allison asked.

Jenny shrugged. ''It's a small town. It's hard to keep secrets around here.''

Libby wiggled out of the chair and walked to the doorway. Allison followed her, not certain what the little girl planned to do. Through the open double doors she saw a woman on a stretcher being wheeled down the hallway beyond the room where Jake had been taken. Her face was bandaged, and even from a distance Allison could see bruises on her arms and throat.

An elderly man in a white coat with a stethoscope around his neck and a clipboard in his hand came toward them, motioning for the policeman to join him as the social worker helped the two stoically silent children into their coats and ushered them out the door. ''Abrasions and contusions,'' he said in the overloud voice of someone who was hard-of-hearing as he and the policeman disappeared into yet another room. "She's lost some teeth and most likely has a slight concussion. We're doing a CAT scan right now. You can talk to her as soon as she gets back."

Allison put her hands on Libby's shoulders to steer her away from the sad scene playing out before them. Riley Creek with its down-home charm and friendly openness had problems, as well, it seemed. "I want my dad," Libby said, starting to cry again. "I want him now."

Julia wasn't even four years old. She couldn't understand all the nuances of the unsettling scene they had just witnessed, but she did understand about children being taken away from their parents and she wasn't going to stand for it anymore. "Daddy!" she screamed at the top of her well-developed lungs. "I want my daddy." She struggled so fiercely to be free that Jenny almost dropped her. She set Julia on her feet and the little girl was off like a shot, black-and-white cow ears flapping wildly as she made a beeline for the last place she'd seen her father. Libby and Michael were only a step behind.

They stopped just inside the doors of the treatment area, confused and frightened by the unfamiliar sights and smells of the emergency room as well as the reappearance of the elderly doctor and the big policeman who had come to see what all the commotion was about.

"Daddy," Libby called, "Daddy, where are you?"

A tall, slight woman, a few years older than Allison, dressed in green surgical scrubs, stepped out of a treatment room. "Kids. Hush. Your dad's right here."

"Margaret, what's wrong? Why are they so upset?" Jake's voice came from inside the room.

"Daddy." Hearing her father caused Julia to cry harder. "Daddy, come and get me."

The doctor spun around, but it was too late. Jake stood in the doorway of the treatment room, shirtless, his right hand outstretched to balance himself, his left arm still cradled against his injured ribs. A trickle of blood seeped from a piece of white surgical tape across the back of his hand, and Allison realized with a shiver that he must have pulled an IV needle out in his attempt to reach his kids. "What the hell is going on? What's got my kids so worked up?" He raked them all with a glance that promised to show no mercy to whoever had caused his children such distress.

Margaret Bostleman paid no attention to his flare of temper. "Jake, get back on that table before you fall and do some real damage to that thick skull of yours." To the children she said, "Settle down. Come and see that he's all right."

Julia reached out her arms to Jenny, and Libby slipped her hand into Allison's. "You come, too," she whispered. "I'm afraid of this place. My mama came here to get Julia and she never came back home."

Allison was pained by Libby's frightened words.

"Your daddy's not going to die. Dr. Bostleman will take good care of him."

Libby nodded slightly, wanting to believe. "I like her," she said. "She doesn't give you a shot unless she really, really has to."

Mike didn't reach for her hand the way Libby had, but he stuck close by as they crowded into the small treatment room.

"There now, you can see he's all right," Margaret Bostleman said with a smile. "But he's still hurt and he has to stay here for a few days to get better."

"No," Julia said fiercely, shaking her head. "Daddy, come home." She held out her arms.

Jake's jaw tightened and he balled his hand into a fist. "You know I can't afford to be laid up here with Mom and Dad in Florida. Who's going to take care of the kids?"

"Jake, you've got two broken ribs and you're lucky you didn't puncture a lung. You're not leaving this hospital tonight, and maybe not tomorrow, either," the physician added uncompromisingly. "Can't Stella watch the kids for you?"

"Lynn's tried to call her place twice. No one answered. I don't know where she's at or when she'll be home."

"The kids and I will be all right, Jake. I can watch them." Jenny looked as if she might burst into tears at any moment along with the others.

"No. That's too much responsibility."

"I've been watching these three since I was twelve."

Jake lifted his head. "I know, Jenny. But this is too much, even for you. Margaret, what do I have to do to sign myself out of this place?"

"I'll be responsible for the children." Allison's heart pounded as she heard herself say the words. *Responsible for the children.* Wasn't that the phrase her cousin had used at Easter when she'd made Allison face her drinking problem for the first time? *I can't let you be responsible for the children. You're a drunk.* What was she doing volunteering to care for these children?

"I don't think we've met," Dr. Bostleman said, watching her with assessing green eyes.

"I'm Allison Martin. Rufina Bremer's granddaughter."

"She's my neighbor," Jake said, suddenly sounding very weary. Allison realized how hard he was working to hide his pain and exhaustion from his kids. "She's been living in Rufina's house this summer."

"Nice to meet you," Margaret Bostleman said with a nod. "Well, if Ms. Martin here is volunteering to watch over Jenny and the kids tonight, I say you'd better take her up on the offer because you're staying here, even if I have to tie you to the bed myself."

Jake glared at the doctor, then turned his eyes on Allison. She made herself return the steady regard. She was a different person now, sober and in control. She could do this. She could watch over Jake's children, keep them safe from harm. "I'll take good care of them," she said.

He continued to hold her gaze. For a moment, she

wondered if he could sense the turmoil and uncertainty inside her. Then he nodded once, slightly, and the spell was broken. ''Thank you,'' he said. ''That would ease my mind considerably.''

IT WAS AFTER ELEVEN before Jake's household settled down for the night. The children had been so wound up it had taken two hours to get them bathed and in their beds. Then Jenny had insisted on playing hostess, making up the bed in the guest bedroom, bringing out the best towels and clearing away the clutter in the downstairs bathroom to make room for Allison's things, although she'd brought nothing with her except her purse and her toothbrush.

''The kids and I sleep upstairs,'' she said, her voice cool. ''Jake's room is right next to yours. This house has six bedrooms. It was built by my dad's grandfather and he had twelve kids.''

''Goodness, what a big family.'' She must have sounded suitably impressed because Jenny favored her with one of her rare smiles.

''I like this house, but my mom said she'd never been so happy as the day they moved into town. We have a nice brick ranch with just three bedrooms and two bathrooms and a basement. My mom loves it, but I think my dad still misses this place. It's where he grew up. My grandparents lived here till they died, then we built our house and Jake and Beth moved in.'' The slight smile disappeared. ''I have a couple of calls to make and then I'll turn in. It's been a wild night.''

"Calls? Isn't it a little late for phone calls?" Allison was sorry she asked before the sentence left her mouth. Even so, eleven o'clock on a school night was late for a fifteen-year-old to be calling her friends.

Jenny's habitual frown returned. "I stood my friends up, remember? They'll still be awake. Don't worry."

Allison backed off. It wasn't her place to be setting limits for Jake's sister. "All right. Good night, Jenny."

"Good night." The teenager started up the stairway. She stopped halfway and leaned over the railing. "Thanks for doing this." Her tone was slightly grudging. "We would have been fine by ourselves, you know. I've been taking care of the kids by myself since I was twelve, but I didn't want Jake to worry about us. So, like I said, thanks."

"I'm only glad there's something I can do to help. It was my clumsiness that got your brother hurt."

"It was an accident." Jenny's expression thawed just a bit. "My alarm goes off at six. I'll wake you."

"Thank you."

"No problemo." Jenny disappeared into the shadows at the top of the stairs.

Allison stayed where she was until she heard the teenager's door close behind her. She wrapped her arms around herself and tried to concentrate on the sounds of the old house settling itself for the night. She'd always been an early riser, even if she was out of the habit now, but she knew there would be no danger of her oversleeping tomorrow. The jittery, anxious feeling she dreaded was back.

She wanted a drink. Needed a drink.

Next thing she knew she'd walked into the kitchen, opened the big refrigerator in the corner by the stove and was staring longingly at the half-full bottle of white wine she'd spied earlier on the back shelf behind the two plastic gallon jugs of milk.

She reached out. She could taste the tart coolness of the wine, feel the tension leave her body as the alcohol coursed through her bloodstream. She remembered how it softened all the rough edges, blurred all the harsh angles of her life, if only for a little while.

She remembered how it had almost destroyed her.

Dear Lord, I'm an alcoholic. I need Your help. Every day of my life, I need Your help. But most of all I need the strength of will to get me through this night.

Allison slammed the refrigerator door, turned her back on the bottle of wine. She could resist. She would resist. She forced herself to walk, not run from the kitchen. She grabbed an afghan from the back of the couch and let herself out onto the big wraparound porch. She sat down on the swing and began to rock.

She thought of her personal talisman, the smooth, round pebble she'd found on a Lake Michigan beach long ago and had kept with her ever since. Though it was on her dresser in the house across the silent, deserted road, she went through the familiar motions of rolling it between her fingers. She would watch the moon and listen for the little owl calling in her maple tree. She would last the night without giving in to her need for a drink. She had given her word to keep Jake's children safe, and she would stay sober tonight for their sake, if not her own.

CHAPTER THREE

"I'M GOING HOME, MARGARET. Today. Now." Jake Walthers and Margaret Bostleman faced each other across the bedside table. The physician was standing, tapping the toe of her shoe on the floor, and Jake was seated on the edge of the bed. But even though she towered over him, there was no mistaking the steely determination in his voice. For the moment, neither of them noticed Allison in the open doorway of Jake's hospital room, an unwilling eavesdropper on the conversation.

"I want you here for at least another forty-eight hours. You've got one broken rib, two cracked—"

"I'm going home." Jake broke eye contact and continued struggling painfully with his shirt. He was wearing the same pair of khaki chinos he'd had on the night before, but his feet were bare and so was his chest, the left side covered with angry purple bruises.

Margaret stepped forward as though to offer her help. "The pain pills are going to make you dizzy. If you stumble and fall, you could do yourself a lot of damage, puncture a lung. You're darned lucky that hasn't happened already."

Jake waved her off and struggled into the sleeve of his shirt. Sweat broke out on his forehead and upper lip, and what little color he had leeched out of his face. "I won't take the damned pills, then." And he wouldn't, no matter how much pain he was in. Allison barely knew the man, but she'd witnessed his strength of will last night when he'd thought his children were threatened and she caught the same implacable resolve in his voice now.

Margaret Bostleman must have heard it, too. "You're going to hurt like hell if you refuse the medication."

"I'll survive," he said grimly, then looked up and gave her a small smile. "I've never heard you cuss before, Maggie Amelia."

"Don't call me that." Her foot tapped faster, but there was a tiny hint of laughter in her high, clear voice. "I hated you calling me that in second grade and I don't like it any better now. And quit trying to change the subject. I can let you go home tomorrow morning if your X rays are clear."

Jake was having none of it. "I'm going home today. My kids need me. I've already called..." For the first time, he stumbled over his words. He gave an angry little shake of his head, wincing at the movement. His eyes narrowed and his mouth firmed into a hard line. "Damned pills. My head feels like a cement block sitting on my shoulders. What's her...? Allison," he said, apparently snaring her name out of his memory. "Allison Martin. She should be here any minute to pick me up."

"I am here." Both of them turned in her direction. Allison felt herself color slightly. Her pale skin with its smattering of freckles and its tendency to telegraph her emotions was the bane of her existence. She shoved her hands into the pockets of her sweatshirt. Summer had been blown away with last night's west wind. Today it was gray and raw and cold, a not-so-subtle reminder that it was November now, and winter was only days away.

"Where's Julia?" Jake demanded.

"She's at the store. Stella is watching her. I...I told her what happened when she came to open the store this morning." Allison had debated bringing the little girl to the hospital with her to answer Jake's imperious summons but had decided against it, even though Julia had fussed about coming along. What if she became as upset as she'd been the night before? What if Jake had to stay and Julia refused to leave when it was time to go? Allison had so little experience with children she'd been second-guessing everything she did, every word she said to them. It was only an hour past lunchtime and she was already on edge.

"Good." His frown eased slightly. "Thanks for coming so quickly. This is the last time I'll impose on you, I promise."

"Jake—"

He cut off Margaret Bostleman with another fierce scowl and went back to buttoning his shirt. As he labored awkwardly with the task, he grumbled, "Just get me the papers to sign so I can get out of here, Doc.''

"I want you on seven days bed rest. Bathroom privileges only.''

His head shot up. Their eyes locked again. "My God, Maggie, I can't spend a week in bed. I've got a farm to run, a business to oversee and kids to take care of. I've got eighty acres of corn to get out of the fields before it rains.''

"You're also risking pneumonia and possibly even more serious complications if you don't do as I say. And I don't want you lifting anything heavier than a coffee cup, do you understand? Who's going to be in charge of the children?'' she asked before he could object again.

"I... Jenny, I guess. She's staying with us while Mom and Dad are in Florida.'' The slight frown between his strongly marked eyebrows deepened.

"She's only fifteen,'' Margaret said, her tone softening. "It's too much responsibility for her.''

"We'll manage.'' He held up his hand to forestall her next suggestion. "I'm not calling Mom and Dad home. Dad's not strong enough for that kind of marathon trip. It's twenty hours from Bradenton and they'd drive straight through if they thought I was really hurt.''

"You *are* really hurt. What about Matt or Kyle? Could one of them fly in for a few days?''

"Get real, Margaret. My brothers have jobs and lives of their own. They can't be taking time off work to come home and baby-sit me.''

"Okay, Stella, then."

"She can't run the store and nursemaid me at the same time." The stubbornness had returned to roughen his voice. "I can take care of myself. I'm going home and that's final."

Allison realized she couldn't remain silent any longer. After all, it was her fault he was hurt. She owed him. But could she do it? Should she do it? *A week.* Allison swallowed the knot of apprehension that had lodged in her throat. "I'll help you watch over the children," she said. "I... It's the least I can do."

"Thank you," Jake said stiffly. "That won't be necessary."

"Oh, yes, it will." Margaret Bostleman's voice was no longer soft. "I wasn't just blowing smoke, Jake. I want you on bed rest. And I want you to take the medication I prescribe for you. For seven days. No farming, no lifting, even Julia. *Especially* Julia. And no driving. Take it or leave it." She gave Allison a long, searching look. "If Ms. Martin is willing to help you mind your brood, I think you should take her up on the offer. That's the only way I'll sign you out of here.

"Let me finish," she commanded, anticipating the outburst even Allison knew was coming. "If I don't dot all the *i*'s and cross all the *t*'s on your discharge papers, you're going to have a hell of a time explaining it to the insurance company." Jake's mouth opened and shut without a sound. She smiled wickedly. "I thought that might do it."

"I can't ask a stranger to move into my house for a week."

"I don't see that you have much choice." The teasing note left her voice, and she crossed her arms over her chest. She was addressing Jake, but her green eyes were fixed on Allison, assessing, appraising.

Allison wondered for a panicky moment if Margaret Bostleman somehow knew of her fear and uncertainty, the desire for just one tiny glass of wine to soothe her jangled nerves. But that was impossible. No one in Riley Creek knew she was an alcoholic, wasn't trustworthy enough to care for children.

"Either Ms. Martin helps you with the kids for a week or you stay right where you are for at least the next forty-eight hours. That's my final offer. Take it or leave it."

"He'll take it," Allison said before Jake could reply. She wouldn't give in to the need. She would do what was right. She would repay Jake Walthers's unselfish actions by taking care of his children. She would do it for him, for them, and for herself. "If we hurry, I can have you home before the school bus drops off the children."

JAKE GRITTED HIS TEETH and tried not to groan. Julia was hanging on to his right hand with both of hers, jiggling up and down on the tips of her toes, trying so hard to be close without getting into bed with him. He didn't have the heart to reprimand her, but it took every ounce of willpower he possessed not to do just that.

"Can I get you something, Daddy?" she asked, bouncing harder. "Do you want a drink of water or some toast?"

"No, baby," he said, shutting his eyes against another wave of pain as she jarred the mattress. "I'm fine."

"Do you want to watch my Pooh tape?" she asked, offering him one of her favorite videos. "Or Mr. Toad? He's funny. Beep, beep," she chortled, imitating the manic frog from the classic children's story. She let go of his hand to take the wheel of an imaginary turn-of-the-century motorcar. "Beep. Beep." She raced around the bed. "Faster, faster."

"Maybe later, baby." He closed his eyes. Dammit, he hurt. He should have taken the pills sooner, but he'd held off until after he could call his parents and let them know he was okay—banged up good, but okay—and not sound like he was half-zonked out of his mind. His mother had kept him on the phone longer than he'd wanted, first to assure herself he really wasn't at death's door and then to grill him, not as subtly as she'd imagined, about the part Allison Martin had played in his fall.

Now he wished he could gobble down a couple more of the high-powered painkillers and get some sleep. But Allison had taken them away with her— so there would be no chance that Julia might mistake them for candy, she'd said—and he couldn't find the strength to call her back into the bedroom.

Julia was back at his side. She tugged on his hand,

none too gently. "Daddy? Are you asleep? Did I wake you up?"

"No, sweetie. I'm awake."

"You're not supposed to be in here," Libby hissed from the doorway. "You're supposed to leave Dad alone so he can rest."

"I'm taking care of him," Julia said, squeezing his fingers more tightly than ever. "I'm taking care of you, aren't I, Daddy?"

"You are," Jake said through clenched teeth. If she'd only stand still it would help, but Julia was almost always on the move, just the way her mother had been. *Beth*. God, he missed her. He felt the old grief and hurt pushing at him, but he fought it. Instead, he tried to conjure up memories of Beth's presence here in this room, which she'd decorated in soft shades of blue and rose and warm touches of gold. The room they'd shared all their married life. But that was harder and harder to do these days. Sometimes he had to look at her picture to remember her face as clearly as he used to.

He wanted to keep remembering. He didn't want to move on. But it seemed that he had no choice; his own body had started betraying him in the past few months. And as much as he hated to admit it, more often than not those feelings of lust had been triggered by the sight of Allison Martin in shorts and a crop top mowing the lawn, or painting the porch trim, or working in her grandmother's overgrown herb garden.

"I've got my homework done, Dad," Michael was

saying. Jake opened his eyes and tried to focus on his son, who was hovering in the doorway. Mike looked just like his brother Matt at that age, round-faced and gawky, still carrying a little baby fat around his middle. Matt had topped out at six foot two, an inch or so taller than Jake, and he'd been the best damned middle linebacker Riley Creek High had ever seen. He wondered if Mike would do the same. He liked soccer as much as he did football, but soccer wasn't a varsity sport at Riley Creek High and—

The phone beside his bed rang, but there was no way in hell he could get himself in position to answer it before less than a dozen rings. Someone, Jenny possibly, picked up on the third. Jake stifled a sigh and tried to relax against the stack of pillows that Allison Martin had arranged behind him.

A soft knock at the door diverted the kids' attention. "Am I interrupting?" His self-appointed guardian angel's voice was as cool and composed as ever, but her smile was warm, if a little tentative, as she entered his bedroom.

"No. Come in," he grunted. "I was just saying good-night to the kids."

She took a half-dozen steps into the big, high-ceilinged room that opened directly off the living room and was originally meant to be a dining room. Despite its awkward location, Beth had insisted on using it for their bedroom because of the big bay window that faced south and framed a view of gently rolling fields stretching off into the distance.

"It's getting time for you to be heading upstairs,"

Allison said, directing her remark to all three children. "Jenny's promised to tuck you in as soon as she comes back."

"Jenny's in Aaron's truck," Julia announced. "Maybe kissing him." She giggled.

"I hope it was all right that she went out to speak to him," Allison said, sounding uncertain.

"It's okay." He didn't like his sister seeing the Masterson boy. He was too old for her, but Jake's parents didn't object so neither could he. Besides, there was nothing he could do about it now. Something in his voice must have betrayed his weariness.

"Your dad's tired and his ribs hurt. I just finished talking to Dr. Bostleman on the phone and she wants him to take another pill and get some rest, so I think you'd all better say good-night and let him do that."

"I want a kiss good-night," Julia insisted. Jake had no idea how he was going to manage that without Julia actually getting on the bed, but Allison solved the problem by picking up the little girl to let her lean over him. Julia framed his face in her small hands and kissed him on the cheek. "Night-night, Daddy. Don't let the bugs bite."

"Night, kitten." He kissed her back and then Allison set her carefully on her feet.

Libby popped out of the rocking chair, bent very carefully over the bed and gave him a peck on the cheek. "Night, Daddy."

"Good night, Bug."

Michael was past the kissing stage, but he came

over for a quick squeeze that had Jake seeing stars. "Night, guy."

"Night, Dad."

"C'mon, Julia, let's go." Libby took her little sister's hand and led her reluctantly away. "I'll read you *Goodnight Moon* and then you have to go to sleep."

"Good night, kids."

Allison stood watching his children as they left the bedroom. She was quiet a few moments longer, staring at the doorway after them. Jake could hear their squabbling voices, punctuated with giggles from the girls and hoots from Mike, as they climbed the stairs. He braced himself against the mattress with his good arm, levered himself upright and swung his feet over the edge of the bed.

The room spun crazily and black spots danced before his eyes. "Hell," he said, swallowing against the sudden nausea that rose in his throat. He wished he could lie down again, but he didn't have a choice. He needed to use the bathroom.

"Here, let me help." She was at his side in a heartbeat. He hesitated a moment, and she must have sensed his reluctance. "If you don't want me helping you, just let me know whom to call."

"I don't like being helpless."

"None of us does. Look, I thought we agreed this is how it had to be."

He did look at her then, really looked at her for the first time. Her red-gold hair hung in waves around her face, but most of it was caught up in some kind of comb in the back. Her gray eyes were shadowed, shuttered so that he couldn't read the emotions she had hidden away behind them, but there was a faint blush of color on her cheeks and he knew he had embarrassed her.

"I'm sorry. I don't make a very good patient, do I?" He was more aware than he wanted to be of the softness of her skin, the blend of citrus and flowers in her perfume. It was nothing musky or heavy, overly sophisticated or sinfully expensive, as he'd imagined her scent to be. This was nice. He frowned a little. He didn't want to notice things like that about her. He didn't want to remember how she looked in a crop top and shorts.

"I'm not used to playing nurse." She surprised him with a smile that was self-mocking, a tad off center and sexy as hell. "I'm probably going about this all wrong."

"No," he said, amazed at the words coming out of his mouth, amazed at the shock of sexual awareness that penetrated even his pain-hazed mind as he reached out and traced the tip of his finger along her cheek. "You're being an angel. Thank you for coming to our rescue."

"No," she said very softly. "Thank you for coming to mine."

JENNY CAREFULLY HUNG her junior high varsity cheerleading jacket on the peg beside the kitchen door—she wasn't eligible to try out for the varsity cheerleaders until next year, and she was only an alternate on the freshman squad, so it was the only one she had. And she was starting to outgrow it. She wondered if her mom would get her a new one when she got home from Florida. Probably not, unless she asked for it for Christmas, and she didn't know if she wanted a new one that bad, at least not until she'd made the squad. She sniffed experimentally at the heavy wool fabric, making sure it didn't smell of smoke. Aaron had only been smoking cigarettes tonight, not pot, as he did once in a while, and she was glad. She didn't like it when he did that, or when he drank too much beer and kept at her to try it, too. But he was the cutest boy in the senior class and he liked her. Plain old Jenny Walthers.

Sure, once in a while he got a little too grabby, wanting to unbutton her blouse and take off her bra when all she wanted were kisses and cuddles. But usually he was nice and smart enough to know that when a girl said no to making out she meant it. That was one of the things she liked best about him. If he'd just quit pressuring her to try pot and drink beer, he'd be just about perfect. She wanted him to like her as much as she liked him. She wanted to be part of his crowd, but he'd told her they wouldn't want her around if she kept on being such a wimp.

She sniffed at her coat again, satisfied she'd stayed far enough over on her side of the truck to keep the smell of smoke off her clothes and out of her hair. She opened the back door and hung it on the covered porch, just to be safe. She couldn't be certain Allison Martin wouldn't notice and say something to Jake. Why the woman would bother, or even get close enough to smell her coat, Jenny didn't know, but she didn't want to chance it. She couldn't be sure Allison wouldn't squeal to Coach Rayle about Aaron or something awful like that. You could never tell with strangers.

Jenny felt a little spurt of shame curl through her stomach, but she ignored it. She had every right to feel a little put out by Allison. She'd just walked into Jake's house and taken over their lives, and Jenny didn't like it one bit. Even if she couldn't come up with a better solution for their problem herself.

She could hear Allison talking to Jake as she moved around his bedroom and knew she was helping him get ready for bed. She felt another pang of regret for her bitchy thoughts. She'd feel really weird helping Jake to the bathroom and in and out of the shower and all. But the kids were her responsibility and Allison Martin was horning in there, too, fixing Mike pizza for supper and reading books with Libby. And Julia. Julia couldn't get enough of being around Allison. That was what really hurt.

Julia was almost like her own kid. She'd taken care of Julia since she was three days old. She was Beth's baby and Jenny meant to keep her safe and happy all her life because Beth had been her best friend and she still missed her.

"Hi, Jenny."

Jenny jumped as if Allison had shouted her name instead of speaking in her regular voice. "Hi," she said back, wishing her voice didn't sound so squeaky.

"The kids are already upstairs. They're waiting for you to go say good-night."

Jenny nodded. "Okay." She looked toward Jake's bedroom door. "How's Jake? Can I go in to see him?"

A little frown made a crease between Allison's eyebrows. Jenny wondered if she darkened them. Most redheads she knew had really light eyebrows and eyelashes to go with their skin. Allison had pale skin, milky white, just like the princess in Libby's favorite book of fairy tales, but her eyebrows and eyelashes were brown. Dyed maybe. She was rich enough for it, or at least Jenny had heard her mother tell Mrs. Christman that Allison had some real fancy Wall Street–type job in Chicago, which made her rich in Jenny's book.

"If you like. But he's almost asleep. Dr. Bostleman said he could take an extra pain pill and they're pretty strong. Maybe it would be better if you waited until morning."

There she went, bossing everyone around again. Jenny bit the inside of her lip to keep from saying something snotty. "Okay. I'll wait."

Maybe Jake needs you, Jenny thought, *but the rest of us don't. We're family and you don't belong.* "Don't worry about the kids. I'll take care of them," she said in her best grown-up voice.

"Jenny? Have I...?" Allison looked upset, as if Jenny had hurt her. Now she felt really bad about her snippy tone, but then she remembered the way Julia had climbed onto Allison's lap and snuggled against her, and she hardened her heart. She didn't look at Allison or smile back.

"Like I said, don't worry about us. Me and the kids will be fine." And then she did do something snotty. She didn't say good-night or anything else, just turned and walked away.

ALLISON SIGHED. Jenny was not happy to have her in Jake's house. She didn't know what to do about it. Just be as pleasant and patient as she could and try not to upset the girl's routine any more than necessary, she supposed. Teenagers were even harder to deal with than younger children she was finding out. But she was sure she'd survive the week. She'd made it through the first day without any major mistakes or confrontations—and without a drink. The knowledge felt good.

She walked through the living room with its big, shabby, overstuffed couch and chairs, turning off the TV, switching off lamps, until she was standing alone with only the sliver of light from the partially open bathroom door to lessen the darkness.

She was tired, dead tired, but sleep wasn't going to come any easier than it had the night before. She curled up on the couch and pulled the afghan around her shoulders. She still wanted a drink, desperately, but she'd managed to ignore the need for one more day. And she would go on ignoring it through the night.

She fingered the smooth pebble in her pocket, cleared her mind and tried to go to her special place, the pristine northern Michigan beach where she'd found the stone. Usually, practicing the meditation and visualization techniques she'd learned at the detox center worked. She would conjure up the blue and gold of sand and water, the heat of the sun on the top of her head, the cool of the pine-scented lake breeze against her cheek. In her mind, she would walk and walk and walk until she was too tired to worry, to fret or to want a drink, and then she would drift off to sleep.

She closed her eyes and strove to clear her mind of turmoil but had little success. Tonight it wasn't her need for a drink that sent her thoughts scurrying in all directions. It was a memory that refused to be banished—the brush of Jake's hard, warm fingers across her cheek, the flash of awareness in his midnight blue eyes—that kept her awake and staring into the darkness long after everyone else in the house was sound asleep.

CHAPTER FOUR

THE SMELLS OF HOT CIDER and cinnamon welcomed Allison as she pulled open the door of the Walnut Hill Farm Market. A few steps inside the big, low-ceilinged room, those scents were overtaken by the tang of eucalyptus and lavender hanging in bunches from the rafters. They in turn gave way to the smell of floral potpourri in jars and bowls placed on lace-covered tables. Allison sneezed. She couldn't stop herself. No matter how much she liked coming in here, the intensity of the smells was always a little overpowering.

"Gesundheit." Stella LaRue was behind the counter. Stuffed animals, so small they could fit in the palm of a child's hand, were laid out before her in orderly rows. There were puppies and kittens and lambs and teddy bears, also a frog and a turtle, a flamingo and an orange orangutan.

Allison sneezed again. Stella pulled a tissue out of a box and handed it to her. "Thanks," she said with a sniff.

Stella laughed. "This place always does that to me, too. Good thing I don't have any allergies or asthma. I'd have to quit my job."

"I love it here," Allison confessed, "but it takes a little getting used to."

"Is it raining yet?" Stella asked. The windows in this section of the huge old barn were original— small, many paned and set up high. In the renovated part, there was a whole wall of big plate-glass windows that looked out over Jake's pear and apple orchards to the fields and meadows beyond, but Stella couldn't see them from where she was standing.

"Not yet," Allison replied. "But I think it will before nightfall."

"How's Jake feeling today?" Stella added two alligators and a family of chimpanzees to her menagerie, then ticked off the newcomers on the shipping invoice beside the cash register. Allison figured the beanbag animals were destined for the children's corner of the store where china dolls and lace-winged angels reclined in wicker chairs with old-fashioned wooden pull toys resting at their feet.

"Sore and...restless."

"Pushing himself too hard, is he? It's only been three days since the accident, but I imagine he's already chafing at the bit to be up and around." Stella's thick, straight eyebrows rose upward until they almost touched the salt-and-pepper bangs she wore cut blunt across her broad forehead. Everything about Stella LaRue was broad and blunt. She was taller than Allison's five foot six—by a good three inches—and she also outweighed her by a substantial amount. But she carried her weight well, and her ready smile and hearty laughter as well as her no-nonsense approach to life made her easy to like.

"He had a bad night and he's worried about the corn still in the fields."

"Had problems with corn borers this spring. Weakened the stalks. But it'll get harvested okay, don't fret about it. How are you getting along with that crew otherwise?"

"Not too badly," Allison said with a smile. "You're right, Jake is hard to keep down. The kids have been great. Jenny especially. And since word started getting out about Jake's accident, I haven't had to cook a single meal. Food just keeps appearing on the doorstep like magic."

"That's one of the good things about living in a town like Riley Creek," Stella said. "People pitch in for each other."

"I've had to put a couple of pies and some of the soups in the freezer," Allison admitted. "There's just so much there's no way we can eat all of it. Everyone's been very generous."

"Jake's a good man. The neighbors will all want to help bring the corn in. And I imagine you've had visits from more than one of the grass widows in town wanting to make an impression on Jake with their cooking."

Stella was right. Several of Jake's gift-bearing visitors had been women alone, and not one of them had worn a wedding ring. "He's had some women visitors," Allison said tactfully.

"Manhunters. Been after him ever since Beth died," Stella said under her breath.

Allison let the last comment pass unremarked. Jake was an attractive man. He was a good catch in anyone's book. It was none of her business that the available women of Riley Creek were interested in him. And she certainly wasn't about to admit to anyone that she hadn't enjoyed standing by holding casserole dishes and pie plates and pans of chocolate brownies while the perfumed and powdered visitors had preened and flirted and coyly wished Jake a speedy recovery, just before adding offers to help out any way he wanted. "Busy day?" she asked instead.

It was less than an hour until closing time and there were only two couples browsing in the store, but the parking lot had been full all afternoon, so Allison expected it had been a good day. In the produce section, one couple could be seen wandering among the colorful aisles of winter squash, red apples and golden pears.

"Not bad," Stella replied. "Sunday afternoons are always good for browsers."

A middle-aged woman wearing a white grocer's apron appeared in the archway. "Stella, I'm sorry to bother you, but there's no price on those tins of hard candies that came in yesterday. The gentleman wants to know."

"Four ninety-eight, Rosie," Stella said without a moment's hesitation. "And leave a note for Angela to price them first thing in the morning, will you?"

"I'll be sure to do that." The woman, Stella's assistant, smiled at Allison and hurried back to her customer.

A growing rumble drew Allison's attention toward the high window behind Stella although she couldn't see anything but the bare branches of a maple and a patch of leaden gray sky beyond. For a moment, Allison thought the sound was the low growl of a late-season thunderstorm.

"Combines," Stella said. "Neighbors must be coming to get Jake's corn out before it rains. I told you it would get taken care of, and the good Lord's proved me right sooner than I expected."

Two of the huge machines were idling in the parking lot when Stella and Allison stepped outside. One red, one green, with the glinting talons of the picking apparatus jutting ahead of them. Behind them, almost as large and noisy as the combines, two tractors with wide-bottomed plows attached were pulling into the driveway. Allison had been in Riley Creek long enough to know that they would follow behind the combines, turning under the corn stubble, allowing the heavy black soil beneath to lie fallow until the following spring. Finally, two pickup trucks drove in, each one pulling a tandem of high-sided grain wagons to receive the shelled corn.

"I'd better set Rosie to making some sandwiches," Stella said. "It'll be supper time before they're done and they'll be hungry." She leaned close to Allison to make herself heard. The noise of powerful diesel and gasoline engines and the smell of their exhaust now filled the farmyard. Stella waved as half a dozen men and two women began climbing out of their various vehicles to mill around in Jake's yard as if waiting for his signal to get to work.

The women—one young, one not so young—were wearing sweatshirts and jeans. Both had scarves tied over their hair to keep out the dust and chaff. They would drive the loaded grain wagons to the elevator that night if the weather continued to threaten. The men wore heavy work boots, jeans and hooded sweatshirts.

As Allison watched, the group began to surround one man. Tall and thin with a ruddy complexion, he looked to be around Stella's age, perhaps nearing fifty, although it was hard to tell from this distance. He began gesturing toward the farm lane that led to the field of yellowed cornstalks.

Just then, Jake appeared at the top of the back porch steps, flanked by his children. Even from across the parking lot, Alison could see the pain lines bracketing Jake's mouth. Margaret Bostleman had given her reluctant okay for him to dress and move from his bed to the big leather recliner in the living room where he felt more comfortable. But she'd said nothing about his going outside. As he started down the steps, she noticed he wasn't using the sling he'd been told to wear but instead had hooked his left thumb through the belt loop of his jeans, providing little support for anything except his ego. He was still a little shaky on his feet, and Allison held her breath, praying he didn't trip and do more damage to himself.

"He isn't wearing a coat. He'll catch his death,"

Stella chided, wrapping her arms around her ample middle. "Temperature's dropped ten degrees since noon."

Jake had on the same blue chambray work shirt she'd buttoned for him after his shower. Her fingers had brushed the warmth of his damp skin as she settled the shirt over his broad shoulders, and now, seemingly of their own volition, they curled into a fist against her side. Once more, she felt the heat of his body. Unsettled by the strength of her reaction, she tried to shake off the surprising and insistent memory. But it wasn't easy.

As she watched, Jake moved forward to greet his neighbors, wincing a little as one of the men pumped his arm with an exuberance that must have caused him pain. The group remained together for a few minutes longer, then at a word from the tall, thin man who seemed to be their de facto leader, the drivers of the combines revved up their huge engines and moved slowly down the lane toward the field. The other men and women stayed behind.

"Better get back inside," Stella said, moving quickly for a woman her size as Jake and the tall, thin man walked toward them.

"Stella!" Jake's companion called before she could get the door open.

Allison thought she heard Stella utter a mild curse under her breath, but she wasn't really paying attention. She was too focused on Jake. He looked ghastly and she was afraid he was going to collapse before he got to them. She hurried forward to help him.

"You really shouldn't be out here," she said. "Dr. Bostleman said you could get up and sit in your chair, not come outside into the cold."

"I'm fine," he said through his teeth.

"You don't look fine. It's time for your medication. I wish you'd go back inside." She hadn't spent the past three days watching and worrying over him to have him fall in a heap at her feet.

He ignored her. "Stella, can you see about getting some coffee and sandwiches made?" Jake asked, his voice as tight as the set of his lips. "I know it's almost closing time but—"

"I'll be happy to. As a matter of fact, I was on my way to do just that."

"Wait up. I'll help you, Stella," the tall man said.

This time, Allison was certain she heard Stella curse. "There's no need of that, Tom Farley. I can manage. The cider's already hot and it won't take me and Rosie more than ten minutes to whip up some sandwiches."

"We've got all that extra food in the freezer. Libby can take some of the pies out to thaw," Jake added. He started to call his daughter to him, turned too quickly and stumbled.

Allison was at his side almost before she knew she was moving, reaching to break his fall. "Jake, please, you shouldn't be out here."

He regained his balance and stepped back so quickly she was left clutching at nothing. "I'm fine." He caught his breath on a gasp of pain. "Quit coddling me."

"I'm...I'm sorry." She felt her color rise and then was angry with herself for letting Jake's sharp words affect her so noticeably.

"Ms. Martin, I'm Tom Farley," the tall man offered when the silence had stretched for just a little too long. "I'm Jake's neighbor across the section. I believe I've seen you around town once or twice this summer."

"Probably more than that," Stella said with a waspishness that surprised Allison. "Seems you spend most of your days drinking coffee at the restaurant."

"I have been known to make an appearance now and then," he countered good-naturedly.

"It's nice to meet you." Allison shook his hand, but her thoughts were elsewhere. What had happened? Jake had never spoken to her that sharply before. It was as if she'd gone too far, crossed some invisible boundary that Jake had placed between them.

"My pleasure." Tom Farley pretended not to notice her discomfort. "Now, Stella, why don't you show me what to do and we'll get a meal laid out for these good people."

"I don't need you barging around in the deli kitchen," Stella said, holding herself very straight. "The health department won't stand for it. Why don't you just go get up in the cab of that big old John Deere you paid a king's ransom and then some for and start plowing before it rains."

He squinted up at the lowering sky. "Plenty of time."

"Well, I don't need help."

Tom Farley tugged at the brim of his hat. He suddenly looked much older and far less affable. "I only offered to make sandwiches, Stella," he said with a hint of what sounded almost like sadness to Allison. "Nothing more."

"I don't need help," Stella repeated, but this time there was no bluster or bravado in her voice, only resolve. She pulled open the door, then hesitated as she overheard Tom's next words.

"Damn stubborn woman." He turned his back on the spluttering Stella. "C'mon, Jake, I'll walk you back to the house."

"I'm staying here," Jake said.

"There's no reason for you to be out here, buddy. Everyone knows what they're supposed to do."

"Mr. Farley's right," Allison heard herself say. "Don't be a fool. You aren't even wearing a coat. What can you possibly do that will be of any help to anyone?"

Jake refused to meet her eyes. "I belong here." He took another step backward, away from her.

"You belong in bed. You look like hell and I haven't spent—" Allison shut her mouth with a snap. Now she knew what line she'd crossed. Standing up to him, arguing with him, had made him look at her as a woman—not as merely a temporary nurse or a slight distraction in his life—and he didn't want to see her as a woman. That was very clear.

"I'm fine," he said, his expression stubborn and uncompromising. "I'm just fine."

"Well, I'm sorry to say I disagree with you there, old pal," Tom interjected. "You do look like hell. Like you've been dragged through a hedge backward, rode hard and put—"

"I get the picture. All right, you win. I'm going back to the house."

"Nice meeting you, ma'am." Tom Farley gave her a satisfied nod and touched a callused finger to the brim of his cap.

Allison nodded, too, not trusting herself to speak.

Jake didn't acknowledge her further. He just walked away.

Allison turned her head and saw the others watching, their eyes friendly but inquisitive. She wondered how many of them were silently comparing her to Jake's wife. Even more, she wondered if Jake was doing the same thing.

"ALLISON? HELLO. It's me, Jenny."

"Jenny? Why are you calling me here?" Allison glanced at the mantel clock, an old-fashioned windup model, that had stopped days ago. She checked her watch. It was a little past eight-thirty. Bedtime for Mike and Libby. Past bedtime for Julia. But the littlest Walthers obviously wasn't in bed. Allison could hear snatches of her favorite *Winnie the Pooh* video playing in the background. And if that video was on, Julia was watching it.

"I...I was wondering if you were going to come

back tonight. I mean..." Jenny stumbled over her words, and Allison glanced out the window of her grandmother's darkened parlor. She could see the lights shining from the windows of Jake's house, warm against the cold dampness of the November night. "You weren't here when I got home and the kids are wondering..."

Obviously she hadn't been as good at pretending nothing had happened between her and Jake as she'd thought. Jake's neighbors had been friendly enough when they'd gathered in his kitchen for sandwiches and pie after the corn had been harvested. No one had acted as if her helping Jake was anything out of the ordinary although, of course, it was. When they left, the awkwardness, the awareness, between her and Jake had intensified, and she'd fled to the dubious serenity of her grandmother's house.

Julia's small piping voice could be heard quite clearly. "Let me talk to her, Jenny! Let me talk!"

Allison pictured Jenny's face and knew the effort it must have cost her to make this call. The atmosphere had been strained between them these past few days. Allison understood Jenny's resentment of her intrusion into their lives, but she wasn't certain how to deal with it.

"Julia wants to talk to you. Is that all right?"

Allison couldn't help smiling, couldn't keep the sound of it out of her voice. "Yes. Put her on."

"When are you coming back?" Julia asked without preamble. Allison had been away less than an hour.

"I want to show you my picture. I stayed in the lines. But Jenny's making me go to bed."

"You should already be in bed," Allison said gently.

"Don't want to go," Julia insisted.

"Of course you do."

"Come tuck me in."

"I'm... There are some things I have to take care of here," Allison stalled, but not without feeling some guilt. "Why don't you let Jenny tuck you in and you can show me your picture tomorrow morning."

"No."

"Sweetie, I'm busy." That wasn't quite true. She'd been doing nothing but standing in her grandmother's bedroom, her room for only a few more weeks, and staring at the summer clothes hanging in the closet, deciding what she would give to the Methodist church ladies for their fall rummage and bake sale this Saturday. All the time wondering how she could possibly go back to Jake's house and continue to care for him as though nothing had changed when it so obviously had.

"Allison?" It was Jenny's voice again. Allison wondered how long she'd been lost in her thoughts. "It's Jake...."

"What about Jake? Is he okay?"

"I don't know. I mean, he's acting a little weird. He...he's on his way over to your place."

"He's what?" Her heart started pounding.

"The kids are fussing and Jake's worried something happened to you."

"I've only been gone for an hour."

"I told him that." Jenny sounded exasperated. "I think it's starting to rain, Allison. And Jake won't let me help him with his coat."

Allison sighed. She couldn't run away from her problems. She should have learned that by now. She could handle this. She could cope. Her hand went instinctively to her pebble. She took a moment to savor its cool smoothness and draw deep, calming breaths into her lungs.

"Allison?"

"It's okay. Don't worry. I'll head Jake off."

It took her only a minute or two to turn off the lights and lower the temperature of the old hot-water furnace. She locked the door, pocketed the key and hurried out into the misty stillness, her footsteps silent on the wet grass. Jenny was wrong. It wasn't raining, but it was cold and there would be frost before morning. The road was a dark ribbon of asphalt, deserted at this time of night. She topped the slight incline on which it was built and spotted Jake on the other side as he moved out of the shadow of the house toward her. As Jenny had said, he wasn't wearing a coat, but he was wearing the sling to support his left arm.

"Go back," she called, a little breathless from hurrying and from the sexual awareness that refused to go away.

"I saw you coming, so I waited here for you. I wanted to make sure you were all right."

"You could have done that over the phone just the way Jenny did."

"Oh, hell, did she call you?"

Allison nodded. "I came to stop you. You shouldn't be out here. You aren't even—"

"I know," he said. And then he did something totally unexpected. He smiled, a real smile that crinkled the corners of his eyes and made goose bumps rise on her skin that had nothing to do with the cold. "I'm not wearing a coat. And I *am* freezing my tail off. But we need to talk and I don't want an audience." He stopped close to her. "I'm sorry for the way I behaved this afternoon, Allison. I'm not good at being on the receiving end of my neighbors' charity."

"No," she said. She wrapped her coat more tightly around her, as much to armor herself against his appeal as to ward off the cold. "That's not what it was." She had learned in rehab, and every day since, that she had to be honest with herself and with those around her.

His head came up. "What are you saying?"

"It wasn't because you were on the receiving end of your neighbors' charity. You would have done the same for them, and probably have. It was because I was there." She gestured toward his house. "Because I'm staying with you. Because today you realized I'm not just some kind of nuisance trying to interfere with your life. That I'm something more."

"I'm not sure what you mean," he said, a frown on his face.

"Out there in the parking lot, in front of your friends and neighbors, you realized you had a living, breathing woman staying in your house, a woman who wasn't your wife. Who wasn't Beth,'' she finished in a rush.

"You don't pull any punches do you?"

"I'm only speaking the truth."

"You're right. I'm sorry. I didn't think I was that obvious." His admission surprised her. "It wasn't your fault. Forgive me. I didn't mean to embarrass you in front of strangers."

"I think it's better if I don't spend any more nights at your place." She had been forced to learn about herself over the past seven months. And that hardwon knowledge told her she could never be indifferent to this man. He had the ability to knock her off center, to make her feel too many emotions—some of which she didn't even want to put a name to yet.

His mouth tightened. "Allison—"

"Daddy! Daddy! Come get me!" Julia was on the porch, barefoot and in her nightgown, hopping up and down. "I sawed you from the window."

"Go back inside, kitten," Jake commanded, swinging around to face his daughter.

"Pick me up. My toes are cold."

"I can't pick you up, kitten." She heard the desperation in his voice as the little girl began to whimper.

"I'm cold, Daddy. Pick me up."

"Allison, please." She saw the anguish and the helplessness in his night-shadowed eyes and she wanted to turn and run from the shock of longing she felt. Instead, she ignored all the warning signals shrieking inside her head and moved past him to gather Julia up in her arms.

"Let's go inside, sweetie. It's late, and you're supposed to be in bed."

"You stay with me."

"Yes, Allison." Jake hesitated only a moment on her name. "Please stay."

"I don't think that's wise."

"For the kids' sake. Not mine. I admit I'm not up to taking care of them alone yet."

Jake had used the one weapon she had no defense against. The children did need her, as unworthy as she might be of that responsibility, and there was no way she could refuse him.

"All right," she said, "I'll stay. For a little while longer."

CHAPTER FIVE

"WAKE UP, ALLISON. I'm hungry. I want cereal."

Allison came awake with a jerk, her heart pounding. She opened her eyes to a blaze of sunlight shining through the high, narrow window beside her bed. She'd slept through the night. She couldn't remember the last time that had happened.

"Wake up. I'm hungry." Julia was on the bed, her face only inches from Allison's ear.

Allison sat up so quickly her head swam.

Julia was obviously pleased to have gotten Allison's attention. She favored her with a megawatt smile. "I want my cereal. I'm being good."

"No, you are not," Allison said before she could censor her thoughts. "It's not polite to wake someone by yelling in her ear."

"I'm hungry," Julia repeated, her smile giving way to a pout. "Nobody else is around. Jenny and Libby and Mike went to school."

"I must have overslept," Allison said, feeling guilty and vaguely alarmed. What had come over her? She never overslept, not even after those nights she'd gone to bed drunk. And there had been more of them than she wanted to count. But today she'd overslept and Julia had been left alone with no one but Jake to look after her.

"Daddy said let you sleep."

"Where is your daddy?"

"Getting dressed." Julia began hopping up and down on the mattress on all fours. She was wearing Winnie the Pooh pajamas and her hair was in pigtails with wisps dancing around her ears. "I let you sleep for a long time."

Allison glanced at the bedside clock. It was only a little past eight. Jenny and the younger children boarded the school bus at seven-thirty. Her alarm usually went off at six-thirty, but last night she must have forgotten to set it. "Didn't Jenny give you cereal before she left?" Allison held out her hand to still Julia, but she hopped sideways out of reach and continued bouncing.

"Libby fixed me cereal, but I'm still hungry."

"I'll get you something to eat as soon as I'm dressed."

"Now!"

"Not until you say you're sorry for behaving so badly." Allison had never disciplined the little girl before. It wasn't really her place, but Julia was out of control this morning.

"Cereal. Get my cereal."

"Not until you stop bouncing on my bed and ask nicely for my help."

"You're mean." Julia sniffed, quick tears spilling onto her cheek. "I'm telling my daddy." She scooted off the bed and ran out of the room.

Immediately, Allison began to have second thoughts. She shouldn't have scolded Julia. She should have been more tactful, tried reasoning with her.

Allison drew her legs up to her chest and rested her chin on her knees. She caught herself up short. She was overreacting. She didn't have much experience with children, but even she knew there was very little chance of success in reasoning with a three-year-old. They needed guidance and limits and it was up to the adults in their lives to set those boundaries. And she was involved in Julia's life—even if it would only be for a short while longer.

"Julia's come to apologize." Allison lifted her head from her knees. Jake was standing in the doorway, holding his daughter by the hand. He looked down at the little girl. "Sometimes Julia forgets her manners. Tell Allison you're sorry, Julia."

"No," Julia said, her face pressed tight to Jake's thigh.

"It's all right." Allison wrapped her arms around her legs. Jake looked slightly rumpled and rakish and sexy with a night's growth of beard on his square jaw. She suspected she looked just plain rumpled.

"It isn't all right. I could hear her hollering even with the bathroom door closed. Julia, tell Allison you're sorry that you woke her up and were rude to her."

"I'm too hungry," she said in a muffled voice.

"You'll be even hungrier if you have to sit in the time-out chair for ten minutes."

"Don't want to," Julia cried, shooting Allison a dark glance.

"Then maybe next time you'll remember not to disturb Allison when she's sleeping." Jake spoke softly but with authority.

"I'm sorry. Won't do it again."

"Thank you, Julia." Allison focused on Julia's unhappy little face. She couldn't quite meet Jake's eyes.

"It's okay." Julia tried out a wobbly smile. "Will you get me some cereal now?"

Jake gave a bark of laughter and shook his head. "She's got a one-track mind. I'll get her something to eat and make us a pot of coffee."

"I can do that." Allison slid a foot out from under the covers, then stopped. She wasn't wearing anything but her panties and a T-shirt, and her housecoat was too far away to reach without getting out of bed.

Jake seemed to sense her discomfort, or maybe he felt some of his own. "I can manage," he said. "I feel better when I'm moving around, and there's no lifting involved in making a pot of coffee." He gave Julia's hand a little tug and they left the room.

Fifteen minutes later, Allison entered the kitchen at the back of the house. Julia was seated at the hand-crafted oak table in the sunny alcove near the back door. There was an empty cereal bowl in front of her and she was sitting with both elbows planted on the table, her chin propped between her hands.

"I want more," she said. Jake was standing with his back to Julia, a coffee cup in his hand, looking out the window. He'd managed to button his shirt and he was wearing his sling, but he still hadn't shaved, and when he turned to face the little girl a wave of dark brown hair fell stubbornly over his forehead.

"No more cereal or you'll be wound up all day. You can have half a banana if you're still hungry."

Jake had a quiet, loving rapport with his children. He never shouted or ranted yet always seemed to get his point across. It couldn't be easy for a man alone to raise three children. Harder even, she suspected, than being a single mom. She had barely known her own father, who'd left his family when she was ten to wander from job to job and state to state until he'd died of cirrhosis three years later. He hadn't been a presence in her life. He'd left her nothing but an empty place in her heart where a father's love should be—and a genetic inability to tolerate alcohol.

"Okay," Julia said, rising to her knees on the high-backed chair. "But can I eat it while I watch TV?"

"Okay. Can you turn on the set yourself?"

"Yep." She took a banana from the bowl of fruit in the middle of the table and slid off the chair. She handed the banana to Allison. "Peel this for me? Please," she added with a sidelong glance at her father.

"Of course."

Jake was silent while Allison dealt with the banana. Knowing he was watching made her feel awkward and clumsy. She sliced the banana as quickly as she could, put half in a small plastic bowl and handed it to the little girl.

"Thank you," Julia said, smiling once again. "Daddy, give me a kiss goodbye."

Jake's answering smile was genuine and breathtaking. "You're only going into the living room."

"I need a kiss."

Julia clearly wasn't going to change her mind, so Jake pulled out a chair and lowered himself stiffly onto it. "Come here, kitten, and get your kiss." He leaned forward, and Julia reached up on tiptoe to plant a noisy kiss on his cheek. Before she moved away, Jake cradled her head in his big work-roughened hand and touched his lips to her forehead.

Allison closed her eyes against the pang of longing that pierced her heart. This is what she'd expected her own marriage to hold—a loving husband, happy children and the simple joy of watching those children grow and prosper. She'd thought her ex-husband had wanted those same things when they'd married. But in the end he hadn't. Instead, by her thirtieth birthday—the date she'd set in her heart to start a family—she'd found herself divorced and alone.

And drinking heavily. A fact she'd hidden from her friends and co-workers for almost two years. Until Easter Sunday, when she'd very nearly caused serious injury to her cousin's little granddaughter. She had drunk far too much wine at dinner and then insisted on taking the child to an Easter egg hunt at a nearby park. She'd carried Mindy outside over her grandmother's protests, stumbled on the flagstone sidewalk and fallen. The toddler hadn't been harmed, but she so easily could have been. And that wine-blurred memory was still strong enough to cause Allison's stomach to churn with dread. It had been the lowest point of her life, and she had entered a detoxification and rehab program the next day.

"Daddy, you're scratchy." Julia's delighted laugh snapped the skein of Allison's thoughts. "You need to shave." Julia left the kitchen still giggling, carrying her bowl with careful concentration.

"She's like a different child." Allison took a bite of the remaining banana so she would have something to do with her hands. They were shaking from the force of her memories, and she didn't want Jake to see.

"Julia's a three-year-old. They're as changeable as the weather." He frowned and looked down at the coffee mug he held. "But she's been getting out of hand lately."

"It must be so hard for her. Have you been taking care of her all by yourself...since Beth died?"

"I try to keep her with me. When she was a baby, Mom came every day. She still helps out when I'm in the field, and Jenny's a brick."

"Julia's a bright child," Allison said. "She really needs more stimulation and structure to her routine. Maybe she should go to preschool."

Jake's frown deepened, and she knew she'd overstepped the boundary again.

"Since when are you an expert on kids?"

Allison didn't allow the pain his words caused her to show. "I'm not an expert. But it doesn't take an expert to see that Julia would benefit from being with children her own age more often.''

''That may be. But Beth wanted to stay at home with our kids, be a full-time mom. I wanted that, too. And we worked hard, did without a lot of things to make that possible.'' He walked over and dumped his coffee into the sink. ''Keeping Julia here with me is my way of keeping Beth's dream alive.'' His voice was rough with anger and grief. He turned back from the sink and she saw the bleakness in his eyes. ''Sending Julia off to day care every day would be one more piece of Beth I'd lose. One more of our hopes and dreams that I'd have to watch slip away. But I'm not going to do it. I'm damn well going to hold on to this one as long as I can.''

IT WAS THE SMELL of apple butter cooking that drew Allison into the farm store later. Jake had installed a state-of-the-art exhaust system in the deli kitchen and good smells were always wafting across the yard. It was cold and blustery and a light snow had dusted the brown fields. And she could hear the thud of an ax splitting wood somewhere far away.

Allison entered the store through the small side door and stood for a moment, trying to dissolve the knot of tension that had been building inside her since her confrontation with Jake. There had been no more strong words between them, no more mention of Julia's being sent to preschool. They had gone about the rest of the day as if nothing had happened, but for Allison it had been a strain.

Stella wasn't behind the counter, but her co-worker, Rosie Dachenhaus, was. "If you're looking for Stella, she's in the kitchen," Rosie said. She nodded and smiled pleasantly before she went back to work on the huge orange-and-gold plaid bow she was attaching to a cornhusk swag, heavy with gourds and miniature ears of red and blue Indian corn.

"Thank you." The swag would look great above the doorway of her grandmother's kitchen, Allison mused, relaxing a little more and feeling the need for a drink, which had been gnawing at her all afternoon, start to drain away. She watched Rosie for a moment longer, then moved away. The swag would be perfect for Thanksgiving, but she'd be back in Chicago by then and her grandmother's house would be empty. There was no place the swag would look right in her minimally furnished and professionally decorated Chicago condo. Reluctantly, she turned away.

Following the aroma of cooking apples, she walked from the lantern-glow ambiance of the gift shop into the brightly lit market section of the store. Allison had never tasted apple butter until a few weeks ago during Walnut Hill Farm's Apple Butter Fest. The children had come knocking at her kitchen door to give her a special invitation. The event was sponsored by the Riley Creek Historical Society, and people had come from miles around to watch how apple butter and cider were made. There were even rides through the woods in a wagon piled with straw and pulled by Jake's shaggy-coated Belgian draft horses, Nellie and Clara. The weather had cooperated perfectly—it had been a beautiful October Sunday, warm and sunny with just a hint of color in the leaves—and Allison had enjoyed every minute.

She thought about sending several jars of the apple butter to her co-workers at Tanner, Marsh and Fairchild, then realized she might as well wait because she'd be back there herself in only a couple of weeks. Allison skirted the pyramids of winter squash grouped in bins down the center aisle and passed the walk-in coolers filled with the Amish-style meat and chicken pies that were becoming the market's signature items to enter the kitchen through the swinging doors behind the meat counter.

"Hi, Stella. Oh! Hello, Tom." Allison was a little surprised to find Tom Farley in the deli kitchen, one hip propped against the deep double sinks, a cup of coffee in his hand. Stella was stirring a big stainless-steel kettle of apple butter on the industrial range.

"Hi, Allison." Tom gave her a friendly smile and lifted his cup in greeting. "Cold enough for you?"

Good manners required that a comment on the weather start every conversation in Riley Creek, Allison had learned early on in her visit. She shivered, shoving her hands deeper into the pockets of her jacket. "It feels like winter's here for sure."

Stella merely dipped her head in greeting. Her cheeks were red, and her lips were set in a tense line.

"More snow coming tonight." Tom set his cup down.

"That's what the weatherman said at noon," Allison replied. Stella remained silent. Evidently, Allison had walked in on something more serious than a discussion of the weather. "Am I interrupting?"

"No. Tom's just leaving," Stella said at last.

"We're finished talking," Tom said. "I've got to be moving along. Markets close in Chicago in an hour, and I need to check with my broker on wheat futures."

Allison glanced at the clock above the door. Tom was right, taking into account the time difference. The fund she managed didn't deal in grain or cattle futures, but not so long ago her entire life had revolved around the opening and closing of the stock markets not only in the U.S. but in Tokyo and Hong Kong and everywhere else in the world. She couldn't help asking, "Buying or selling?"

He grinned back at her before turning to empty the remains of his coffee into the sink. "A little of both. Small potatoes compared to what you're used to." He smiled more broadly as he made the pun, but Allison wasn't fooled by his facetious comment. There was a fierce, quiet pride in his eyes. He was proud of his farm, which, like Jake's, she knew had been in his family for four generations. She had seen that same look in Jake's eyes more than once this past week. "Can't just plow and plant and harvest anymore. Have to keep on your toes in this business."

"It's not a business," Stella muttered. "It's a gamble."

"Some of us like taking risks," Tom said, ignoring her bad temper. "Sure you won't change your mind about the movie Saturday night?"

"I told you, I'm busy Saturday night." Stella gave the bubbling kettle of apple butter such a vigorous swirl with her long-handled spoon that some of the dark brown sauce oozed over the rim and down the side to land with a sizzle on the open flame of the gas stove. "Damn," she said. "Look what you made me do."

"Think I'll mosey over to the house and see how Jake's feeling." Tom pulled a cap out of his back pocket and set it on his head.

"He's working in his office," Allison said, trying to break the tension that had settled over the room as thickly as the smell of burned apple butter.

"Maybe I can get him to take a break." Tom nodded goodbye and started toward the swinging doors.

"Julia's down for her nap," Allison cautioned.

"I promise to be real quiet." He touched his finger to the bill of his cap and disappeared from view.

Stella kept on stirring.

"I'm sorry I interrupted your conversation," Allison said, taking Tom's place at the big sinks.

"Don't be sorry. I've been trying to get him to leave for the past fifteen minutes. The man just won't take no for an answer." Stella turned away from the kettle and began removing sterilized jars from a big Dutch oven on the back burner of the stove. She set the old-fashioned jelly jars carefully on a stainless steel cart and started ladling apple butter into them.

"I think he cares for you," Allison said. She'd kept her feelings inside for most of her life, and that reticence had contributed to her drinking problem. She didn't want to see anyone else suffer as she had. Especially Stella, whom she considered a friend. And in the male-dominated world of finance that she lived in, she didn't have many of those. "I take it you don't feel the same way."

"I do care for him. That's the problem."

"He seems to be a good man."

"He's a farmer," Stella said as if that settled the matter. "I won't have another farmer." She wiped the edge of the jars with a clean cotton cloth and then screwed on the lids.

"I don't understand."

"My late husband was a farmer," Stella said. "We lost our farm in the early eighties when times were really bad around here. He couldn't accept the fact the farm that had been in his family for a hundred years was gone. He couldn't find work. One day, he went out into the garage and shot himself with his daddy's rifle. He left me with barely enough money to pay for his funeral and three kids to raise myself. It wasn't easy, but I did it. Got two of them through college and the youngest is a junior at Ohio State. When she graduates, I'm out of here. I'm going—" she stopped abruptly "—I'm going where it's always sunny and there are bright lights and lots of restaurants. Where no one has ever seen a soybean in its natural state. I don't care if I ever set foot in Riley Creek again in my life."

"But you have friends here. Riley Creek's your home."

"I didn't say I wouldn't miss the place some. But not enough to stay."

Allison had dreamed of a husband and children and a home in a place like Riley Creek, fantasies built on memories of long-ago visits to her grandmother and a deep and heartfelt longing for roots. Stella had lived that dream and lost it, and she didn't want to try for it again.

"And Tom?" Allison asked softly. She realized now she hadn't come in on just any conversation but a lovers' quarrel.

"I won't fall in love with another farmer," Stella said bluntly. "Didn't I just say that? He's as rooted to this place as deeply as one of those oaks in your grandma's front yard. If times get bad again, I can't be sure he wouldn't react the same way my husband did. I won't take that chance." She set one of the jars down so hard the others rattled in protest.

Allison wanted to tell her that all of life was a risk, but she wasn't certain how to say it without admitting to her own problems. She had never been comfortable turning the focus of a conversation on herself, but she'd learned it was necessary sometimes. Allison looked down at the water-smoothed pebble she hadn't even realized she'd taken from her pocket. Maybe now was one of those times.

"Stella!" Jenny poked her head around the edge of the swinging door. "Help me. I'm desperate."

Allison and Stella turned in unison. Jenny didn't look desperate. She looked as happy as Allison had seen her since Jake's fall. She was smiling, really smiling, a feminine version of her brother's devastatingly sexy grin.

"Desperate about what?" Stella asked, apparently unfazed by the pleading in Jenny's voice.

"I have to get to the mall in Lima. Today. Now." Lima, a city of about forty thousand people, was an hour's drive west of Riley Creek.

"What for?"

"I *have* to buy a dress."

"What for?" Stella repeated, her frown giving way to a wary grin that crinkled the corners of her eyes and made her look ten years younger.

"I'm going to be Freshman Harvest Dance attendant. Marcie Courtney failed two midterms and her mother grounded her. I was runner-up. The dance is Friday night and I'll curl up and die of shame if I don't get a new dress."

"Wear your confirmation dress," Stella suggested.

"That old thing? No way. I've just got to get to the mall and Jake can't drive yet. Can you take me?"

"Sorry, Jenny. Not tonight. Tonight's the night the Altar and Rosary Society meets and I'm president."

"Then I'll call Aaron."

Stella snorted. "Good try. That's a date in Jake's book and you know he won't allow a date on a school night. Can't this wait until tomorrow? I could probably take you then."

"I'll drive you," Allison said, folding her fingers around the smoothness of her stone. "I'd be happy to." Maybe this was a chance to put their still tenuous relationship on a more solid footing.

"I..." Jenny's smile faltered just a bit, then returned. "Thank you, Allison. Thank you very much," she said politely. "Would you mind if I asked a friend to come along?"

CHAPTER SIX

THE SHOPPING TRIP turned out to be quite an adventure. Jenny invited not one but two of her friends, then Libby and Julia got into the act, demanding to be included. When it became apparent that it would take five females to purchase one dress, evening bag and pair of shoes for Jenny, Jake suggested she drive his van. Allison accepted the offer since there was simply no way all of them and Julia's car seat would fit into her Lexus.

Salads and sandwiches at the mall fast-food court would take care of dinner. Jake and Michael were left to fend for themselves, and when Allison and the girls headed out the door, they were busy adding their own special toppings to a frozen pizza and discussing whether to watch a video or the sports channels on satellite TV.

Allison enjoyed the drive to the mall. The roads were dry and clear of the light snow that had fallen earlier in the day. The three teenagers in the back were chatty but not too loud—at least not loud enough to be heard over the Garth Brooks tape they'd popped in the player before they'd left the driveway—until in the sudden silence between songs, she heard Aaron Masterson's name in combination with the words "drinking" and "beer." Allison glanced into the rearview mirror, meeting Jenny's eyes for a split second before the girl turned away to hush her friends. Had she heard correctly? Was Jenny becoming involved with a boy who was already into drinking and who knew what other risky behavior?

Allison was all too aware exactly how dangerous underage drinking could be. She had started drinking at the age of sixteen. She was torn between saying nothing and requesting an explanation for what she'd heard, ruining not only the shopping trip but any progress she'd made in her relationship with Jake's sister. But Garth started another song and a huge corn picker loomed out of the darkness ahead of them on the county highway, and by the time Allison had maneuvered safely around the hulking machine, the moment to confront Jenny and her friends had passed.

They all vowed to remember where they parked the van, and since Julia was too hungry to be put off for very long, they ate first and discussed what kind of dress Jenny would look for. The consensus was that it had to be sexy enough to knock Aaron Masterson's eyes right out of his head, even though her escort for the evening was actually another freshman, Sam Watchman. Sam was okay, at least two inches taller than Jenny, but "just a boy." No way did he compare to Aaron Masterson, a senior who was on the football and basketball teams and drove his own truck. Allison bent her head over her fries to keep her smile hidden.

Jenny also lamented the fact that Jake had given

her what she considered far less money than necessary for the purchase of such a dress. Allison didn't have to say anything to counter Jenny's remark; Libby beat her to it. "Dad gave you a hundred and fifty dollars!" Her eyes were round with incredulity. "I saw him count it out. That's a *lot* of money."

Julia nodded wisely in agreement. "A lot," she echoed, her mouth full of a chicken nugget.

Jenny made a face as she poked through her salad to find the bits of hard-boiled egg. "Not when you have to buy a dress and shoes."

"And a purse." This from Ashley Reimund, the granddaughter of Jake's neighbors.

"And a push-up bra," Maria Pedroza added, with a naughty grin. "Or maybe even a strapless one, if the dress is really, really hot."

Libby snorted inelegantly. "A strapless bra. That's a good one. Jenny doesn't even have boobs."

"I do, too."

"Do not."

"Do, too," Jenny fired back before she remembered she was too old to trade insults with an eight-year-old. "Be quiet or I'll make you sorry you came along," she threatened.

"I think we'd better finish up here and get started," Allison said with the same firm voice she used to quell boardroom discussions that were in danger of getting out of hand. "I want to have Julia and Libby home by nine."

Maria glanced at her watch. "Then we'd better move."

"Let's try that great little boutique down by Penney's," Ashley suggested. "They have the most adorable clothes."

"Didn't you hear?" Maria said, dumping the remains of her hamburger and fries in the waste bin beside their table. "They're going out of business."

"Oh, no. I love that place."

"But they're having a great sale. Let's check it out."

"Ready, Julia?" Allison asked, wiping ketchup off the little girl's chin.

"Uh-huh. What's a push-up bra?"

"Will everyone kindly stop talking about my underwear?" Jenny demanded. "It's gross."

"No boobs," Libby muttered, then sucked very noisily on her soft drink to drown out any retaliatory words from her aunt.

Julia took Allison's hand without a moment's hesitation as they started down the concourse toward the boutique, their altercation of the morning long forgotten. Allison didn't think Jake would forgive her well-intentioned interference as quickly as Julia had. Libby hesitated only a heartbeat or two longer before she, too, slipped her hand into Allison's.

"I'd like to stop at the bookstore if we have time," she said shyly. "I like to look at the books."

"We'll make time," Allison assured her, smiling down at the child. She used to walk like this with her little cousin, before that disastrous Easter Sunday. For a moment, a panicky ripple of nerves raised the hair on her arms. Maybe Jake was right. She didn't know enough about raising a child to offer him advice. And there was still the specter of her alcoholism hanging over her, shadowing everything she did. What if she lost control and harmed a child, or another person, or even herself.

"Oh, God, Jenny. Look at that dress in the window. It is so hot. It's you," Maria squealed, clutching Jenny's arm. They'd arrived at the store and Allison hadn't even noticed. "Try it on, girl. Try it on."

"I don't know..." Jenny stopped in front of the plate-glass window of the boutique. A Going Out of Business sign obscured half the display area, but in the other half a cadaverous mannequin was dressed in a short—very short—satiny black tube dress with spaghetti straps and a scandalously low neckline accented by fiery red sequins.

"Everything's fifty percent off." Ashley pointed to another, smaller sign. "Think of all the money you'll save. At least try it on."

"It is beautiful," Jenny breathed, unable to take her eyes off the dress.

"Come on. See how it looks," Ashley urged, leading the way into the half-empty store.

Allison didn't know what to say. The dress was totally unsuitable for a girl Jenny's age. Especially to wear to a dance held in the Riley Creek High gymnasium and chaperoned by the Lutheran minister and his wife. It was by far too tacky and cheap-looking. But Allison was not Jenny's mother or even an older sister. She was only a neighbor who had volunteered to drive her to the mall. She could only hope the dress didn't fit.

But it did. And it was perfect or it would be, according to Maria, once Jenny bought a strapless bra and a pair of spiky black heels. When Jenny emerged from the changing room in the dress, with her hair pulled high on her head in what Allison was convinced the three teens considered a sophisticated swirl, there was a flush of excited color in her cheeks.

"What do you think, Allison?" Jenny asked, looking at herself in the mirror. She shifted this way and that, observing the effect of the light catching the satin at her every movement, accentuating her slight curves. It was obvious Jenny had fallen in love with the dress. "It's beautiful and it's on sale." A fact that appealed to Jenny's deep-rooted practicality.

"It's a little…too formal…for the Harvest Dance, isn't it?" she suggested tentatively. Allison was used to navigating the treacherous waters of high finance where millions of dollars were at stake with every decision she made. But this was different. This was the ego of a fifteen-year-old girl who was going to her first grown-up dance.

"Oh, no," Ashley gushed. "It's just perfect. Jenny, you look at least eighteen!"

Inwardly, Allison groaned. That was the clincher. She didn't have a chance of talking Jenny out of the dress now. Even though she gave it her best shot when she saw the All Sales Final sign at the cash register.

Jenny did pass on the stiletto sandals Maria urged

on her when Allison pointed out that if she wore her hair up—an absolute *must*—four-inch heels would make her half a head taller than her escort, and more importantly, an inch taller than Aaron Masterson. Jenny chose black velvet pumps instead, and Allison sighed with relief. Ashley ferreted out a black satin purse with a rhinestone clasp that was twenty percent off. And because they'd gotten such a bargain on the dress, Jenny had enough money to buy the strapless push-up bra Maria insisted was necessary to complete the look.

They stopped for a Coke and fries at the drive-through window at McDonald's, and the girls giggled and whispered in the back seat of the van all the way home. But Allison heard no other mention of Aaron Masterson or drinking. Libby curled up on the bench seat beside Julia and went to sleep, still clutching the picture book of fairy tales Allison had bought her. Julia stayed awake all of five minutes longer, humming to herself and playing with the knockoff fashion doll she'd purchased in the dollar store with money she'd sweet-talked out of her father.

Allison still thought the dress was not a good choice for Jenny, but she also knew she could have talked the girl out of it if she'd tried. The truth was she'd been enjoying herself too much to play the bad guy. She'd never really had girlfriends herself. There'd been no one to go shopping with, to giggle with, to talk about boys and the mysteries of sex and what the future held. She'd been too studious, too focused on making good grades and getting a full scholarship to the University of Chicago business school so her mother could stop working two jobs to keep her in the prestigious private school where she had always felt out of place—the poor scholarship girl dropped among the daughters of Chicago's elite.

Jenny moved into the front seat of the van after they dropped off Ashley and Maria at their homes. She was still talkative, still full of excitement and the wonderful sense of accomplishment that came from finding the bargain of a lifetime.

"I have twenty-five dollars left," she said, sliding down in the bucket seat and propping her sneakered feet on the dash. "Jake will like that." She sounded very pleased with herself.

"You're a good bargain hunter," Allison said, smiling.

"I get that from my mom. She never, *ever* pays full price for anything." Jenny smiled and laid her head against the back of the seat. "I'll be glad when they get home. I miss them."

"You've taken on a lot of responsibility the past couple of years."

Jenny was immediately on the defensive. "I love Jake's kids," she said, her smile disappearing in an instant. "And I loved Beth. She was like my own sister. I would have done anything for her. Taking the best care of the kids I can is my tribute to her. That and not letting them forget her."

And keeping Jake's loss achingly alive, even though it was time for him to move on?

Allison believed that with her whole heart but knew

she couldn't say it. "It's a wonderful, loving thing to do. I don't think you could have found a more meaningful way to honor Beth's memory."

"Thanks," Jenny said, then turned her head and looked out the window, not saying anything more.

Jenny prodded Libby awake when they pulled into Jake's garage and made her help carry packages. Allison unbuckled Julia from her car seat and lifted her into her arms. It never failed to amaze her how good it felt to carry the little girl. Julia didn't wake up, just turned her face into Allison's neck, her soft breath tickling.

"I'll take Julia upstairs and tuck her in."

"Thanks. I want to try on my dress for Jake," Jenny said, her eyes shining in the glow of the porch light. "Then I'm going to call Mom and tell her what a bargain I got. I wish they'd be home in time for the dance, but Dad's doctor wanted him to stay in Florida until after Thanksgiving. He works too hard at harvest time and all that dust and dirt and chemicals aren't good for him."

"Take lots of pictures," Allison suggested.

"Yeah, and I'll ask Jake if I can borrow the video camera. Are you sure you don't want me to help you tuck Julia in?"

"No, I'll be happy to do it." It was the first time Jenny had willingly delegated the task to Allison.

Libby had already opened the door and gone inside the kitchen. Allison followed, stopping just over the threshold, blinking as a rush of light and warm air spiraled out to meet her. Julia stirred but didn't waken at the sound of the food processor Mike was operating at the kitchen island.

"Shut it off, Mike," Jake cautioned his son, turning away from the sink where he was straining cooked pumpkin though a colander. He was surrounded by baking pans and discarded pieces of pumpkin shell.

"Pumpkin?" Allison asked, putting a name to the pungent, slightly earthy smell that filled the kitchen.

"For the Thanksgiving pies," Mike explained. "We use the leftover pumpkins from Halloween."

"Family tradition. My dad usually does this," Jake said, wiping his hands on a kitchen towel he'd stuck in the back pocket of his jeans. "He always makes the pumpkin pies from scratch. I don't have his touch with pastry dough," he said with a grin that twisted one corner of his mouth a little higher than the other and sent Allison's pulse racing. There were still pain lines around his mouth, but his color had improved and he was moving more easily than before. "But since Mom and Dad aren't due home until the week after Thanksgiving, I'll give it my best shot this year."

"Grandpa's pies are awesome," Mike informed Allison.

"Awesome," Julia mumbled against her throat.

Allison smiled. "I think I'd better get her to bed."

"And I'm going to go try on my new dress for you guys," Jenny said breezily as she headed for her bedroom carrying her packages.

"I got a new book," Libby said, holding up her

treasure and taking an uncertain step toward Jake. She was still half-asleep, her blue eyes glazed.

"We'll read it tomorrow night," Jake said, smoothing her tumbled curls. "Sleep tight, Bug."

"Night, Daddy."

"Mike, you'd better be heading upstairs, too."

"But I'm not done grinding up my pumpkin guts."

"They aren't pumpkin guts," Jake said. "And the term is puree."

"Hammerhead would call them pumpkin guts."

"That isn't very appetizing."

Mike lifted the lid off the food processor and took a sniff. "*This* isn't very appetizing."

"It will be when I get done with it. Now off to bed. There's school tomorrow and it's after nine."

"I'll be back down as soon as they're tucked in," Allison said after Libby and the reluctant Mike left the kitchen.

"Thanks for taking Jenny and the girls shopping tonight."

Allison considered saying something about Jenny's dress—to prepare Jake for it. But didn't. Maybe she was being too critical. Maybe Jake wasn't as conservative as she'd thought him. Maybe he wouldn't find the low-cut dress objectionable. Fat chance! "Jake—"

"Daddy! Mike's got my new book. He won't give it back." Libby's anguished cry echoed down the stairs. Jake took a step toward the living room.

"Never mind. I'll take care of it," Allison said, whisking out of the room with Julia still cuddled in her arms. A sibling brawl in progress upstairs wouldn't help the sibling brawl that was about to occur downstairs.

The kids were all tired, even Mike, and they were bundled into pj's and in their beds in less than ten minutes. But even though she'd hurried as fast as she could, steering Julia through the bathroom, helping Libby find her school clothes for the next morning and turning Mike's light out for him, she still wasn't back down in time to avert the disaster she'd feared from the moment Jenny had set eyes on the black dress.

"You are *not* wearing that dress to the Harvest Dance." Jake was standing with his back to the kitchen counter, his arms folded across his chest. "Mom and Dad would have a fit if I let you be seen in public in that getup."

"You don't know any such thing!"

"Oh, yes, I do." He took a deep breath. "It's much too old for you. I'll drive you back to the mall tomorrow to exchange it."

"You're not supposed to drive." Jenny put her hands on her hips, hiking the short skirt even higher on her slender hips.

Jake's mouth tightened into a thin, straight line. "I'll get you there," he said shortly.

Jenny tossed her head. "I can't take it back. It was on sale. No refunds. It says so right on the receipt. Doesn't it, Allison?"

"Yes," Allison said, wishing she was somewhere else, wishing she'd taken the time to warn Jake.

He turned on her. "Why in hell did you let her buy such a trashy-looking dress?"

"It's not trashy. It's *hot*," Jenny wailed, sounding more like Libby than she would ever admit.

"It's trashy."

"I'm sorry you don't find the dress suitable...." Allison began diplomatically.

"You shouldn't have let her buy it," Jake stated bluntly, fixing her with an angry gaze.

"Allison didn't want me to buy it," Jenny said, unexpectedly coming to her defense. Tears shimmered in her blue eyes, eyes so like Jake's. "She tried to talk me out of it. But it was so...elegant. And I want to look special. I'm second choice for freshman attendant—everyone knows that. I want to knock their eyes out."

"You will in that thing," Jake said, but his voice had softened. "I'm sorry, Jenny. You can't wear it."

"Allison..." Jenny looked at her in despair. "What can I do? I don't have enough money left."

"There's your confirmation dress," Jake reminded her.

"No." This time, Jenny did start to cry.

Jake looked bewildered by his sister's tears. "You look very nice in that dress."

"It's my *confirmation* dress." For Jenny that said it all.

"Then you'll have to stay home."

"I will not." Jenny fled the room, and a few seconds later they heard the bathroom door slam.

Jake shook his head. "I didn't handle that very well, did I?"

"You two sounded exactly like Mike and Libby quarreling over a toy."

His head came up slightly. "I didn't know you were an expert on teenage girls."

"I used to be one." Allison stood her ground. Jake had a forceful personality and was sure of himself and his actions in most things, but he didn't have a clue about how to handle the emotions of a fifteen-year-old.

"Jenny is my sister."

"Jenny is a woman."

"She's still just a girl."

"Not in this day and age."

Jake digested that, but she could tell by the set of his mouth he wasn't going to back down. "My sister is not wearing that dress to the Harvest Dance. She looks like a hooker. I'll take her to the store tomorrow. Going out of business or not, they'll take that dress back. She's a minor. They took advantage of her."

"They didn't. The clerk explained the no-return policy. Jenny was determined to have that dress and no other."

"Then it will just have to hang in the closet until hell freezes over."

"Jake, please. You're handling this all wrong. I think I can—"

He moved so quickly she didn't have time to get out of his way. His hands shot out and wrapped around her upper arms, just below the shoulder. His touch wasn't gentle, but it didn't hurt. "This is the second time today you've lectured me about my relationship with my family. I'm raising my kids the best damned way I know how. I'm handling *this* fiasco the best damned way I know how. That's what I do with everything that comes up around here. I try to handle it. I try to get through one damned day after the other. It's hard, damned hard. But it's living and it sure as hell beats the alternative. You wouldn't know anything about that, would you, Ms. High-and-Mighty Stock Market Wizard?"

"I know," she said quietly, seeing the misery and loss lurking just below the anger in his eyes.

His grip tightened for a moment, the space of a heartbeat or two. He leaned closer, his breath warm on her face. The anger went out of him as quickly as it had come. "How do you know?" he asked, his voice surprisingly gentle.

Tell him, her heart whispered, *tell him why you know.* But she couldn't be that selfish. It was Jenny's happiness that mattered now, not her own.

"It's not important now. What's important is Jenny." She could see the fine lines that crinkled the corners of his eyes, lines that testified to days spent out in the sun and wind. This close, she noticed a hint of auburn fire in his dark hair. He needed a haircut and she longed to reach up and run her fingers through the slight wave above his ear. She took a deliberate step backward, away from his heat and her need to be warmed by it.

Jake was looking at her mouth as though he wanted to kiss her, and heaven help her, she wanted him to. No one had looked at her that way in a long, long time. She didn't want to fight with him. She didn't want him to be angry with her. She wanted to help him, console him. She wanted him to want her just as badly. She swallowed hard, made herself take a deep, steadying breath. Jake blinked, looking slightly dazed. He, too, moved back, a hasty step that put more distance between them.

"I'm sorry. That's twice today I've taken out my bad temper on you. It must be the damned pain pills."

Or was it because she had made him face issues he wasn't willing to deal with?

"I... I'll make it right with Jenny," he said. "But the dress—"

"I'll help with the dress." Allison knew her voice had a hollow ring. She'd seen the truth in his eyes when he'd stared at her. Just as it had happened on Sunday, she'd seen the exact moment he'd realized he was arguing with a woman, feeling passion for a woman, about to kiss a woman—a woman who wasn't Beth. "I think I can fix it. Make it more suitable. I'll try to get Jenny to let me work on it tomorrow."

"Thanks." He shoved his hands in his pockets. He had shut himself away, sealed himself off from whatever emotions he'd experienced. "I'll go try to talk her out of the bathroom. I'll tell her you'll help her. And Allison...?"

"Yes."

"Thanks for coming to my rescue. Again."

CHAPTER SEVEN

"YOU LOOK FINE, GIRL." Maria was staring at her with a big smile plastered on her face.

"It can't be the same dress." Ashley was grinning too, shaking her head in wonder.

"It's the same dress." Jenny turned to look at herself in the wavy mirror that hung over the tiny fireplace in Allison's grandmother's front room. Rufina Bremer had never called this her living room, always the front room or the parlor. Jenny remembered that from when she had visited the old lady when she was a little girl, not much bigger than Julia.

She swiveled left and then right, checking herself out. It was the same black dress, all right. At least most of it was, but it was also very...different. A whole knot of cold, ugly tightness that had curled around her heart and stomach ever since she'd brought it home two days ago started to unwind and melt away. "Thank you, Allison."

"You're welcome." Allison got up from the old-fashioned dining room table where she'd been working on the dress on her grandmother's little black sewing machine. Jenny had been skeptical when Jake told her Allison could fix the dress. She'd never expected someone like Allison with a big-time job that made big-time money would know how to sew.

"It's awesome. Like some kind of designer dress right from New York or Paris." Ashley perched herself gingerly on the very edge of the hard-cushioned velvet couch.

"That's where Allison got the idea," Jenny couldn't help boasting. "She has a Bonnetti just like it."

"A genuine Reynoldo Bonnetti? He's the hottest designer in New York." Ashley was addicted to fashion magazines. She was always checking them out of the library and going on and on about this or that designer, and the fashion shows in Paris and New York

"A real Bonnetti?" Ashley was staring at Allison, openmouthed. "It must have cost a fortune."

"Ashley." Maria warned. "That's rude."

"Sorry." Ashley shrugged. "It's really bitchin'. I wish I could wear it." She stared ruefully down at the last bite of the Snickers bar she held in her hand. "Well, one like it in a size 12," she said, and smiled a little sheepishly.

"I can't believe you found the stuff to fix it at Hagemeyer's." Maria walked a circle around Jenny, her head tilted to one side, her brown eyes round with amazement.

Hagemeyer's was the dry goods store in town. They sold a lot of fabric, mostly cottons in little patterns and plain colors for the quilts that the various church organizations made to raise money. But Jenny had forgotten they also carried more expensive fabrics for wedding gowns and prom dresses because she never went in there unless her mother made her.

Allison had taken her there yesterday after school. Jenny had figured it was a wasted trip. She'd wanted to go back to the mall and try the sewing store there, but she'd been afraid to say so for fear Jake would just make her return the dress. And she would have died of embarrassment if that had happened. So in the end, she hadn't had much choice. But, thanks to Allison, it had all worked out. She'd helped Jenny, just as Beth would have.

Sometimes Allison reminded her a little of her dead sister-in-law. Not in her appearance. They didn't look the same at all—Beth had been blond and round and cuddly, while Allison was tall and a little on the skinny side with beautiful red-gold hair—but in other ways they were alike. Allison never raised her voice or scolded for no reason. She listened to your opinion, then gave her own. She explained why she wanted something done and she asked you, never just told you to do it. She treated you like a grown-up, and Jenny knew Beth would have done the same.

Allison had found a white ruffled organdy trim that she said was just what she wanted. Jenny had gritted her teeth, unable to picture how six yards of that stuff was going to fix her dress. She had begun to trust Allison's judgment and style so she'd tried to smile and look enthusiastic, but inside she'd been really nervous, picturing herself being introduced at the Harvest Dance in her confirmation dress with all the other kids snickering behind her back.

Allison had carefully removed the red sequins from the satin band and replaced them with two rows of the stiff organdy. Jenny had watched silently, then had obediently put on the push-up bra and tried on the dress. The bra and the ruffles made Jenny's boobs look bigger and covered just a little more skin. Jenny didn't mind that if she told the truth, and it didn't look bad. The contrast between the black satin and the white organdy was striking and very grown-up looking. Far more sophisticated than she could have possibly hoped for. That's when she'd started to believe Allison could pull it off.

An hour ago, while she'd been trying on the dress, Maria's brother had dropped her and Ashley off, and they'd waited while Allison had added two more rows of the trim to the bottom to give the dress some length. "Enough to satisfy your brother's reactionary standards," Allison had said with a smile that was more mischievous than any Jenny remembered having seen before.

Now Jenny just stared at herself in the mirror. She did look great. She was going to knock Aaron Masterson dead. Not to mention Sam Watchman. But he was just a freshman and already had a crush on Melinda Rohrs, so he didn't count.

"I didn't think you could do it," she said, turning to Allison with a sheepish smile. "I didn't think someone like you, someone who had enough money to buy a real Bonnetti, could *sew*."

Allison just laughed. "I went to a Catholic girls' school. Everyone had to learn the basics, but you're right. I never had time to sew in Chicago."

"Now all you need is black net stockings," Maria suggested.

Allison answered before Jenny could open her mouth to speak. "I don't think so. With a Bonnetti, less is always better. What do you think, Ashley?"

Ashley blushed a little, pleased to be consulted. She was silent a moment, considering her answer. "Sheer black stockings," she agreed. "Silk if you can get them."

Maria snorted. "In Riley Creek?"

"They have some that look like silk at Hagemeyer's. I'll get those," Jenny said, determined to give her hometown store a second chance. She spun around. "I have to show this to Jake. He won't believe it's the same dress."

"He's at the store," Ashley informed her. "We saw him go in with Julia when Lupe dropped us off."

A horn sounded in the driveway. "And there he is back again. C'mon, Ashley. Lupe can't be late for work again. He'll drive off and leave us if we keep him waiting." Maria hastily threw on her coat. "Thank you for inviting us into your home, Ms. Martin." Maria had the best manners of any of them.

"Yes, thank you," Ashley seconded hastily.

"You're very welcome, and please call me Allison."

"Okay, Allison. Later, Jen." They headed into the kitchen and out the back door.

"Will you come to the store with me to show Jake the dress?" Jenny hadn't been very nice to Allison at first and she regretted her behavior. Allison was a friend, and a good one. She'd proved that by fixing the dress. Jenny smiled and spread her hands to show off Allison's creation. "Jake will have a cow when he sees how great this dress turned out."

Allison laughed. "That I have to see. And if Maria saw him go over there an hour ago, I think I'd better go along just to rescue him from Julia."

"Oh, sh—" Jenny clapped her hand over her mouth. "Sorry! Julia will have the doll display ruined by now. She never leaves them alone. Stella probably had to tie her to a chair to make her behave."

"Better change your shoes," Allison cautioned as she took her coat off a peg on the kitchen wall and handed Jenny hers. "You'll scuff the heels in the parking lot."

"Yeah." Jenny hadn't thought of that. She didn't wear heels often. She didn't find them all that comfortable, but they did make her legs look longer, and for some reason guys thought they were hot.

She slipped out of the velvet pumps and wiggled into her sneakers. She didn't bother to tie the laces, and Allison, cool woman, didn't say a word about it.

"What is it with guys and high heels anyway?" She spoke her thoughts aloud, dangling the footwear from two fingers. She'd never have the nerve to ask her mother a question like that. But Allison was way younger than her mom. She might know.

"Fantasies," Allison said, opening the back door.

It took Jenny a moment to figure out what Allison was alluding to. Then she felt her face turn red and wished she hadn't said anything. But Allison was smiling at her as if they were two girlfriends talking about guys, not a woman stuck with giving a birds-and-bees speech to a dorky teenager. She remembered what she'd been thinking—about the shoes making her legs look longer. Guys were a hundred times worse about stuff like that. A thought popped into her head. "They probably all wish we'd been born with Barbie doll feet."

Allison laughed. A real laugh, soft and merry. It echoed across the yard and over the frozen fields like sleigh bells ringing on a snowy day. "Exactly," she said. "I think you've solved one of the mysteries of the universe, and before your sixteenth birthday, too. I am impressed. Jenny, you are a very smart lady." They were still laughing when they walked into the barn.

"OH, DADDY! JENNY LOOKS like a princess." Julia was dancing around the gift shop, endangering the bisque figurines on the lighted display case behind her. Stella had given her a caramel apple a while ago and she was on a sugar rush of monumental proportions. He'd barely gotten her to stand still long enough to wash the sticky residue from her hands and face. There was no way he could get her down for a nap. She grabbed his hand and pointed toward the door. "Look!"

Jake turned. Jenny was standing on one foot putting

on a pair of black heels. She was wearing her Riley Creek letter jacket, but she slipped it off and handed it to Allison as he watched.

"What do you think?" she asked, spinning around.

He just stood there. *God, Jenny was growing up. She looked like a woman, a very lovely woman, not his gawky baby sister.*

"I—I'm going to wear my hair up. And Maria's mom has a rhinestone choker and earrings she's going to lend me. Allison says that shouldn't be too much. Jake?"

"Where did you get that dress?"

"It's the same dress, Jake." Jenny giggled. "You said Allison would fix it and she did. It looks like a Bonnetti now. She has one just like it back home in Chicago."

"A Bonnetti?" He'd been on his feet for over an hour. His ribs hurt, he was cold and hungry and he'd never heard of a Bonnetti, whatever that was.

"He's an Italian designer," Allison said.

"Naturally." The word came out pretty close to a snarl.

"I—I needed it for my work. I have obligations." She stopped talking and shut her mouth, her lips thinning.

"I'm sure you do." He was acting like a jackass again. It seemed he couldn't say two words to her without insulting her or causing an argument. What the hell was the matter with him? He wished he could still blame his poor judgment on the painkillers, but he hadn't had a pill for six hours.

"Jake? My dress."

He tore his eyes away from Allison's flushed face and concentrated on his sister's shining one. What business was it of his if Allison had half a dozen Italian designer dresses in her closet in Chicago? She probably did need them to entertain the financial hot-shots she worked with. He ignored the jabs of pain Julia's swinging on his arm caused and kept talking. "It's great. It's hard to believe it's the same dress."

"Allison bought the trim at Hagemeyer's and took those awful sequins off the dress and—" she twirled around again "—here I am. Isn't it elegant?"

"It certainly is."

"You look like a princess," Julia agreed. "But I like the red sparklies. I want them to make a pretty dress for my doll." She stuck out her lower lip and started swinging again.

Allison must have noticed the pain that was causing him because she held out her arms. "Come here, sweetie. I still have the red sparklies."

"How did you get them off the dress?" It was a stupid question, but he felt stupid at the moment, blindsided by Jenny's transformation from duckling to swan, and by the woman standing beside her. Allison made his heart beat hard and his gut tighten. He wasn't used to feeling like this about any other woman but Beth.

"A very sharp pair of scissors and a great deal of patience," Allison said, lifting Julia up into her arms. "Have you been good while I was busy with Jenny's dress?"

Julia wouldn't meet Allison's eyes. She reached out toward her aunt and touched her fingertip to the stiff white organdy ruffle that rimmed the neckline of the dress. "I was good," she said slyly. "Real good."

"Julia?"

"I didn't break nothing."

Allison laughed, and the sound was sweet and clear and sexy. She rubbed noses with the little girl. "I'm glad to hear that."

"Sounds like another miracle to me. C'mon, brat," Jenny said. "Let's go show Stella my dress."

"Okay." Julia's smile came out again like the sun coming out from behind a storm cloud. "She's in the kitchen. I'm hungry. I smell cookies."

"You can't be hungry again," Jake said.

"I am."

"Make sure she doesn't have any more sweets, Jen," Jake said.

"Will do. No, Julia. I'm not carrying you. You'll muss my dress. Walk. You're a big girl. Where are Libby and Mike?" Jenny asked, taking Julia's hand after Allison set her down.

"Watching a video. Homework's done."

"I wish mine was. I have a family science test in the morning."

"Then you'd better be getting at it," Jake said.

"Yes, Master," Jenny said grinning, making a mocking little curtsy to show she wasn't intimidated by his tone. "Allison?"

"Yes, Jenny."

"Will you help me dress…for the dance? I—I want to make sure everything's perfect."

"I'd like that," Allison said, and this time he thought he saw sadness in her smile.

In another moment, he was alone with Allison. The store had been closed for an hour. Only Stella and Rosie were still in the building, baking pumpkin cookies for the Thanksgiving rush, although the real draw at this time of year was the maple-cured Amish hams and free-range turkeys. "I haven't seen her this happy in weeks. Thanks for salvaging the dress, Allison. She—" he spread his hands at a loss for words "—she looks great."

"She's a very pretty girl." A tiny frown had appeared between her eyebrows. They were a couple of shades darker than her hair, softly arched and touchable. He wondered what it would feel like to trace their curves with his lips.

"Is there something wrong?" He was very close to her now although he wasn't exactly sure how he got there. She had to tilt her head back a little to meet his eyes. Her mouth was slightly open, her lips a warm, sweet red. There was a scattering of freckles across her nose and cheeks that he'd noticed before. They were as kissable as the rest of her.

"I could ask you the same thing," she said with the faintest hint of a smile curving her mouth.

"Why?"

"You're frowning."

"So are you."

"No. Nothing's wrong. I'm just tired, I guess. It's

been a long day." She took a step backward. Cool air moved between them, but it did nothing to cool the blood in his veins.

"You've made Jenny very happy. I'm in your debt once more." He closed the gap again, though he wasn't sure it was a good idea.

"I was happy to do it for her."

Her lips were soft and moist, and he was drawn to them. He put his hand behind her head, twining his fingers in her hair, holding her still. He wanted to kiss her. He wanted a woman in his arms again, to feel her softness and warmth against him, the way he'd held Beth so many times. He touched his mouth to hers. She didn't resist. Her lips were warm beneath his as he'd known they would be. But she didn't kiss him back. He lifted his head, looked down at her.

"No." Allison raised her hand and placed her fingers against his lips. "Please, don't." Her eyes were full of lantern light and secrets.

"Let me kiss you." Maybe if he kissed her, the restlessness she stirred in him would go away. She made him feel so many things. She made him laugh and challenged him to look inside himself. She was dangerous to his peace of mind, to the still, hard coldness that allowed him to keep all the pain locked away.

"No," she said quietly. "You don't want to kiss me. You want to kiss Beth."

"Beth's dead." Even now, after a thousand days and nights of its being true, he could hardly say the words.

"Not in your heart, I think."

He wanted to deny her words, but he couldn't. He stepped back. The spell was broken, except he still wanted to kiss her. Not because he could pretend she was Beth. But because she was Allison, calm and steady and burning with a quiet inner fire. The thought made his head spin.

"I think it's time for me to go."

"Back to Chicago?" He spoke before he could stop himself. Maybe if she went away, the tornado of conflicting emotions spinning around inside him would go away, too. The cold stillness was better. He didn't want to come back to life, to living, because then losing hurt too much.

She wrapped her arms around herself, protecting herself, shutting him out. "No, not Chicago. Not yet." Shadows hid her face, hid her feelings. "I can't leave until I arrange to sell my grandmother's house. But soon. Very soon. Until then, I think it would be better if I spent as little time as necessary at your house."

"Allison, don't take it out on the kids because I've acted like a jerk."

"I wouldn't do that. Of course I'll be here for them. But you can take care of yourself now. I'm certain Dr. Bostleman will tell you the same thing tomorrow. I need some space. And so do you." She turned her head, refusing to meet his eyes. "Especially at night."

ALLISON DIDN'T LOOK BACK as she crossed the road and walked up the gravel driveway to her grandmother's house. It was cold. The moon was high and far away, no bigger than a dime and the same silvery white. She lifted her cold fingers to her mouth. Her skin was tingling from the touch of Jake's lips against hers. It had been hard to put the children to bed and then pack her bag and walk out of the big old house, but she had. She had no other choice.

She should have known how much it would hurt to have him kiss her and sense that his thoughts were still with Beth. His body might want her, but his heart did not.

She hadn't wanted to admit to herself that she was beginning to care for Jake Walthers more than she should, but after their kiss she could no longer avoid the truth. She wasn't good at picking men. She had loved Brandon Martin more than he'd loved her. She'd known that from the beginning, but she'd thought if she was patient and giving she could change him. But it hadn't worked. He'd left her, and her heart had cracked, leaving only alcohol to dull the pain.

Well, this time, at least, it was different, she thought as she watched her shadow be swallowed by the bigger one of her grandmother's house. She'd caught herself before it was too late, before she needed to turn to alcohol.

Her fingers closed around her sobriety stone, and she smiled a little, even though a tear spilled out of the corner of her eye. Her heart ached because she was honest enough to admit that she was already much too close to falling in love with Jake Walthers, a man who was still in love with his dead wife. But for the first day in so many, many days, she hadn't once thought about taking a drink.

CHAPTER EIGHT

A LITTLE OVER A WEEK after Jake's accident, on a dreary November afternoon, Allison found her grandmother's wedding dress. It was in the back bedroom, in the big dark closet built under the eaves that she'd put off clearing out for as long as she could. She knew what it was the moment she saw it because she kept Rufina's original hand-tinted wedding photo on the dressing table in her bedroom in Chicago.

The dress was blue silk with mother-of-pearl buttons, a lace collar and French cuffs, a nipped-in waist and gored skirt. In the photo, Rufina was wearing white lace gloves and a hat with blue feathers and a veil. The gloves were with the dress, pinned to the lining, but their lace, like the collar and cuffs, had deepened with age to a pale ivory. The hat was nowhere to be found.

Allison closed her eyes and saw the picture once more. Her grandmother had been a war bride, her young marine husband standing tall and solemn at her side. Her mother had had his eyes and the strong jut of his chin. Allison didn't look like him at all; she favored her father's side of the family. She had never met her maternal grandfather, heard him laugh or speak her name. Donald Bremer had died on a faraway Pacific atoll in the waning days of the Second World War when Allison's mother had been a baby. Rufina had never remarried, raising her daughter alone. Twenty-five years later, Candace Martin had followed in her mother's footsteps, but by her own choice, leaving Allison's father when his neglect and heavy drinking had become too much to bear.

Allison held the fragile silk in her hands for a long time. For some reason, the dress made it all real somehow—her heritage, this house and the two acres of land that went with it. All that was left of her great-grandparents' homestead. Eighty acres of rich, fertile black soil, cleared and drained and made productive through years of hard work and commitment. The rest of the legacy was gone now.

Jake had bought the land when her grandmother had first become ill.

Now Allison was preparing to sell her grandmother's possessions and cut her ties with Riley Creek. Even though she had not been in this house since she was a child, it was much harder than she'd thought. But her life and future were in Chicago and the financial world she knew so well. There was no place for her here.

"That's a pretty dress," Julia said, coming over to stand beside Allison. She reached out and touched the fragile silk. "It's blue like my crayon. Like the sky."

"Like your eyes," Allison said. She'd almost forgotten Julia was with her, she'd been so good and so quiet, playing with her crayons and the stuffed dinosaur she'd wheedled out of Stella that morning at the store. She was continuing to help watch over Jake's children although she'd seldom been alone with him since the night he'd kissed her in the gift shop. And it was better that way. She spent far too much time thinking about that kiss...and him. "They're the same color as the sky."

Julia wasn't interested in the color of her eyes. She was interested in the dress. "Are you going to try it on?"

"No," Allison said, smiling down into the little girl's inquisitive face. "It belonged to my grandmother and she was much smaller than I am."

"Like if I tried to wear baby clothes," Julia said, making a connection she could understand.

"Yes," Allison said, surprised at how bright she was. "Like you wearing baby clothes."

She put the dress back in the muslin bag that had protected it, fumbling a little with the snaps. She couldn't wear the dress, but she couldn't bear to give it away. She would take it with her to Chicago when she returned.

She didn't want to think about leaving Riley Creek right now. "Let's go see what Stella's doing," she said.

"Okay." Julia started shoving her crayons into the plastic carrying case she'd brought to Allison's house with her. "I'm hungry."

"You're always hungry."

Five minutes later, they walked into the gift shop.

"Hi," Julia called to Rosie. "I'm back. Where's Stella?"

"She's in the storeroom." Rosie gestured toward the back of the big room before she turned her attention to a customer's question about an antique child's desk that Jake had for sale on consignment.

Allison gave Julia a little nudge. "Thank you," Julia said. Allison smiled her praise and they headed into the shadowy corner where the entrance to the storeroom was partially concealed behind a reproduction of an antique Victorian screen. The wall on either side of the door was lined with Christmas trees, their branches stiff and unadorned. Julia plopped into a child-size rocker and began to rock.

"Be good," Allison cautioned. "Leave the dollies alone."

"Okay," Julia said, rocking harder. "I'll be good."

Allison pushed open the door and stepped into the chilly storeroom. Stella was muttering under her breath, standing on a step stool and pulling boxes off a metal shelf.

"Here, let me help you with those," Allison said.

"Thanks," Stella said, sounding breathless. "These darned boxes are heavier than I thought." She turned halfway and handed over a big plastic storage box.

Allison took it and felt its weight drag at her arms. She frowned a little. "What's in here?"

"Christmas lights. Time to start decorating. We always have the gift shop stocked and ready the weekend before Thanksgiving. That way we get the turkey shoppers and the early-bird Santas in one fell swoop.'' Stella snorted. ''Besides, the snow puts me in the mood.''

It had started to snow while Allison had been cleaning out her grandmother's closet. Now, it frosted the tree branches and rooftops and covered the dark, plowed earth in a blanket of white. The second snowfall of the season, unusual for Riley Creek this early in the winter. Allison smiled to herself. She was becoming a weather watcher like everyone else in town.

''These are the full-size lights for outside. We outline the barn roof, the foundation plantings. Jake's pretty traditional that way. But not until after the first of December,'' Stella was saying. ''That's another tradition. Inside, we only use white minilights. They're on the next shelf up.'' She reached higher and brought down another box that Allison stacked on top of the first. ''Jake can probably get Tom to help him with the outside stuff, but I'm stuck with the trees.'' She looked down over her shoulder at Allison. ''Do you do trees?''

''Do trees?''

''Decorate Christmas trees,'' Stella said, dusting her hands on her ample hips before she climbed down off the step stool. ''You know, lots of gold bows and crystal ornaments for a Victorian one, Santas and nursery-rhyme figures for the children, calico and straw braids for a country theme. Don't tell me you didn't notice six naked Christmas trees right outside the door.''

"I noticed." Allison laughed. "I've never heard anyone call a tree naked."

"What else can you call them? They're made out of plastic or some such and have no other purpose than to be covered up with frills and fancies. If they were real, they'd still be growing in God's green earth giving shelter to birds and bunnies as the Almighty intended."

"I never thought of it that way." Allison shook her head, a smile she couldn't seem to stop spreading across her face. She loved Christmas. She loved holidays even when she spent them by herself, although she realized now they were a very dangerous time for a recovering alcoholic, with their added stress and the strain of not joining in holiday libations. But she suspected Stella had a serious Scrooge complex. "How many trees do you decorate?"

"Just the six for the store." Stella made a face. "I hate decorating Christmas trees."

"I'd love to help. But I'm watching Julia while Jake is down at the new barn." He'd gotten the okay from Margaret Bostleman to drive and to work his way back into as much of his normal routine as he could. Which meant he wouldn't need Allison's help with the children much longer, either. Not today, not this minute, but inevitably the time she felt she owed them would be over. All too soon she wouldn't be needed anymore.

"Great. You're in charge of the lights. It doesn't matter how carefully I pack the little monsters away every January, come the next November they're tangled into knots Harry Houdini couldn't untie.''

"It's a deal," Allison said, trying not to think about being alone again. "I never have problems with the lights."

ALLISON WAS ON HER hands and knees, wrapping lights around the lower branches of one of the Christmas trees, her rounded bottom, encased in a pair of soft, faded jeans that were just tight enough to make his pulse pound, moving enticingly to and fro as she worked. Jake stopped dead in his tracks for a moment, and Tom, who was following him, almost walked into him.

"Hey, what gives?" Tom demanded.

"Sorry," Jake muttered, stepping aside and pulling off his work gloves as if that's what had occupied him. He thought about Allison too damned much as it was. He couldn't get her or the memory of kissing her out of his mind.

"No problem." Tom shoved his own gloves into his back pocket and took off his cap.

They'd been checking on Nellie's left rear fetlock. It was supposed to snow enough before the weekend to make it worthwhile getting out the sleigh, but he didn't want to go to the trouble of having Mark Wilhelm, who also taught fourth grade at Riley Creek Elementary, drive out here and then have the Belgian come up lame.

"Saw Nellie running through the pasture like a filly a couple of days ago," Tom said, his mind still on the horse's problem. "Could be she kicked herself then."

"Could be," Jake agreed. That sometimes happened to draft horses when they were running or pulling a big load. "I'll try liniment and hot dressings for a day or two. If that fetlock's not looking better by then, I'll call the vet."

"Good idea." Tom had been helping out with a lot of the heavier work around the farm. Jake suspected the older man's being available so often was as much from wanting to be around Stella LaRue as it was friendship.

By the time they'd stomped the snow off their boots and unbuttoned their coats, Allison was sitting demurely on her heels, her hands resting on her knees. She smiled at Tom and then, with a little more reserve, at him.

"Hello, Allison," Tom said.

"Hi. Want to help? There are still two more trees that need lights." She was talking to Tom now, although she had included Jake in her greeting.

"Sure," he replied. "I'm pretty good with Christmas trees."

"Hi, Tom." Julia appeared from behind one of the trees, a cookie in hand. "Want to see my tree? I have my own."

"Hi, kiddo. Sure I want to see your tree. Whatcha eatin'? Can I have a bite?" He pretended to lunge for her, leering at her cookie. Julia danced out of his way.

"You gotta get your own."

"Which tree is yours?" Jake wanted to know. Julia

wasn't old enough to be decorating Christmas trees, especially with delicate spun glass and other fragile ornaments.

"Don't worry," Allison said, smiling as though she'd read his mind. "She has a little tree over there that Stella scrounged up for her. She's decorating it with some old ribbon and lace Rosie found in the storeroom."

He smiled back. He couldn't help himself. "Good. I don't want my profit margin taking a header because Julia's into the inventory."

"She's fine. She's been good as gold since lunchtime."

"Stop flapping your arms like a windmill. You're going to knock over one of these darned trees," Stella grumbled from the door of the storeroom as Tom continued to pretend he was going to steal Julia's cookie.

When Tom did what she'd ordered, Julia scampered back to her tree. "Hello to you, too, Stella," he said affably.

"Hmm." Stella barely acknowledged him. The woman was stubborn when it came to men. Jake wondered sometimes why Tom kept trying as hard as he did.

"I put all those trees together and got them straight in their stands last night," Tom said. "It'll take more than me having a little fun with Julia to knock one over."

"Well, I don't want to find that out the hard way. But I appreciate you doing it," Stella said, reaching high to put a lace-covered china angel on top of a tree that was already crowded with Victorian ornaments of all shapes and sizes.

"You do?" Tom asked, moving closer.

She looked down at him. "If you hadn't done it, I would've had to. Don't you have something more important to do than watch me work?"

Tom laughed, ignoring her tart comment. He handed her a smaller lace angel from the box on a table nearby, and when she took it from him, their hands touched and color rose in Stella's cheeks. Jake began to wonder just how far the relationship had developed. He liked Tom and hoped he wouldn't lose too much blood getting pricked by all the thorns growing out of Stella's hide.

"I do need help picking out my Thanksgiving turkey," Tom admitted, choosing a frosted crystal icicle for Stella to fasten to one of the top branches. "When we get done here, can I count on your expert advice in getting just the right one?"

Stella snorted. "What's a single man like you doing making a whole turkey for himself."

"I didn't say I was spending the holiday alone, did I?" Tom asked innocently.

"Who are you spending it with?" Stella betrayed her interest by speaking too quickly.

"You, I hope."

"Not if you're fixing turkey. I can't abide the stuff." She took another ornament from Tom's outstretched hand and stuck it on a branch with so much force it wobbled alarmingly. Jake bit his tongue to keep from pointing out to her that those ornaments were handblown German imports and cost twenty dollars a dozen wholesale.

Allison had given up all pretense of putting up lights and was listening to Tom and Stella's sparring as openly as Jake was. He braced one hip on the edge of a solid walnut Hoosier cupboard he'd found in the back corner of the old chicken coop and restored himself and watched the play of emotions across her face.

He leaned toward her. "What do you want to bet she ends up spending Thanksgiving with him."

Allison looked up, her gray eyes shot through with silver sparks from the myriad tiny lights on the tree. He tried to see something of the seven- or eight-year-old girl he barely recalled visiting her grandmother when he was not much older and spending summer days at the farm, but he could not. Girls hadn't been something he was very interested in twenty-five years ago. His only memories were of her with her nose in a book. In those days, reading a book was the last thing on earth he'd wanted to do. He doubted she remembered him at all.

"Do you think so?" She met his gaze for just a moment, then seemed to focus on a spot somewhere near his chin. "She seems so adamant." Allison lifted a string of lights from the storage box and studied them carefully. He wasn't sure what she was looking for—bare wires, broken bulbs, or just an excuse not to meet his eyes.

Suddenly, he wanted that very much. He wanted her to look at him, to see her gray eyes darken with passion and desire. He swallowed hard and began to study the lights in her hand as intently as she did.

"How do you know Stella doesn't have other plans for Thanksgiving?" she asked softly so that neither Stella nor Tom could hear.

"Her kids aren't going to be home for the holidays," he said at last. It had been hard to concentrate on her words. He couldn't stop thinking about her as a woman, a warm, sexy woman whom he wanted... wanted very much.

"She'll be alone?" For a moment, she looked stricken, or he thought she did. It was hard to tell in the uncertain light. He didn't know her well enough to be able to read her emotions, he reminded himself. She was a wheeler-dealer in the world of high finance. People like that didn't worry about whether or not near strangers would be spending holidays alone. "I'm sorry to hear that. I—I wish I was still going to be in Riley Creek for the holiday. I'd invite Stella to have dinner with me." She looked down again, and her red-gold hair brushed the soft curve of her cheeks, and his stomach tightened with desire. "Why won't her children be with her?"

"The two oldest can't get time off work. They're in Atlanta and Jacksonville. Her in-laws spend the winter in North Carolina. Stella never got along with Dick's mother so she won't go there. Her youngest is driving their car down for the old folks when she finishes her classes at Ohio State and then she'll fly home on the Sunday after Thanksgiving."

"Stella told you all this?"

"No. I heard it at the restaurant this morning when I stopped for coffee after I went to the bank. Stella's mother-in-law told Linda Panning at the Cut and Curl before she flew down to Myrtle Beach last week. Linda told Hank Johnson's wife, and Hank told everyone at the table that he'd put money on Tom talking Stella into having turkey and all the trimmings at his place." He smiled, hoping she'd smile, too, but she didn't. "It's the Riley Creek grapevine. Not always accurate, but fast."

"Oh," she said. She nodded and set the string of lights aside. "I know about grapevines. The one at Tanner, Marsh and Fairchild functions at warp speed. You won't let Stella spend the holiday alone, will you?" she asked with what sounded like a catch in her voice.

"No," he said, and held her gaze. "Stella and her children have a standing invitation to share Thanksgiving dinner with us. There's always a place at Walnut Hill for friends, for anyone who has nowhere else to go for the holiday."

"I'm glad."

She smiled then, and he knew what it felt like to come back from the dead. Jake swallowed hard. He felt so alive around her. He didn't want to, had fought it for days, but now there was no denying the fact. No going back to his careful solitude.

"Holidays are meant for friends and family to be together. I've always dreamed about a big Norman Rockwell family Thanksgiving."

"You've never had one?"

"No," she said. "I don't have any family left, only my mother's cousin. And my ex-husband's family all live on the West Coast. It...it just never worked out."

"When Beth was alive, our house was always filled over the holidays."

"I'm sure those are wonderful memories."

"They are." She looked surprised that he had mentioned Beth. He was a little bit himself. He almost never talked about her to anyone. Maybe it was easier now because he'd stopped thinking about her as he used to, dreaming of her beside him in their bed, waking hard and hurting with loss and need. Her memory had grown softer, sweeter, still loving but no longer everpresent. It was as if the cold ache inside him was melting away like the last snow of winter, freeing him from his grief. With a sense of wonder, he realized he wanted to feel again.

He wasn't sure what or how much he could offer. But Allison Martin stirred his senses, and he didn't think he was too far wrong to believe he did the same for her. What harm could come of their spending some time together? In less than two weeks she would be gone. But that wasn't what he wanted to think about now, not with Allison so close.

"Excuse me, Jake," Rosie called from behind the counter. "It's Angela. She's got Levi Yoder on the other line. He wants to know how many more hams we'll need for the weekend."

"Hams?" Stella broke off her conversation with Tom. "If that's Levi on the phone, I'll talk to him." Levi Yoder was one of the cantankerous and independent Mennonite farmers who supplied Jake with many of his Amish delicacies.

"You're busy here. I'll talk to him," Jake said. "Just tell me what we need."

"At least three dozen more hams. And four dozen or so turkeys, sixteen to twenty pounders, don't you think?"

"Three dozen and one hams," Tom said, adding a green blown-glass pickle, an old German symbol of good luck, to the mostly white-and-gold tree. "I'll be serving ham this Thanksgiving. Stella doesn't like turkey."

"Three dozen and one it is." Jake didn't let his surprise show on his face. He had figured Tom was going to have to work a lot harder than this to get Stella to spend Thanksgiving with him. Evidently he'd underestimated the older man's powers of persuasion. He pushed away from the Hoosier cupboard he'd been leaning against and began to head for the phone and a bargaining session with Levi Yoder when a flash of light and the crackle of sparking wires made him stop.

As the lights flickered and dimmed, the stench of burning wires overpowered the scent of cinnamon and potpourri. Then he heard Julia scream.

CHAPTER NINE

"My God. it's Julia! Something's happened to her." Allison scrambled to her feet in a blur of movement. Her face was as white as the lace angel on top of the tree. "Julia, sweetie? Where are you?" She whirled away, already lost among the forest of artificial trees, before Jake could take another step.

Julia was huddled against the back wall of the store, looking dazed and scared, clutching her left hand with her right. A small artificial tree, only a foot or two high, adorned with tired red bows and bits and pieces of lace lay toppled at her feet. A string of Christmas lights, which she must have taken when no one was looking, was sparking and sputtering around her. Smoke curled out of the receptacle where she'd plugged it in.

"Daddy." Her voice was small and wavering.

"Don't move, Julia," Jake cautioned. He wanted to rush forward and snatch up his child, but his injured ribs hampered his movements, and Julia was still within inches of the live wires. Tom, who was a step ahead of him, leaned forward and yanked the half-melted plastic plug from the wall.

"Sweetie, are you all right?" Allison dropped to her knees and gathered Julia into her arms.

"These lights are defective," Tom said. "Look at the bare wires."

"Yes, that's why I laid them aside," Allison said, fear in her voice. "It never entered my mind she would take them."

"I'll check the wiring and the fuse box. Just to be on the safe side. You stay here and take care of Julia." Tom walked away just as Rosie hurried over to find out what had happened.

Jake stared down at his little girl's pale face. *God, not Julia!* He lowered himself clumsily to his knees. Allison was holding Julia so tightly, sheltering her in the curve of her body, that he couldn't tell how badly she was hurt.

He put his hand on her shoulder. "Let me see if she's okay." Allison didn't respond to his touch. She rocked Julia back and forth, murmuring under her breath. "Allison," he said more sharply, "let me take her."

Her shoulder stiffened beneath his hand. "I'm so sorry." She lifted her head and looked at him with eyes that were filled with misery, the irises big and dark. "It's my fault. I let her wander away. I'm so sorry, Jake. Forgive me."

"There's nothing to forgive," he said, holding out his arms for his daughter, although what he really wanted to do was wrap them both in his embrace and make everything all right. "Julia, let Daddy see where you're hurt." His heart was still beating like a sledgehammer, but he could see that Julia wasn't seriously injured, and his terror receded a little. "What happened, kitten?"

"My fingers..." Julia sobbed. "They bit me." Still cuddled against Allison's breast, she held out her hand to him. "The Christmas lights bit me," she repeated in an aggrieved tone. "They're bad."

Jake turned her hand over. There were small blisters on her thumb and first two fingertips. "Baby, you're gonna be okay. But how many times has Daddy told you you're not supposed to play with things that take electricity." It was a miracle she had escaped being more seriously burned or, *God help him,* electrocuted.

"My fingers hurt." Julia wasn't in the mood for lectures no matter how well deserved, and her sobs escalated.

"Take her into the kitchen and let's get some cold water on those blisters," Stella said, almost making Jake smile. She'd raised three rambunctious and headstrong children. Nothing rattled her calm and stolid approach to life.

"That's a good idea," Rosie agreed, nodding like the banty hens in the pen outside the store. "Oh dear. Here come some customers. I'll head them off." She hurried away to steer three blue-haired matrons who'd just entered the store in another direction.

"Yes," Allison said. "Cold water. Cold water is good for burns, isn't it?" Her voice sounded almost as forlorn as Julia's.

"Sure is." Stella held out her arms to Julia.

"C'mon, kiddo. Let's get you fixed up." Reluctantly, Allison allowed Stella to take the child from her arms.

Jake pulled himself to his feet, wincing at the strain the move put on his ribs. Allison stayed where she was, looking slightly dazed. He held out his hand. "It's all right, Allison. She'll be fine."

She gazed up at him. He could see she was trembling all over. "I never thought she would take those lights and try to plug them in. I—I don't know how I could have been so careless. I'm so sorry, Jake."

"She's okay, Allison." He pushed aside the last vestiges of his own fear at the sight of her. He wanted to pull her into his arms and comfort her—just as any man wanted to do for the woman he loved when she was frightened or in pain. The thought brought him up short. He wasn't in love with Allison Martin, but the idea wasn't as foreign, as unimaginable, as it would have been just days before.

"Are you sure?"

"I'm sure. It's nothing a little first-aid cream and a cookie won't cure. Thank God." He held out his hand to help her to her feet. "Come on, see for yourself."

"I HAVE POOH and Eeyore and Tigger," Julia said with great satisfaction, wiggling her bandaged fingers in front of Jake's nose. "I want to show them to Libby and Mike."

"After your nap," Jake said.

"I'm not sleepy."

"You will be if you lie quietly and shut your eyes."

Julia never gave in easily. "My fingers hurt. I think I need another cookie."

"You've already had three, one for each owie," he reminded her. He pushed her gently but firmly back against the pillow. "Go to sleep, kitten."

"Don't want to."

"If you don't take your nap, you can't stay up and talk to Grandma and Grandpa when they call tonight. You'll fall asleep before you get to tell them about your bandages." Jake's parents called from Florida twice a week to talk to the children and Jenny and catch up on the news from Riley Creek.

"Still don't want to," Julia said, her lower lip jutting out in a practiced pout.

Jake changed tactics. "Want me to lie down beside you until you fall asleep?"

Her little round face brightened. "Yes," she said, patting the bedspread where all the Pooh Corner characters cavorted among the trees of the Hundred Acre Woods. "Take a nap with me."

"Okay, kitten. I could use a snooze."

"Allie, too."

"I don't think there's room for all three of us." Allison avoided meeting Jake's eyes as he settled himself against the headboard, half-reclining with his feet in their heavy work shoes still on the floor. How many times over the years had she fantasized herself in Jake's place, her own child cradled in her arms, warm and sleepy? Julia snuggled against him, carefully avoiding his damaged ribs, and Jake folded her in his arms. Allison's heart contracted with a sharp pang of remorse. Children were so precious and so fragile, and she had let harm come to this one. Even now, an hour later, her heart pounded whenever she thought back to the terrible moment. *She needed a drink. She had to have a drink. She had to make the echoes of Julia's scream go away.* "You take your nap," she said, willing her voice steady, forcing her lips into a semblance of a smile. "I'll go downstairs and make some popcorn so we can have a nice snack when Mike and Libby and Jenny get home from school, okay?"

Julia's eyes were already heavy. She smiled and nodded. "Popcorn and apples."

"Okay, apples, too."

"And caramel dip." Her eyes drifted shut.

"Allison, are you all right?" Jake asked, his voice barely more than a whisper as he smoothed Julia's flyaway hair from her cheek with a gesture that was both casual and protective.

"I'm fine," she said, and fled down the stairs.

But she wasn't fine. Her nerves were stretched so tightly they hummed in her ears. She'd been given the task of watching Julia and she'd been inattentive. As a result, the little girl had been injured. It was a miracle she hadn't been electrocuted by those lights. It didn't matter that Jake and Stella and Tom had also been there. In *her* mind, she was responsible for what had happened and no one else. She couldn't stop trembling. And she couldn't stop thinking about the bottle of wine in Jake's refrigerator. Her ex-husband had been a wine snob. There was no way in the world he would have been caught drinking a grocery-store domestic white. But Allison was an alcoholic and she had no such scruples.

She found herself standing in front of the refrigerator. *Just one glass.* Just to silence her conscience. *No.* She spun away and walked blindly to the pantry, a room that dated back to the original homestead. Half-sunk in the earth, its limestone walls lined with jars of homemade preserves and its floor crowded with bushel baskets of pears and apples and winter squash had made it seem like a haven, and Allison enjoyed going in there. But not now. Now it seemed more like a cell, the kind of place in which a woman who would let a three-year-old play with defective lights deserved to be locked up. *You can't be responsible for a child. Your own or anyone else's.* She sat on the top step and buried her head in her hands, breathing in the earthy, musty scents, aware of nothing but the bottle in the refrigerator.

She would not give in. She could call her AA mentor, but at some point, Allison had come to realize that she must fight her craving, her addiction, on her own. For her, it was the only way to feel in control of her life again. She stood up, filled her hands with crisp red apples and walked back into the kitchen. The room was quiet with midafternoon stillness, too quiet. She turned on the radio. It was oldies hour on the local station and a Beatles tune filled the room. Automatically, she washed the apples and put them in a bowl. She stared at it, seeing nothing. The Beatles were singing, but all she could hear were Julia's sobs.

What had she promised Julia? Popcorn. Yes. Making popcorn would give her something to do. She couldn't open the popcorn container. She yanked so hard that when the lid finally came off kernels went flying in every direction, bouncing off the countertop and skittering across the floor. She looked at the mess in horror. That was all she could take. She gave up the struggle and opened the refrigerator door.

Allison watched herself reach for the bottle of wine as though her hand belonged to another woman. *Just one glass. Just enough to steady her nerves. She could stop after that.* She watched herself open the cupboard and take out a glass, pour it full of the pale amber liquid. Felt the coolness of the glass as she picked it up and held it to her lips.

"That's not a bad idea," Jake said. "I'm not a big wine fan, but I could use a drink right now."

She dropped the glass of wine in the sink and it shattered. The acrid scent of wine filled her nostrils. She almost screamed with frustration. Tears clogged her throat and pushed at the back of her eyes.

"Oh, God, I'm sorry," she whispered.

"No problem," Jake said. He reached around her and took a glass from the cupboard. "I'll pour you another glass."

"No!" She backed away from the sink. "I...I don't know what I was thinking. I'm...I'm allergic to wine." She should just come out and say it. *I can't drink. I'm an alcoholic and you just caught me falling off the wagon.* But somehow the words wouldn't come. She had no strength left for confessions, for explanations. It took every ounce of willpower just to stay away from the wine, to stay sober. "Look at this mess," she said. "I couldn't get the lid off the pop-corn container. Let me get the broom and sweep it up."

Jake regarded her silently as she worked, then took a cloth and swept the spilled kernels from the coun-tertop into the wastebasket. From the corner of her eye, she watched as he poured the rest of the wine down the sink. "This stuff's probably turned, any-way. It's been sitting in the fridge for months." He picked up the broken pieces of glass and dropped them into the trash. "I could use a beer, though."

"Go...go right ahead." She hated the taste of beer, but that hadn't stopped her from drinking it in the past. It wouldn't stop her now if Jake actually set a bottle in front of her. *Tell him. He won't judge you.* But she couldn't be sure and she couldn't face Jake's censure. She swept the last kernels into the dustpan and emptied it before putting the broom back into the narrow closet between the sink and refrigerator. Then she moved as far away from the smell of spilled wine as she could.

"What I really need is a cup of coffee," Jake said, running water into the sink, dissipating the smell. "To tell you the truth, I can take alcohol or leave it. But caffeine, that's another story."

Allison almost sobbed aloud in relief. *A reprieve. Time for her to pull herself together.* "Coffee sounds fine," she said wrapping her hands tightly around the back of one of the high-backed chairs grouped around the big oak table.

"Allison, what's wrong? You look as if you've seen a ghost."

"I'm fine." Her voice cracked and broke on the words. A tear spilled over and trickled down her cheek. She lifted a trembling hand and tried to brush it away. To her horror, two more followed. She never cried. Never.

"Allison?"

"I never cry," she said. "Tanner, Marsh and Fairchild doesn't allow it." In her old life, she never lost control of anything but her drinking. Here, it seemed her emotions were always too close to the surface.

"I can understand that," he said with a smile, trying to coax one from her. "No one wants a stock analyst—"

"Fund manager," Allison corrected automatically.

"Fund manager, then, who makes like a watering can at the drop of a hat."

She tried to smile back, but she couldn't. The tears just kept coming. "I... It's just nerves." And terror, terror of losing control.

"You're still beating yourself up over Julia's accident, aren't you? It wasn't your fault. Three-year-olds are the sneakiest animals on the face of the earth."

He smiled again, but she couldn't make light of what had happened. "She could have been electrocuted. She could have suffered terrible burns or brain damage or..." She lifted her hand to her mouth to stifle a sob.

"Hey." Jake was across the room in half a dozen steps. "Don't dwell on what might have been. You'll drive yourself crazy if you do that. It's survival rule number one for parents."

"I'd make a terrible mother," she said, not daring to look at him. The words came from deep inside her and could no more have been held back than the tide. "Beth would never have let anything like that happen to Julia." It was a measure of her distress that she spoke the thought aloud.

"Things like this did happen when Beth was alive," he said after a moment. "Mike fell off the slide at the park when he was four, and Libby found a juice can filled with kerosene and came so close to drinking it that my skin still crawls when I think about it. It happens to every parent. Even the best. You can't keep your eye on them every minute of every day no matter how hard you try."

Even with her own pain she saw how hard it was for him to talk about Beth. But she had to know, had to be reassured that other women—even mothers— made the same mistakes she had. Suddenly, she felt trapped, and Jake was blocking her way. She couldn't get past him so she turned to the window. She could sense him behind her, the heat of him, the strength of him, and it comforted her. She felt the burning need for a drink start to ease.

"Thank you for telling me that. It helps to know

that other people make the same mistakes. Even a wonderful mother like Beth.''

"Beth *was* a wonderful mother, but she was also human.'' His voice roughened a little, but he kept talking and Allison drew more comfort, gained more resolve, from the sound of his voice. "Sometimes she got frazzled and frustrated. Sometimes she lost her temper or let her attention wander for a moment. God, so did I. I still do, but it doesn't mean I don't love my children with all my heart and soul. I'd give up my life for them if the choice had to be made.''

Sadly, Allison realized Beth actually *had* given up her life for her child. "I hope I would be able to do the same for my children.''

Jake reached out and took her by the shoulders, turned her gently but implacably to face him. "You would. I'm certain of that.'' He was watching her with a steady regard that made her heart beat faster. "You'll make a wonderful mother, Allison. Don't ever let yourself think otherwise.''

He was paying her the highest of compliments by comparing her to the woman he had loved. Fresh tears slipped down her cheeks. "Thank you,'' she whispered.

"No. Thank *you*.''

"How did Beth die, Jake? What went wrong?'' It was a question that came from her innermost soul. Dying in childbirth—every woman's darkest fear.

He dropped his hands and closed his eyes. For a moment, she thought he wouldn't answer her. "It was an aneurism. A weak blood vessel in her brain. Later, the doctors said it had probably been there all her life. It ruptured after the delivery. She was holding Julia, laughing at her scrunched-up little face and talking about what we should name her. And that she wanted at least two more children. Beth was an only child.'' He raised his eyes, held her gaze with his. ''Like you.''

She nodded. She'd never expected him to volunteer this much and she wanted him to keep talking—wanted to know more about the woman whose home she was beginning to wish was her own, whose children she was coming to love as though they were her own...and whose husband she was falling in love with.

''Her parents were killed when a freight train hit their car at an unmarked crossing a year after we were married. She was devastated. Family meant everything to her. Julius was Beth's father's name so we decided on Julia in his honor. She said she had a headache, a terrible headache. I buzzed for the nurse, but it was already too late. She died about an hour later.''

''I'm sorry.''

''So am I. But we had almost eight good years together. And I have the kids and a lot of memories. Good memories, wonderful memories. I'd forgotten that, but lately...''

His hands moved back to her shoulders, pulling her closer. She held herself very still. The battle within her took a new direction. His mouth was mere inches from hers. She closed her eyes, wanting to feel the touch of his lips, but knowing he was using her as a substitute for Beth.

"Jake, don't..." She put her hand on his chest to hold him away. Beneath her palm she felt the beat of his heart quicken at her touch. She made herself open her eyes. As much as she longed for the intimacy of his kiss, she wouldn't be a stand-in for a dead woman.

He must have read her thoughts. "I'm not kissing Beth," he said. And she saw that was the truth. His eyes held no ghosts, but there was confusion and an uncertainty that matched her own in their depths.

"Don't kiss me because you're grateful." She was winning her solitary battle, but the temptation to lose herself in his arms, in his strength, was even more compelling than her need for alcohol. She couldn't afford to let herself lean on him. She had to make it on her own.

"You're wrong there, too, though I am grateful for what you've done for us," he said, but he let her go when she attempted to put some small distance between them. "More grateful than I can say."

"I've enjoyed every minute of being here with the children." She grasped the chair back to keep herself from returning to the sanctuary of his embrace. She couldn't add the complication of a love affair to her still-shaky grip on sobriety.

He frowned slightly but didn't try to take her in his arms again. "And you were right about Julia's needing more structure in her life. Today was a wake-up call for me. There were four adults standing right there and she still managed to take those lights and plug them into the socket. She's getting to be a handful. I've been letting her get away with too much. She needs someone to watch over her full-time. I'm going to make arrangements for her to attend preschool. I've been selfish to keep her so much to myself."

She knew how hard that was for him to admit. "If you do that, you'll be giving up Beth's dream. Your dream."

Sadness and regret darkened his eyes to the color of the midnight sky. "No dream is worth a child's safety. A child's life."

Allison curled her fingers around the chair until her knuckles turned white. She wanted so badly to hold him. But, of course, she couldn't do that. It wouldn't be fair. She would be gone in a matter of weeks, days. But until then, until Thanksgiving came, she could do something for him, something that his faith in her made possible. Something that he would remember long after she was gone.

"Go ahead and arrange things at the preschool. But not right away. I'll take care of her for you as long as I'm here. I'll help you keep Beth's dream alive a little while longer."

CHAPTER TEN

ALLISON LOOKED OUT the kitchen window as Jake walked the two big draft horses, Clara and Nellie, up the lane. She assumed Jake had decided Nellie was well enough to pull a load because both horses were harnessed to a big, high-sided green wagon filled with golden straw.

A hayride? Jake usually didn't book them for the middle of the week. Perhaps he was just going to drive Clara and Nellie along the lane and back to exercise Nellie's healing fetlock. Yes, that was probably it. She turned away from the window, not allowing herself to watch him any longer. She spent too much time doing that these days, watching Jake work or read to the kids in the evening, enjoying his air of quiet competence, his low, growling laugh…his maleness.

She glanced at the clock. It was half past three. The children and Jenny would be home from school soon and she should be thinking of what to fix them for dinner. The time she had here now was very short. In just over a week she had to return to Chicago. She didn't want to spend a minute of it alone in her grandmother's house when she could be storing up memories of being part of a family, Jake's family, to see her through the lonely times ahead. Julia had been coloring quietly at the kitchen table. Now she got up and wandered to the window to see what Allison had been looking at.

"It's the horsies," she squealed. "Daddy's going to take us for a ride. I'm going outside."

"Not until you put your crayons and coloring book away. And not without your hat and coat." Allison no longer had any problem infusing her voice with the authority necessary to command the three-year-old's attention. After the weekend, Julia would start going to preschool for the full day on Mondays and Fridays, the busiest days at the store, and on Wednesday mornings.

"Okay. A hayride. We're going on a hayride." She hopped up and down, clapping her hands. The burns on her fingers were almost healed, but she insisted on wearing bandages anyway.

"Do you think so? Where would you be going today?" Allison asked. It was a beautiful afternoon, warmer than it had been for several days, with the sun shining and a slight breeze pushing big, fluffy white clouds through the sky.

"I don't know. Allison, where's my coat?" Julia hurried back to the table to shove her crayons into their plastic carrying case.

"Right here." Allison took her purple parka from the low hook beside the back door. "Do you think you should go potty first?" It was amazing how natural and right all of this seemed, being in Jake's kitchen, getting his child ready to go outside. Allison tried vainly to ignore the vision of herself alongside Jake and Julia, waiting for Libby and Mike to get home from school.

"I just went. Hurry. I want to ride in the wagon."

"Okay, kitten. You're all set." Allison zipped Julia's parka and settled a purple hat over her blond ponytail. "Do what your daddy tells you and have a good time."

"Come with us," Julia begged. "Come ride in the wagon with me."

"I...I have to see about getting the pot roast on for dinner." They ate early so that the children would have plenty of time for homework and baths before bedtime. In her other life, five nights out of six, she stayed at her desk at Tanner, Marsh and Fairchild until long after the dinner hour—rather than eat alone. A return to that life seemed less appealing every day. But then she would think of the afternoon of Julia's accident, her near brush with a lapse from sobriety, and harden her resolve. She wasn't ready for this. She wasn't strong enough. She had to return to Chicago and gain the strength, the stability, she needed to face whatever the future held.

"Please, Allison. Come with us."

Julia's enthusiasm was infectious, and Allison wanted to be out in the sunshine, away from thoughts of having to leave Riley Creek and Walnut Hill Farm. "All right, sweetie. I'll come. We'll wait for the school bus together, okay?"

"Hooray!" Julia danced over to the door. "All the

big kids will see my horsies and wish they had some, too. You can ride beside me," she said magnanimously. "There's room for you and me and daddy up there."

Allison laughed. She couldn't help herself. Julia's delight at one-upping the older children was wonderful. "Thank you," she said, while they walked outside. "I'd like to sit beside you."

"Hey, kitten, I figured it wouldn't take you long to get out here." Jake looked up as they approached. "Want to go for a ride?"

"Yes," she squealed. The big Belgians' heads came up. They snorted and whuffled through their noses, lifting their big hooves to stamp the ground. "Put me up,"

Before Allison could obey the little girl's command, Jake took her carefully in his arms. It was the first time since his accident that he'd attempted to lift her. He swung her up onto the seat, then leaned against the high side of the wagon, an expression of pain visible on his face. "I think that might've been a mistake," he said with a rueful grimace. "Is it just me, or has she gained weight in the past two weeks?"

"You're pushing yourself too hard," she said before she could censure her tongue.

Instead of arguing with her, he grinned. "Yes, Nurse Martin. I'll take a couple of aspirins and sack out in the recliner when we get back. I won't even volunteer to help with the dishes."

"The kids always take care of them anyway."

"It builds character," he said. "How do you think I grew up to be such a paragon of virtue."

"By bullying your little brothers into doing your share of the kitchen chores?" She tilted her head a little to one side to better see his expression beneath the brim of his baseball cap. She didn't often tease him. It felt good.

He laughed and held out his hand to help her up onto the wagon seat. "You know me too well."

On the contrary, she didn't know him well at all. There had been quiet times the past few days when they'd sat around the kitchen table and talked of this and that over a cup of coffee—discussions of favorite movies and TV shows, a little about politics and what went on in the world beyond Riley Creek. They hadn't talked about Beth again, or themselves. And she hadn't told him of her drinking problem. She knew she should, but somehow she hadn't been able to find the right way to start. "I'm learning," she said instead. Which was the truth, although time for that was running out on her, as well.

The big yellow school bus pulled up alongside the driveway as Jake adjusted Clara's harness. Mike and Libby tumbled off the bus the moment the double doors whooshed open and came running toward the wagon. Jenny followed more slowly.

The horses threw up their big heads and flicked their tails but stood still in their harnesses as Mike reached up to pat their velvety noses. "Are you taking them for a ride?" he asked eagerly.

"Tom needs acorns for the turkeys. Run in and

change your clothes. We'll go out to the woods and see if we can scrounge some up for him. How about you, Jen? Want to come along?''

The teenager shrugged, but the smile hovering about her lips and the way she patted Nellie on the neck made a lie of her show of disinterest. "Sure, why not? I haven't got anything else to do until dinnertime." She hurried off to change her clothes at a pace that further displayed her enthusiasm.

Libby stayed behind and asked, "Are we going to take the acorns over tonight? I want to see Tom's turkeys."

"Turkeys?" Allison was completely lost. The only time she'd heard any mention of turkeys was the day of Julia's accident. Tom had said he was going to have ham for Thanksgiving dinner because Stella didn't want turkey. She remembered that distinctly.

"Tom Farley's got a flock of wild turkeys at his place. He's got a special license from the Department of Natural Resources to keep them." Jake went on checking harness and tack as he talked. "There haven't been any wild turkeys in these parts for a hundred years. They like woods, lots of them, and oak trees, not open fields and plowed ground. Acorns are their favorite food. Tom has nearly twenty acres that are still forested with some native timber, the last in these parts. He wanted to try to bring the birds back, but it hasn't worked out very well. A coyote or feral dog got at them. Killed a couple of the hens and beat up on the male pretty good. Now Tom's got them penned up in an old coop by the barn. Trying to decide what's best to do with them.''

"Do with them?" Thanksgiving was only two weeks away. She hoped that didn't mean what she thought. "Is this a last meal we're taking them?"

Jake laughed at her. "Don't worry. They're in no danger of becoming anyone's dinner. Tom just isn't sure if he wants to have another go at acclimating them here, or send them back to southern Ohio where they came from and where there's plenty of habitat."

"Good. For a moment there, I thought I might be paying a visit to a condemned man."

"MORE ICE CREAM?" Tom asked Allison. As payment for the two bushels of acorns they'd brought with them, Tom had asked them all to stay for spaghetti and meatballs—his specialty.

"Thank you, no. I couldn't eat another bite." She smiled up at him as she refused another scoop of the fudgy chocolate chip ice cream. "Everything was delicious."

"Good company makes good food." Tom smiled back. He'd been halfway flirting with Allison ever since they'd pulled into the yard, and Jake felt a surprising twinge of jealousy. It took him a moment to recognize the sensation. He hadn't been jealous in years, and never over any woman except Beth. But he couldn't blame Tom for flirting with Allison. He'd been pretty much wanting to do that himself lately.

"If you're right, Tom, then this meal was gourmet fare," Allison said.

Tom bowed his head in a courtly gesture. "Thank you, ma'am. And the turkeys thank you, as well. They are most grateful for the excellent acorns you brought with you."

"Raking acorns was a pain," Libby said, looking down at her hands. "I think I got a blister and those old turkeys didn't look like they were all that grateful."

"Turkeys are proud birds. When the male strutted around the pen and dragged his wings along the ground, he was telling us how much he liked the gift."

"Really? I thought he was just showing off for the lady turkeys."

Jake grinned. "Well, that, too."

"I want more ice cream, Tom," Julia announced, holding up her bowl. "Please."

"Just a spoonful."

"Only a spoonful."

Jake spoke in unison with Allison, just as he used to do with Beth. She caught his eye for a moment, colored slightly, then looked away. He couldn't tell what she was thinking, what she was feeling, but he wanted to know. She was always so calm. The day of Julia's accident was the first time he'd seen her display any emotion, yet underneath that composure and self-assurance he knew there was passion.

"Kids, why don't we help Tom with the dishes?" Allison said, getting up from the table. "It's the least *we* can do to say thank-you for this great dinner."

"I'd rather walk around with my arms out like the turkey," Libby said, scowling down at her plate.

"Wish Tom had a dishwasher," Mike groused under his breath, but he picked up his plate and headed for the sink. When Libby didn't follow, he glared at her until she started to clear the table.

"I don't need a dishwasher," Tom informed Mike as he put the ice cream back into the refrigerator. "Besides, they don't make them in harvest gold these days and I'd hate to spoil the decor." Tom's kitchen was a monument to the seventies, gold-colored stove and refrigerator, orange brickwork linoleum on the floor and a heavy, carved table and chairs that were vaguely Mediterranean—and downright ugly.

"Too bad," Jenny said, piling up plates and silverware. "This place is seriously retro. I wouldn't change a thing, but a dishwasher is an absolute necessity of life."

"The world has gotten along for thousands of years without automatic dishwashers," Tom observed mildly.

"Just barely," Jenny countered, making a face.

"For that you dry," Tom said, and handed her a towel.

"You could buy a white one and I could paint it gold for you," Mike offered, and Tom told him he might consider doing just that if he got a good enough price for his soybeans.

The next half hour slipped by in a flurry of small household chores and conversations that ranged from the Riley Creek Warriors basketball team's ranking in the first statewide poll of the preseason to the possibility of rain in Columbus on Saturday when Ohio State played Michigan. Allison debated the latest Washington scandal with Tom, then listened when he regaled her with stories of his years as a county commissioner. Small scandals versus big ones. Jake and Julia were excused from KP duty, so Jake sat at the big, ugly table and held Julia on his lap while they watched the others work.

The moon had risen by the time they were ready to say their goodbyes, and the silvery globe gave off enough light so they didn't need the battery-powered headlight Jake usually used. The kids crawled into the back and cuddled under the old woolen blankets he'd thrown on top of the straw before they'd left. Julia nodded off in Jenny's arms almost before they pulled out of Tom's yard.

Jake kept Clara and Nellie to a walk. The creak of the wagon wheels and the jingle of harness bells were all that disturbed the stillness of the evening. His great-grandparents had ridden like this on their way home from visiting neighbors and friends. The past was close tonight.

"I wonder if my grandmother ever did this when she was a little girl." He wasn't surprised anymore that Allison's thoughts often paralleled his own.

"Didn't she ever tell you what it was like living on a farm when she was young?"

"No, at least not much that I remember. She and my mother spent most of our visits arguing about my father. I...I never had a chance to know her better after I was grown. I only remember bits and pieces of being here. Gathering eggs. Playing with the kittens in the barn. How hot and still and sultry it got before a thunderstorm.''

"I remember you," Jake said. "You hair was redder then, and you were always so serious. My grandmother used to try to get me and Matt to come over and ask you to play when we were out here to visit.''

"You never did," she said. "I would have remembered that.''

"I was nine," he said. "And you were a girl.''

She smiled, and it rivaled the moonlight. "It's beautiful out here tonight," she said softly. She was sitting beside him on the hard wooden seat, and the faint scent of her perfume and the warmth of her skin mingled with the cold night air. "The stars are so much brighter than in the city, and the moonlight on the fields almost makes me think we're on the ocean instead of in the middle of Ohio.''

"I get that feeling, too," he found himself saying. "When the wheat is young and the wind is blowing, it's like watching waves.''

"Amber waves of grain," Allison said, and he could hear the smile in her voice although her face was hidden as they passed through shadows of the apple trees at the edge of the orchard.

He clucked for Clara and Nellie to pick up the pace. The wagon wheels rolled over the last of the windfalls and the scent of cider filled the air. "When the wheat's ripe enough to be classified as amber, I'm usually not looking for the wind to blow that hard,'' he said only half-jokingly. "It's damned difficult to make a profit on a field of wheat that's beaten into the ground by the wind."

"Yes," she said, "I suppose it is. I'm not quite thinking like a farmer yet, am I?" She turned her head to look at him. He caught the gleam of moonlight on her hair as they left the orchard behind, and he was surprised by how natural it felt to have her there beside him.

"Do you want to learn to think like a farmer?" he heard himself ask.

She didn't answer for a moment. "Yes," she said. "I'd like to learn to know the land well enough to think in its terms." She shook her head and laughed a little self-consciously. "I'm not making a bit of sense."

"No. I understand." He thought about the question he'd been going to ask her since the evening before. "Pastor LeVeck called me last night after you left," he said.

"The Lutheran minister?"

"Yeah. He and his wife were supposed to chaperon the Harvest Dance Friday night, but their daughter's having a baby and she's having some problems."

"I'm sorry to hear that."

"The doctor has decided to do a caesarean on Friday to be on the safe side, so the LeVecks have bowed out. My parents' names came up next on the list of chaperons."

"And you've been asked to take their place?"

"You guessed it." He caught her gaze with his

own. She had bullied him back to life. His heart
hadn't died with Beth. He didn't know if it was ever
going to be whole again, but it was still beating. He
could feel desire again. And he desired Allison Martin
with every fiber of his being. "I said yes. I hope
you'll do the same. Allison, would you be my date
for the Harvest Dance?"

CHAPTER ELEVEN

"I TOLD YOU YOU'D LOOK hot in that dress," Ashley said. "Didn't I tell you? Sam can't keep his eyes off you. I'm surprised Melinda Rohrs hasn't come over here and tried to scratch your eyes out."

Jenny just nodded. She didn't care about Melinda Rohrs. Or Sam Watchman—even though Sam looked really good in his new suit and wildly patterned tie and he'd helped her up to the stage when the Harvest Dance queen and her court had been presented, just like a real gentleman. She didn't even care that Aaron Masterson had danced two fast dances and one slow dance with her. She only cared about the scene Jake and Allison Martin were making.

Well, it wasn't exactly a scene. In fact, they hadn't even danced together. Right now, they were standing over by the punch bowl talking to Coach Rayle. It was just that they *were* together. She'd heard Jake ask her to be his date the night they'd gone to Tom's in the wagon. But she hadn't thought he actually meant it *that* way. How could he? People would talk. They'd think he didn't love Beth anymore. That he'd forgotten her.

To be fair, she liked Allison. And her mom had

said Jake was too young to spend his life alone, which was true. Even Jake must have stopped hurting quite so much. She had, when she admitted the truth. But she would never forget Beth, or stop loving her. And she thought Jake felt the same way.

Maybe she was just making too much of this one date. Allison had been great to Jake and the kids, to all of them. She didn't have any friends around here. She wasn't even going to be staying much longer. What was wrong with the two of them coming to the Harvest Dance? It wasn't like he was falling in love with her or anything. They were only in the Riley Creek school gym drinking punch and eating cheese and crackers because Pastor LeVeck's daughter had had her baby today, and Mom and Dad were still in Florida and couldn't be chaperons. Some date. She relaxed a little.

"Here comes Aaron. I suppose I'd better take my cue and go get something to eat." Ashley gave Jenny a wink before slipping away.

"Want to dance?" Jenny looked up. Aaron stood there, one knee cocked, his hand on his hip. He'd taken off his tie and unbuttoned the top button of his white shirt. He had hair on his chest and a shadow of a beard on his chin. He was seventeen; two whole years older than she was, almost a man. His eyes lingered just a second too long on the skin above her white ruffles and she felt her cheeks get red. It always amazed her that he'd want to spend time with a no-body like her.

"Yes."

She couldn't say anything more. Somehow when Aaron was around, her throat always seemed to tighten up. So she just let him take her by the hand. She wound her arms around his neck, and he put his around her waist. Then they swayed to the music. It was really old, like World War II old. All brass and woodwinds, no guitars or drums at all. Mr. Hartwood, the principal, must have been after the DJ to play it. He liked all that ancient stuff.

"Hey. Where you at?" Aaron asked, lifting his hand to tip her chin up so he could see her face.

"Just thinking." She liked the touch of his hand on her face. He pulled her a little closer. She stepped backward a tiny bit. It wouldn't do to get too close together. "People are watching," she warned, scanning the perimeter of the dance floor, looking for the chaperons. Coach and Mr. Hartwood were over at the buffet table. Mrs. Bachleman and Maria's parents were stationed at the entrance to the gym, which had been turned into a wisteria bower, dotted with tiny gold and orange lights. Wisteria didn't bloom in the autumn. It didn't even grow anywhere around Riley Creek that Jenny knew of. But it didn't look too bad.

"Let 'em watch," Aaron muttered, and pulled her closer again. Jenny's breath caught in her throat. She felt hot and cold at the same time, happy and a little bit afraid because she smelled cinnamon on his breath and knew he'd been drinking again. Aaron and his friends mostly drank beer, which they paid Aaron's older brother, Nick, to buy for them. But tonight he must have been drinking cinnamon schnapps. Jenny knew a lot of the kids drank schnapps. There were all kinds of flavors. It didn't smell like booze. It tasted good. But she wished Aaron wasn't drinking tonight. Jake might find out, and if he did—well, this would be the last time Aaron held her in his arms.

"Have you been drinking?" she whispered, making sure there wasn't anyone near enough to overhear.

"Yeah," he said. "Want a taste? It's cinnamon schnapps. I snuck it in right past old Hartwood and Coach and all the rest of them."

"No, I don't want a taste. And you shouldn't be drinking it, either. If you get caught, you'll be off the basketball team for the season and you know we've got a good chance to go to state tournaments this year."

"No one will rat us out." Aaron looked down at her, his brown eyes narrow and hard. "At least they'd better not, if they know what's good for them."

"I won't tell." She lifted her chin and looked him straight in the eye. But she should tell, she knew. This was wrong. Aaron and all his friends were too young to drink.

"I know you won't tell, Jen Jen." He always called her Jen Jen. It was a baby name, and no one had called her that since she was six. But it sounded so different when Aaron said it—lower, sexier. She shivered a little, glad it was so dark in the gym because she knew there were goose bumps standing up on her arms. Tonight when he took her home, she would let him kiss her, and maybe—she shivered again with half scary, half delicious excitement—maybe even a bit more than a kiss. "I'll give you a taste of my schnapps. It'll keep you warm on the drive home."

The excitement abated. Now she felt wary. "I don't want anything to drink."

"Oh, come on, Jen Jen," he said in that wonderful teasing way he had. "Quit being such a little Puritan."

"I'm not a Puritan." He always called her that when she insisted on putting a halt to their kissing and petting.

"Yes, you are." He was grinning, and it was hard not to respond in kind. He had such a great smile.

"You shouldn't be drinking," she said once more to show him she hadn't completely given in.

"It makes me feel good," he said defensively. He wasn't smiling anymore. "And it's a hell of a lot better than smoking pot."

"You do that, too," she reminded him.

"Not lately."

"I'm glad."

"Don't worry, Jen Jen. I won't get caught. And I can handle my liquor. I don't get drunk. Just a little buzz. You'd like it. It's great. Christmas and your birthday and the Fourth of July all in one."

"I…" She'd like to feel that way. "I'll think about it."

That seemed to satisfy him for a moment. He reached up and urged her head down on his shoulder. "You look hot in that dress."

"Thanks," she said, not caring now who saw them this way. "Allison made it for me." It wasn't precisely the truth, but close enough. Too much explaining would spoil everything.

"Allison Martin?"

"She's living in her grandmother's house across the road and has been helping us out since Jake's accident. She's from Chicago. I've told you about her."

"I know who you're talking about. I'm not that drunk. I've seen her around town...." It sounded as if he was going to say more and Jenny waited, but he didn't, so Jenny went on talking.

"She's been great. A real friend."

"Looks like she's getting friendly with your brother, too."

Jenny's head came up with a jerk. Aaron leaned back so they didn't bump heads. She looked over his shoulder. Jake and Allison were dancing, moving as slowly to the music as she and Aaron were. She closed her eyes for a moment. *Oh, Beth.*

Aaron moved her in a half circle so they could see better. "It must not bother your brother much."

"What?"

"Drinking." He sounded as though he was scoring a point. "It must not bother him as much as it does you. Don't you know she's an alcoholic?"

"Allison?" She stopped right in the middle of the dance floor. "No. I don't believe you."

"Yeah. My uncle Norbert got picked up for drinking and driving again. He has to go to Alcoholics Anonymous. He saw her there, at a church in Lima, a couple of times early in the summer. Didn't you know?"

Jenny shook her head. "No. No, I didn't." Allison was an alcoholic. She didn't look or act the way Jenny thought an alcoholic should. She'd never slurred her speech, or walked all wobbly, or passed out on the couch. Jenny had never seen her drink anything stronger than iced tea. "Are you sure?"

"I told you he saw her there. And then my uncle and my mom went out to the farm market a couple of days ago. She was there and he recognized her. She didn't see him."

Jenny wasn't sure what to do next. Should she tell Jake? Did he already know?

She looked at Allison, so pretty and sophisticated-looking in a cream-colored shell and black silk shirt over slim-legged pants. She didn't look drunk now. Of course she wasn't, Jenny berated herself. She wasn't drinking or she wouldn't be going to Alcoholics Anonymous meetings. She didn't know much about AA, but she did know that.

The music stopped. Aaron let go of her, and when he stepped back she felt cold. She felt a coldness in her heart, too. She'd thought that Allison was her friend, that they were *real* friends who talked about important things with each other. But all along, Allison had been keeping secrets, big, earthshaking secrets. From everyone.

"DO YOU HAVE THE FEELING someone is watching us?" Allison asked. She couldn't quite relax in Jake's embrace. She didn't dare. Her need to be in his arms was a growing compulsion that she feared could rival her addiction to alcohol.

"Everybody probably," Jake said, leaning his head back a little to look at her. "Does it bother you?"

She laughed. It was a little tremulous, she realized, betraying her nerves, but she didn't think he noticed. "Yes, it does a little."

His next words surprised her. "I'm sorry," he said. "I should have realized this would happen. You're the first woman I've been seen in public with since Beth died. I should have guessed it would cause a stir."

"I...see." She managed a smile that felt more than a bit forced. "Then I'm not paranoid. There really are two hundred pairs of eyes trained on me."

"Not all two hundred. Most of the kids are more interested in each other than in us."

She looked past his shoulder. "Isn't that what we're here to forestall?" She was all too aware of the strength of his arms and the solidity of his chest as they danced. She was thirty-two years old. She had known passion, but nothing like what she felt when Jake took her in his arms. She was playing with fire and just as likely to get burned as any of the hormone-riddled teenagers sharing the dance floor.

"Yes, dammit. I guess we are. I'm sorry I subjected you to this." He stepped back and raked his hand through his hair. He still hadn't gotten a haircut and the dark waves just brushed the top of his collar, its silkiness begging to be touched.

"Don't be. People are curious. I'm a stranger from the big city after all." She tried another smile and thought she had it just about right, if no one looked too closely. "And you did say this is the first time you've been seen with a woman who's not your wife. Your friends are naturally going to wonder."

His expression was rueful. "Riley Creek is a very small town."

"And Beth was well liked."

"Yes, she was. She lived here all her life. Everyone knew her. Everyone liked her." They had almost stopped dancing even though the music was still playing. A big band tune, Glenn Miller, she guessed, one small corner of her mind remaining stubbornly occupied with mundane thoughts while the rest of her concentrated solely on the man before her.

"And you loved her from the time you were children."

"Tom Sawyer and Becky Thatcher."

She would give everything she owned, everything she would ever have, to be loved that way. "You were very lucky."

"Yes, I was. Most people never get to experience the kind of love I shared with Beth."

"I know."

"Your marriage wasn't a happy one?" It was the first time he'd asked her such a personal question. It caught her off guard.

"We were too different," she said. "We should never have married."

"Do you want to talk about it?"

She looked into his eyes. "No. I'd rather not."

"Okay." He didn't press her further. "How about a glass of punch? This paranoia thing must be catching. I'm beginning to feel eyes boring into the back of my head, too."

"I'd like that." She didn't know how to tell him she'd married the wrong man for all the right reasons. Not here, not now.

He glanced at his watch. "Actually, this should be the last set. Thank God Pastor LeVeck didn't pull cleanup committee, too. We'll be home in twenty minutes if we're lucky. Oh, hell, here comes Merrit Hartwood. He'll want to thank you for filling in and grill you about your family tree. He's a genealogy nut. Look, give him that million-dollar smile of yours, say 'You're welcome and I'd love to talk family history someday,' and let's get out of here. The kids are staying with Stella tonight. I gave Jenny permission to be out until eleven-thirty. And I'd like to spend the next hour alone. With you."

"I..." Being alone with him, even for an hour, was a huge risk. This wasn't playing with fire. This was standing on the edge of an erupting volcano.

"Please. An hour alone. Is that too much to ask?" He reached up, touched her cheek with the tip of his hard, callused finger, and she was lost. She knew he was asking her for more than an hour of pleasant conversation and she accepted that, too. Attraction had been building between them for days, and it wouldn't be denied. Love wouldn't enter into what might happen between them later, but banishing loneliness did.

She could consider making love with him if she was very careful and didn't allow herself to dream of a future with him.

"No," she said, "it's not too much to ask."

They spoke very little on the drive back to his house. Once more, he commented on how beautiful Jenny had looked in a proudly bemused big-brother kind of voice that tugged at Allison's heart.

She murmured in agreement and turned her head to watch the frosty, moon-washed landscape roll by. They pulled into Jake's driveway and drove by the store, dark but for the big security lights mounted on each corner, then continued on down the lane toward the "new barn," which was now the heart of the working farm.

"Do you mind? I need to take a look at Nellie. She was out running in the pasture today and I want to make sure she didn't reinjure her fetlock."

"No, I don't mind." But neither did she want to be alone with her thoughts. "May I come inside with you?"

"Sure. But this isn't the place for high heels."

"Oh." She couldn't keep the slight note of disappointment out of her voice. She'd never been in the barn before.

"What size shoe do you wear?"

"An eight."

"Jenny keeps a pair of tennies down here for mucking around. I'll see if I can find them."

He came around and opened her door before she could find the handle for herself. He held out his hand to help her down from the van, and when his big, warm fingers closed over hers, she felt the heat of his touch all the way to the center of her soul. He didn't step back immediately and she remained seated, their eyes level, her hand in his.

"I'm really sorry about exposing you to all that curiosity tonight."

"It wasn't surprising since I was your first date."

"That's what it felt like." His breath was a wreath of smoke around his head, blurring his strong, angled features just a little. It was cold but still and calm with no wind.

"Was it that awkward for you?" she asked as she got out of the van.

"No. It was that wonderful." The bemused note was in his voice again. "Be careful here. Don't twist your ankle on the stones."

"I won't." Her throat was too tight to say anything more. She waited for him to open the small door. Once inside the barn, he flipped a switch and a row of fluorescent lights flickered into reluctant compliance.

The building was weather tight and well laid out but lacked the character of the big red barn that housed the farm market. Along one wall were the tractors and other equipment that Jake needed to work the fields. At the far end, a loft, half the size of the long, low building, was filled with bales of straw and sweet-smelling timothy hay for the livestock. She could just catch its summery scent above the stronger odors of motor oil and manure.

Allison slipped into Jenny's grungy tennies while Jake set her heels on a bale of straw by the door. The chickens had come awake with the artificial dawn. The bantam rooster crowed and ruffled his feathers in greeting while the hens clucked and fussed. Just as they did for the children who visited the store, the pygmy goats came to the edge of their pen hoping for a treat. But Jake walked past to open Nellie's stall and stepped inside, patting the big horse and reassuring her with soothing words as he hunkered down to check her left hind leg.

Allison walked to the next stall and raised her hand to scratch the other horse on the nose. "Is she okay?"

Jake ran his hand up and down Nellie's leg. "Seems to be. Still no swelling and she's not favoring the leg that I can see." He stood and wiped his hands on a cloth that had been hanging on a peg. He ought to look out of place standing in the middle of the barn in his blazer and tie and charcoal gray dress slacks, but he didn't. "She'll be raring to go by the time there's enough snow to pull the sleigh."

"I'm glad."

"So am I. These horses were bred to work. They don't like when there's nothing to do but stand in their stalls and eat." He smiled when Clara demanded some of his attention by nuzzling him with enough force to make him take a step backward. "Besides, they're real hams. They love the attention."

"But you don't spoil them. Do you?" she asked, pleased at the light tone she managed, thinking of the times she'd seen the horses being fed a treat of carrots or sugar cubes.

Jake looked slightly embarrassed the way men did when they were caught doing something sensitive or sentimental. "They earn their keep."

"No higher praise from a farmer," she said, then laughed. Jake laughed, too, but instead of lessening the tension between them, it seemed to heighten it even more.

"Allison." He lowered his head, blocking out the fitful light, and brushed his lips across hers. "I've been wanting to do that again for days."

Heat pulsed deep inside her. She'd wanted to feel his lips on hers again, too. And more.

He deepened the kiss as though her thoughts had communicated themselves to him without words. She kissed him back, learning the feel of his mouth on hers, the taste and texture of him. She wanted him to make love to her. She wanted him to love her and she was afraid that could never happen.

She broke the kiss. "I think I should go."

"No. Stay." He looked as dazed as she felt. Her heart was pounding. She was dizzy and light-headed with desire.

"Jake." She took a deep breath. *Honesty. Be honest with yourself and with others.* "I don't think this is going to work."

He shook his head, dismissing her words. "There's something between us. You know it. And it's not going to go away."

"I'm not denying that, but..." She lifted her eyes

to his. She knew no other way to say it. "I'm not good at...casual affairs."

He bracketed her face with his hands. Steel threaded his words. "There's nothing casual about what I'm feeling right now."

"I know that. I'm sorry. I didn't express myself very well."

"I didn't think either of us wanted commitment."

How wrong he was. It wasn't that she didn't want commitment. She couldn't *risk* commitment. But she only said, "Yes. That's true."

"Is it so wrong? Neither of us wants to be alone. We could find something meaningful together, if only for a little while."

"But Beth?"

"Shhh." He put his fingers to her lips. "I loved Beth. A part of me will always love her. But it's time to move on with my life." He smiled and brushed his thumb along her cheek. "You've told me that often enough. I want to be with you, Allison. I can't say it more plainly than that. You and me. No ghosts. No regrets."

She looked at the shadowed planes of his face. She knew that if he kissed her again she'd be lost. She'd been alone for so long. She wanted desperately to be part of something vital and caring.

"No regrets," she said so softly he had to bend his head to hear. But she would have regrets, a small voice inside her insisted, a lifetime of them. She ignored it, desire and anticipation overruling caution. Loving Jake, even if only for one night, was worth the regrets...and the pain.

CHAPTER TWELVE

"JAKE? SON. IT'S ME, DAD. Are you in there?" The handle of the small door through which they'd entered started to turn.

"Jake." Allison moved her head slightly. His breath warmed her already flushed cheeks. "Someone's calling your name."

"It's my dad." He shook his head as though trying to clear it. He laid his forehead against hers, and she slipped her arms around his waist, letting herself stay in the circle of his embrace for one moment more. "He's not supposed to be home for over a week."

"But he's obviously here."

"Allie, I'm sorry..." *Allie*. It was the first time he'd used the children's nickname for her. The sound of it went straight to some lonely place deep inside her and nestled there. "I wanted this to be special. I—"

"Jake?"

Now a woman's voice could be heard on the other side of the wall. "Your mother's with him." Allison couldn't keep the horrified note from her voice and it made him smile.

"Sounds like it." Jake looked endearingly confused and off balance. He raised his voice and called out, "Mom. Dad. We're back here with the horses."

Allison took a step sideways. "What will they say when they find us here together?"

He cleared his throat and raked his fingers through his hair. "They'll say, 'Hello. Nice to meet you and thanks for taking such good care of our boy.' And ignore the rest. I hope."

"The rest? Oh dear. Is my makeup smeared?"

"No. Not a smudge."

Not thinking, she caught his face between her hands. "You don't have any lipstick on you."

"No. But what's wrong with me is just as obvious," he said ruefully. "Good thing the light's so bad in here." He turned his head and touched his lips to her palm, then moved away to check that the latch on Nellie's stall was secure as his parents entered the barn. "Mom. Dad. What are you doing home?"

Jake's father was as tall as he was, slightly stooped and thin as a rail fence. His hair—which she saw when he took off his John Deere cap in a courtly gesture—was gray and thinning some on top, but thick and dark on the sides. It was hard to tell the color of his eyes in the blue-white fluorescent light. They were either dark blue like Jake's, or brown like Mike's. His mother was half a foot shorter, wide-hipped and heavy bosomed like a lot of women in Riley Creek. Her hair was light brown frosted with gray, and her eyes were a lighter blue than the rest of the family. Her round, good-natured face was wrinkle free, and her complexion peaches and cream, although she had to be nearing sixty.

"Your mother wanted to come home for Thanksgiving," Jake's father said, then looked startled at the sight of Allison.

"Me? You're the one who's disobeying the doctor's orders, driving that bus seventy miles an hour all the way through Georgia just so you could be home to watch the Ohio State— Oh, hello." Jake's mother stopped in midsentence and midstep to stare at Allison. Her mouth formed an O as she looked from Jake to her husband and back again.

"Hello," Allison said, managing a smile.

"Hello?" Jake's mother looked as if she could have been knocked down with a feather. She stared at Allison a moment longer, then turned inquiring eyes on her son.

Jake stepped into the breach. "Mom, Dad, this is Allison Martin. I don't think you've actually met before. Allison, my parents, Roger and Darlene Walthers."

Jake's introduction gave Allison time to compose herself. Allison held out her hand, calling on countless boardroom introductions to carry her past the awkwardness. "It's nice to meet you."

"Yes, of course." Darlene squeezed her hand briefly, then let go. "I'm sorry I never got out here to welcome you to Riley Creek. I knew your mother. Candy was several years younger, of course, but I remember her from school. She was closer to Roger's youngest brother Alvin's age. Wasn't she, Roger?"

"Yes, I think she was." Roger's handshake was brisk, but his smile was friendly.

"It's nice to meet you," Allison said, smiling, too. "I've heard a lot about both of you these past couple of weeks."

"Same here. Didn't expect to find you in the barn with my son at near eleven o'clock at night, though."

"Roger." Darlene's voice rose a couple of notes.

"Nellie's got a bruised fetlock," Jake said. "I wanted to check on her before I went to bed."

"Uh-huh." To his credit, Roger Walthers kept his eyes firmly on his son's face, but it was easy to see he didn't buy the explanation for a moment.

Jake turned the tables. "You still haven't answered my question. What are you doing here almost two weeks before you're supposed to be."

"Your mother hates Florida." He tilted his head toward his wife. "Made me bring her home for Thanksgiving."

"Roger, that's not true."

He shrugged. "Okay, I hate Florida. And I hate living in that RV no matter how much it cost. Farming's done. No reason for me to stay away from my home any longer."

"The RV's a little cramped when it rains," Darlene said, shrugging apologetically. "And it rains so often in Florida. Roger's used to being able to get out and about—"

"Like living in a crate with windows. If I wanted to go splashing through puddles day and night in the cold and damp, I might as well be here. Do you know how much it costs to rent a car down there? Besides, you weren't calling down the grain futures like you said you would."

"Dad, you were supposed to be on vacation," Jake reminded him with equal parts of affection and exasperation in his tone. "You had heart surgery less than three months ago."

Jake's father went right on talking. "Stay there with all those damnable old coots driving thirty-five miles an hour in the passing lane two more weeks, and I'd have had another heart attack for sure."

"Roger! Don't ever say that again. We were homesick," Darlene explained. "And Roger's right. I did want to be home for Thanksgiving. Matt called from Texas the other day and said he and Ginger and the kids could make it home for the holiday after all. Did he call you yet?"

"No," Jake said, barely getting the word out before Darlene was off again.

"Oh, well. I'll call him tomorrow evening and tell him we're safe home. And Kyle and Janet. They'll be surprised to find they won't have the house to themselves like they thought they would have. So many things to do. You know, Bette Gerschutz is vice president of the Women of the Church Guild and I just don't think she's up to the job of getting out the holiday baskets. A lot of people depend on us for their Thanksgiving meal."

"I know, Mom. We donate a dozen turkeys and a hundred pounds of potatoes for the baskets, remember?'' There was no censure in Jake's voice, only loving acceptance.

"Of course we do, but that still doesn't mean Bette's up to the job."

"Keeping Bette from getting credit for your mother's hard work is only half of it," Roger interjected smoothly, probably thanks to long practice. "'Fess up, Dar."

Darlene gave him a misty smile. "All right. I confess. I missed Jenny and the children so much I couldn't stand it any longer. Are they already in bed? We didn't even stop at the house when we saw the van in front of the barn. Your dad figured something must be wrong for you to be down here this late."

"The kids are spending the night with Stella. Jenny should be home soon. It was the Harvest Dance tonight."

"And I want to see Jenny in her dress. We tried to be home early this afternoon, but the alarm didn't go off this morning and the construction and traffic around Cincinnati were just awful. Then when we finally got home, the furnace wouldn't start..." Darlene bit her lower lip. Her eyes were liquid with tears of exhaustion.

"It's the pilot light gone bad, far as I can tell," Roger finished for her. "Can you put us up for the night, son? I'll call Riley Spangler first thing in the morning and have him over to work on the furnace."

"We can go back to town and sleep in the RV if..." Darlene's voice trailed off. She lowered her eyes, two spots of color darkening her cheeks.

"I was just leaving," Allison said hurriedly.

"We were just on our way back up to the house for a cup of coffee," Jake said firmly. "And of course there's room for you to spend the night."

"A cup of coffee sounds wonderful. Decaf?"

"Sure, Mom."

"There, Mother. That's settled. We have a place to sleep that doesn't require us running an extension cord from the garage to the RV. Are you happy?"

"Yes. I'm happy."

"Good. Then so am I. Now, what did you say was wrong with Nellie?" Roger asked, walking toward the stall.

"Bruised fetlock, left rear leg," Jake replied. "It's coming along okay. You can have a look at her in the morning."

"Will she be ready to pull the sleigh?" Roger asked, taking his son's word for the horse's condition. "Weather report said snow's coming this weekend. A little early in the season, but good for the tourists." The last was said in a carefully neutral voice. Allison wondered what Roger Walthers thought of turning his family farm into a tourist attraction, then decided if he was anything like the other farmers she'd met around Riley Creek, he would shake his head at the foibles of city people and take their money with a smile of welcome.

"I think so. Tomorrow should tell. It's iffy that we'll get enough snow to handle the sleigh anyway."

Roger nodded. "Wheat up yet?"

"You can see for yourself in the morning if the

wheat's up or not," Darlene said as she headed for the door. "It's too cold to stand out here talking shop when we could be doing it in the comfort of Jake's nice, warm kitchen. You will join us for a cup of coffee, won't you, Allison? I haven't even had a chance to thank you properly for helping Jake when he had his accident."

"I... Yes, thank you, I will." If she went running off to her grandmother's house, it would look as though she and Jake had something to hide.

"You two go on up to the house," Jake said. "Allison and I will follow you in the van."

"I'll start the coffee, then. I suppose it's too late to call Stella's house and say hello to the kids?" Darlene asked, clearly hoping Roger wouldn't agree with her.

"It's way too late. You can spend all day tomorrow with them." Roger's voice drifted back to them as the heavy metal door swung shut leaving Jake and Allison alone again.

"Allie, we have to talk."

She was already heading toward the door. She didn't turn around, just slipped off Jenny's sneakers and put on her own shoes. "Not now, Jake." She softened her words with a smile. "I don't want your parents thinking we're up to something in here. I have my reputation to consider."

He wasn't so easily put off. "Allie, we can't just walk away and ignore what just happened."

"Jake, please. It was only a kiss."

"What was happening between us wasn't going to end with a kiss and you know it."

She couldn't argue with that, so she said nothing at all.

The short ride to the house was completed in silence. Jake had placed electric candles in each of the big windows, upstairs and down. The house looked even more welcoming with the soft glow of candlelight shining out into the darkness. Jake drove the van into the garage so she wouldn't have to walk along the gravel driveway in her high heels. He held open the mudroom door and she stepped into the kitchen to be enveloped in light and warmth and the tantalizing smell of brewing coffee.

"Here, take your coat off and sit down," Darlene said, bustling forward as though it was her kitchen and not Jake's. "The coffee will be ready in two shakes."

The door opened again and Jake's father stepped inside carrying two suitcases. Jake attempted to take the cases from the older man. "I'll put these in the bedroom."

"No, you don't. Your mother packed enough for a week. You shouldn't be lifting anything this heavy with those busted ribs."

"You shouldn't be lifting anything that heavy with a busted heart."

Roger rolled his eyes. "Clean bill of health from the doctor at the clinic down in Florida. I can lift anything I want. Now out of my way."

Jake studied the older man's lined face a moment

longer, then obviously satisfied with what he saw, he shrugged and did as his father commanded. "Mom, Stella made coffee cake for the weekend crowd. There's one in the cupboard if you want a sample."

"That sounds good. Did she use Grandma Dachenhaus's recipe?"

"Would she dare make any other kind?" he asked with a grin. "I'd better wash up." He left the room before she could form a retort.

"That boy." Darlene giggled, an infectious chuckle far younger sounding than her years. "Well, he isn't a boy anymore, of course." She looked up from the sugar-and-cinnamon-dusted coffee cake she was cutting into squares. "I really can't tell you how grateful we are you were here to help with Jenny and the children after Jake's accident." She shook her head slightly. "I could hear the strain in Jenny's voice and Jake's, too, whenever we talked on the phone, although they both did their best to hide it. Caring for the children to that extent was just too much for a girl Jenny's age."

"I was glad to help."

"I honestly didn't know what to do. I had Roger's health to think about as well as everyone here. Roger insisted we come home as soon as we heard Jake had been injured. He would have had to do all the driving and, of course, he would have tried to make the trip nonstop. I had nightmares thinking about what might happen. I cannot drive that monstrosity of an RV." She pursed her lips and stuck out her chin just like Julia. "Not that I'm helpless. I can drive a tractor and a tandem of loaded grain wagons as good as any farmer in the county. But that RV—I hate it. From now on, if we go somewhere, we drive our own car. Or fly and stay in a nice hotel like civilized human beings."

She waved the knife she'd been using to cut the cake in an apologetic gesture. "Listen to me ramble on. Anyway, what I really want to say is thank-you for everything you've done for me and mine. I know a little about Jenny's dress and how you fixed it—"

"What are you complaining about now, Mother?" Roger asked, coming back into the kitchen. He went directly to the big freezer, opened the lid and looked inside. He picked up a clear plastic container and studied the contents.

"I'm not complaining. I was thanking Allison for all she's done for Jake and Jenny and the children."

"I'll add my gratitude to Darlene's," Roger said. "If you ever want or need anything from this family, don't hesitate to ask."

"Yes, I will," she said, touched by the sincerity in his voice. "Thank you." She took the plate of cake and the cup of coffee Darlene handed her, relaxing a little as the easy, friendly acceptance of Jake's mother and father washed over her.

"Roger, what are you doing over there?" Darlene demanded.

"Just checking to see if Jake's pumpkin filling passes muster."

"Well, does it?"

"Looks good," he conceded. "But we won't be sure until the big day now, will we?"

"I'm sure the pies will turn out just fine. I taught Jake to cook, you know. Cream or sugar?" she asked Allison in the same breath.

"Black is fine."

"Only half a cup, Dar," Roger said, sitting down at the round oak table, which Allison knew had been there since the house was built. "Too late for coffee, decaf or not. Doesn't agree with my stomach," he confided to Allison. "Used to be able to eat or drink anything, day or night. Not anymore. When you get older, you pay attention to your stomach."

"Coffee, Jake?" Darlene inquired as her son came back into the kitchen.

"No, thanks, Mom. I've had my limit for the night." He pulled one of the chairs away from the table and turned it around. He straddled the seat and rested his forearms along the carved back. "I'll just wait for Allie to finish and then run her home in the van."

Allison felt heat rise to her cheeks. He'd called her Allie in front of his parents. To her, it sounded special and intimate. He'd taken off his blazer and tie, and she watched as he rolled up the cuffs of his shirt.

She could see the strong bones and tendons of his wrist, an enticing glimpse of tanned skin and crisp hair at his throat, and her pulse raced in a way that had nothing to do with sugar or caffeine. Her palms were suddenly so sweaty she held on to her coffee cup with both hands because she was afraid she might drop it. If that happened, Jake's mother would realize she was sitting there at the table lusting after her son.

Roger and Darlene continued to ply Jake with questions about the children and the farm while Allison ate every bite of her coffee cake. She'd only been around Jake's mother for thirty minutes, but she was under no illusion that Darlene would be anything but offended if there was more than a stray crumb or two remaining on her plate.

When she looked up at last, Jake was watching her with a half smile on his face. "Want seconds?" he asked. The corner of his mouth quirked up a little more, turning his smile slightly roguish, which told her he'd read her mind.

"No." She swallowed hard. Brandon had never known her so well, even after two years of marriage. "No, thank you. I really must be going."

Jake rose from his seat and swung the chair around to slide it back under the table. His movements were strong and masculine, without the slight hesitation and stiffness she'd come to expect since his accident. He was almost fully recovered. The thought brought a little lump to her throat. He didn't need her anymore. None of them needed her anymore.

"I'm ready. Let's go," she said, the tiny quaver in her voice so slight she hoped no one noticed.

Just as Jake reached for her coat, the door burst open and Jenny rushed inside. "Mom! Dad! When did you get back?" Tendrils of dark blond hair had escaped from the knot of curls on top of her head. Her face was flushed and her eyes sparkled; the wrist corsage of tiny pink roses and baby's breath her escort had provided held in her hand. "You weren't supposed to start home for days and days yet."

"We came because your father wouldn't stay in Florida any longer, doctor's orders or no doctor's orders," Darlene said, holding out her arms for a hug. "Oh, baby, you look so beautiful. And so grown-up."

"Thanks, Mom." Jenny wrapped her arms around her mother's plump shoulders and hugged her tight. "I've missed you guys so much."

"We've missed you too, sweetheart. Let me see your dress."

Jenny obediently stepped backward and slipped off her coat. She held out both arms and pirouetted so that Roger and Darlene could get the full effect of white organdy and black satin. Allison waited for Jake's parents to pass judgment on her work. Somehow their approval meant more than it should.

Roger whistled. "Jenny girl. You've grown up."

"Hasn't she though." Darlene hurried forward for another hug. "It's just beautiful. You're beautiful." She sniffed and rummaged in the pocket of her slacks for a tissue. "Just beautiful."

"Allison did it," Jenny said, but there was a hardness in her voice that Allison had never expected to hear again.

"Yes. The dress is lovely. Thank you again, Allison. I'm sure it was a lot of hard work. I really have to find some way to repay you for all you've done for us."

"I was happy to do it, Mrs. Walthers." Allison

looked at Jenny, but the teenager wouldn't quite meet her eyes.

"Darlene. You must call me Darlene. Mrs. Walthers was my mother-in-law, may she rest in peace."

"Darlene," she said. Her mouth formed a smile, but her thoughts were elsewhere

Why wouldn't Jenny look at her? When she'd helped her with her hair and dress only a few hours ago, she'd been chattering like a magpie, excited and happy. As far as Allison could tell, the evening had been a total success for Jake's sister. She'd danced with Aaron Masterson and a couple of other boys. Her escort had been polite and attentive. The girls had flocked around to compliment her on her dress and hair. She'd been allowed to stay out an hour past her curfew. Allison watched her closely for another few seconds, looking for telltale signs of drug or alcohol use. There were none. Jenny simply didn't want to look at her. Allison couldn't think of anything she'd said or done that might have hurt Jenny's feelings or made her angry with her. Perhaps she was reading too much into this. It was late. Everyone was tired. Tomorrow would be soon enough to find out what, if anything, was wrong and make it right.

She let Jake help her into her coat as she said her goodbyes. He opened the door and she preceded him through the mudroom and into the garage. She forgot about Jenny's odd behavior, about everything but the man beside her in the van as they backed out of the driveway and headed across the road. It was only a hundred yards to her house, but it would have been hard walking in her spindly heels.

Jake pulled up parallel to her kitchen door and put the van into park. "Thanks for being such a good sport about Mom and Dad showing up out of the blue that way."

"I enjoyed meeting them," she said. "They both seem very happy to be home."

She could just see his mouth curve in a smile by the faint glow of the dash lights. "My dad isn't going to take well to retirement. I can see that already. But God willing, by spring he'll be strong enough to help with the planting. And this winter he can bug the heck out of his cronies at the Country Kitchen every morning and play penny-ante poker at the American Legion in the afternoon. Mom will be available to help out with Julia when she's not at preschool. I've been relying too much on Jenny." He shook his head. "I didn't want the evening to end with a conversation about my parents."

Allison remained silent. Her heart was beating too fast again. She could see the hard line of his jaw, envision the dark shadow of beard on his chin. She let her gaze wander to his hands. She knew the strength of those hands, and the gentleness. She took a deep breath, but it didn't help because she just inhaled the scent of his aftershave. "I didn't, either," she whispered before she could stop herself.

He reached across the bucket seat and touched her cheek. "I'm not going to kiss you again. I don't think I could stop if I did." His smile was tinged with regret. "And even if I did have that kind of self-control, I don't want my mother checking the clock every five minutes until I get home."

Allison managed a smile, too. "Don't tell me she keeps as close an eye on you as she does on Jenny?"

"Closer. This is all new to me, Allie. I haven't even wanted to make love to another woman since Beth died. But I want you. I want to make love to you very much."

"I want you, too," she said, knowing that he wouldn't believe her if she tried to lie. "But I don't think it would be wise."

"Why not?" He slid his hands along her throat, curved them over her shoulders as though to draw her closer. She resisted the gentle pressure.

"I don't belong here, Jake. This isn't my world. This isn't my life." *Tell him the truth,* a small voice inside her begged. *Tell him why you have to go back to Chicago. Why there can't be a future for you in Riley Creek.*

"It could be."

"No." She shook her head, trembling with the need to let herself be pulled into his arms. "No." She did her best to keep the desperation she felt out of her voice. "It won't work, Jake. It can't."

"I know this all seems sudden to you. I feel as blindsided as you must. But I'm not some teenager with a hard-on for the prettiest girl in the senior class, Allie. I care for you. I know the difference between love and lust." He let go of her abruptly and dropped his head back against the seat. "God, this isn't coming out the way I want it to. I'm making it worse, aren't I?''

"Yes. No," she amended hastily. "Not because of Beth." Jake's feelings for his dead wife had been overtaken by her other concerns. She wasn't so selfish a woman that she begrudged him what he'd shared with the mother of his children. "It's because I'm not staying, Jake. I'm going back to Chicago in only a few days, a week at the most. I thought I could take what you offered tonight, make love and then turn my back and walk away when the time came." She had to be very careful how she said this. She swallowed hard to keep tears from clogging her throat and affecting her voice. She hadn't known it would be so hard. "Now I realize that would have been wrong, for both of us."

"Yeah, you're probably right." His voice had roughened with anger and hurt. "What the hell is there for you in Riley Creek? What the hell is there for you with me? A farmer with three kids to raise and a load of debt that would make your hair curl."

She reached out, unable to stop herself. He'd made a fist on his thigh and it took both her hands to cover his. "That's not it, either, Jake."

He made a sound of disbelief deep in his throat. "You can probably buy and sell me twice over."

"No, Jake. You're just using money as an excuse. You're not any more ready for what's happening between us than I am."

She felt the tendons in his wrist and arm tighten. He moved quickly, uncurling his fist, capturing both her hands in his big one. "Promise me you'll stick around long enough to give us a chance."

There were tears in her eyes. She blinked hard to keep them from spilling over. That was the one thing she dared not promise. She had to go back to Chicago, prove to herself that she was strong and whole again. Prove she had beaten the demons inside her. But even as she admitted that, she was also admitting she was still too weak, too small a person to tell Jake the truth about herself. "I can't promise to stay."

CHAPTER THIRTEEN

THE WEATHERMAN WAS WRONG. It didn't snow. The next morning dawned clear and bright. It had been days since Jake had seen the sun, a not uncommon occurrence at this time of year, and he spent almost half an hour he could ill spare leaning against a fence post watching Nellie and Clara munch the last of the summer grass in the small fenced pasture beside the pond. Nellie wasn't limping, and the bruised fetlock seemed to have healed completely. He turned and walked up the gentle rise to the store with the morning sun warming the back of his neck. There were already half a dozen cars in the parking lot. It was going to be a busy day.

"Where's Allie?" Julia demanded, rushing out of the house. His mother watched her from the kitchen doorway, but when she saw him, she went back inside and returned to whatever she'd been doing. The purple pom-pom on Julia's hat bounced up and down as she ran. Her face was wreathed in smiles. She was always smiling lately.

He hunkered down beside his daughter, and put his arm around her. "I don't know where she is. Is her car in the driveway?"

"Yes," Julia said, sticking out her lower lip. "Look. There it is. Why isn't she here watching *the game?*" Jake hid a smile. Even at three and a half, she was adding emphasis to the words. In this part of the world, when Ohio State played Michigan, there was no other football game worth mentioning.

"Did you ask her to come and join us?" he asked, smoothing back a stray wisp of hair. Beneath her parka, Julia was dressed in red sweats with an Ohio State University logo embroidered across the front of the shirt. Jenny had painted a Buckeye emblem on her cheek and braided her hair with red and gray ribbons. Mike and Libby were also dressed in red and gray to show their support for the Bucks. Jake and his brothers had attended Ohio State and the Walthers clan were all loyal Buckeye fans.

"Grandpa made candy," Julia informed him, not bothering to answer his question.

"I bet they were buckeyes." The chocolate and peanut butter fudge candies were one of Roger's specialties. He'd left for town an hour ago to oversee the furnace repairman and then watch the game at the American Legion hall with his buddies, just as he'd done for almost forty years. If Jake had had any doubts about the wisdom of his parents' early return to Ohio, they'd disappeared when he'd seen the spring in his father's step as he worked in the kitchen that morning, humming the Ohio State fight song and listening to the game show on the radio.

"Grandma says no more candy." Julia had apparently been sampling Grandpa's goodies. There was a smudge of chocolate at the corner of her mouth, and she was clutching a plastic bag with three more buckeyes tightly in her left hand. "Grandpa's gone to fix the furnace. Then Grandma and Grandpa can go home and they won't get poisoned. Dead on the floor with their faces all black and their tongues sticking out like this." She puffed up her cheeks and stuck out her tongue.

Jake nearly choked trying to keep from laughing out loud. "Who told you that?"

"Mike," she said. Julia was suddenly very serious. "I don't want Grandma and Grandpa to die like Mommy did. Did Mommy look like that?"

Jake shook his head, serious, too. "No, Mommy looked like an angel. Just like you." He gave her a little kiss on the cheek. *Beth, she's so great. They're all so great.* He waited for the pain, but it wasn't there. Only the whisper of happy memories. "Don't worry. Mr. Spangler will fix Grandma and Grandpa's furnace good as new. And we won't let them go until everything's working just fine at their place, okay?"

"Okay." She smiled and put her arms around his neck. "I want Allie to come and watch the game with us. I miss her."

"So do I, kitten," Jake said softly.

He hadn't slept well last night. He wasn't sure exactly what had happened to him. He was falling in love again—that much was certain. But just how and when it had happened, he had no idea. The thought of it still scared him. What did he possibly have to offer Allison Martin? A patched-together heart, three kids and a farm that was mortgaged to the hilt to convert a perfectly good barn into a barely breaking-even farm market. She bought and sold millions of dollars of stocks and bonds at a time. Lived a life-style he could only imagine.

"Come with me to ask Allie to watch the game with us," Julia begged. "Please."

"Honey, I'm going to be here helping Stella with the store." There were a lot of football widows in this part of the country when Michigan played Ohio State, and a good many of them liked to shop.

"I want Allie to watch the game with me." Julia was starting to whine. Tears were sure to follow if she didn't get what she was asking for, and she knew he was still a soft touch when she cried. "I think I'm big enough to cross the road by myself today," she added craftily.

"Okay. I'll go across the road with you, but, kitten, she might be too busy. She's going to be moving away." He needed to start getting the kids used to the idea of Allie's leaving Riley Creek. Hell, *he* had to get used to the idea.

"No, she's not," Julia said with a three-year-old's confidence. "I'll tell her to stay here."

Jake leaned down and put a double knot in her shoelace so she couldn't see his face. "Let's not worry about it today," he said. "Let's just have a good time."

He looked up. Julia was watching him intently, not at all fooled. "I don't want her to go," she said once more. "You're the dad. Tell her to stay."

If only it was that easy. But he knew this argument could go on indefinitely. "All right, I'll ask her to stay."

"Good," she said, satisfied that he would make everything right.

ALLISON WAS IN the front parlor, trying to decide whether she could take down the big gilt-framed mirror from the mantel by herself or whether it would require a man's help when she saw Jake and Julia heading for her kitchen door. Her palms instantly became sweaty. She wiped them on the legs of her jeans. *Concentrate.* That's how she controlled her need for alcohol. Surely it would work as well to curb her need for Jake.

She looked at the mirror again, willing her thoughts away from the man approaching her house. She'd decided to take the mirror back to Chicago with her. It would look woefully out of place in the high-tech, off-white living room of her lakeshore condo. But there was a space for it in her bedroom above the stark white marble fireplace that bisected the wall across from her bed. That room was decorated in warm earth tones with bright splashes of copper and gold, and the mirror was just what she needed to soften that cold expanse of marble, which so far had defied her attempts.

Her Martha Stewart exercise wasn't working. Her breathing was still too fast and too shallow, her stomach full of butterflies. She'd lain awake all night. Not because she craved a drink but because she craved a touch—Jake's touch.

A knock sounded at the back door. She was still standing in front of the mirror, seeing nothing, feeling everything. "Just…just a moment," she called, hearing the catch in her voice, hoping it couldn't be detected through the inch-thick walnut door. She pasted a smile on her face as she crossed the worn kitchen linoleum and swung the door open. "Julia!"

There was a smudge of chocolate at the edge of Julia's mouth and Allison couldn't resist going down on one knee and wiping it away with the tip of her finger.

"Hi, sweetie. I've missed you. Did you and your grandparents have a good time today?"

Julia nodded so hard the pom-pom on her hat bounced up and down. "And guess what! Grandpa made candy." She giggled and held up a small plastic bag filled with round chocolate candies. Buckeyes, Allison guessed. She hadn't seen them since her college days. "We came to get you so you can watch *the game* with us."

"*The game?*" Allison repeated the emphasis she'd heard Julia put on the words.

"The Buckeyes and those damned Wolverines," she said, smiling sweetly.

"Julia, you know that's a bad word."

"That's what Grandpa called them," Julia said with another angelic smile. "But I won't say it again."

Allison enfolded the little girl in her arms and

looked up at Jake. His expression was as wary as she knew her own must be, but there was a dark spot of color high on each cheekbone and she guessed he was remembering what had happened last night.

"It's the Ohio State–Michigan game. Kickoff's at noon. I hooked up a TV in the small staff room off the deli kitchen. Libby and Mike are already there. Julia would like—" he caught himself "—we'd all like you to join us if you haven't got any other plans."

"No," she said, shifting her gaze to Julia's excited, happy little face. "I don't have plans. I—I was only starting to pack the things of Grandmother's that I want to take back to Chicago with me."

"Then come with us," Julia cried.

What choice did Allison have? The lure of spending a day with Jake and the children was too great a temptation for her to resist. "I'll get my coat."

"Yea!" Julia sang out, hopping up and down. "Allie's coming! Allie's coming."

"You don't have to do this," Jake said as she stood. There was so much unsettled between them, so much he didn't know. With Jake, she would have everything she'd ever wanted—a home, a family, roots. But she would never have peace of mind, forever wondering if some crisis she hadn't anticipated would cause her to drink again. She couldn't commit to anyone or anything until she proved to herself she could survive in the world she knew best.

"I want to," she said.

"All right!" Julia pumped her fist up and down the

way Allie had seen Mike do so often. Jake looked down at the little girl and smiled. He was still smiling when he looked at Allie, and her heart twisted a little, a sensation caused by both desire and despair.

"We'll make you the designated Michigan fan. Otherwise, poor Tom will be outnumbered ten to one."

"Tom's going to be here, too?"

"Stella's working. Tom will show up."

"I suppose you're right. Okay. Go Blue!" she said. "How's that?"

"Go Bucks!" Julia responded at the top of her voice. "Want to hear me yell it louder?"

"No," Jake said forcefully. "Save it for the game."

Julia held tightly to Allison's hand all the way into the store, but the moment the big glass doors of the market side of the barn swung shut behind them, she broke free and made a mad dash for the gift shop. "I want to see the new Beanie Babies!"

"Julia, slow down." Jake's tone brooked no argument. She did as she was told, looking back over her shoulder with a grin.

"I'll be good."

"Words to strike fear into a father's heart," Jake said, following her. "All I need is chocolate finger smudges on those da— On those Austrian lace angels we just got in. I'll bring her into the lounge when I catch her. She can't do as much damage in there."

About a dozen customers were browsing through the aisles of candy and maple syrup, inspecting the pears and squashes, standing in the checkout line or ordering from the deli cases. The parking lot was full of cars, so Allison suspected there were at least that many women to be found on the gift-shop side of the barn. And they were all women today, she noticed, football widows, just as Jake had predicted. Stella was busy behind the meat counter and acknowledged Allison's wave with a harried nod of her head.

The moment Allison stepped into the kitchen she was greeted by the noise and laughter of children, the smells of meat and cheese and pastries, and the bustle and energy of a prosperous business. Tanner, Marsh and Fairchild had never been like this. Even the most frantic trading days on the market were translated into low-keyed conversations and consultations. No voices were ever raised. "Never let them see you sweat" had been the words she'd lived by. And nearly lost her soul because of. Was she ready to step back into that life? It was an answer she would have soon enough.

"Hi, Allie." Mike came running from the small staff lounge that was connected to the kitchen by a low archway.

"Hi, guy," she said, wanting to reach down and catch him in her arms for a big hug. But she would be leaving soon, so it was best to start putting a little distance between them. God! She hadn't realized it would be so hard to withdraw from Jake's children. "How's your day been?"

"I've been real busy," Mike said seriously. "Lots to do. I wish you could still stay with us."

"But there isn't room for me with your Grandma and Grandpa here."

"It is kinda crowded," Mike agreed. "But you could come over for supper, couldn't you?"

"I'd like that," Allison said, unable to lie.

"I'll tell Grandma you're coming tonight."

"I... We'll see," she said. "Where's Libby?" She made herself smile.

"She's in the staff room coloring. She doesn't care a thing about the game."

"She doesn't?"

"She's a girl."

"Girls like football."

"Not as much as guys. My uncle Matt played for Ohio State," he said proudly.

"He did?" Allison made certain she sounded suitably impressed.

"Well, yeah." Mike was scrupulously honest. "He never got to play on TV or anything, but he was on the team. We've got pictures. I'll show you sometime."

She followed Mike into the staff room. It was low-ceilinged with the same pale green walls as the kitchen and industrial-grade linoleum squares covering the concrete floor. Jake had literally built a building within a building to bring the kitchen and storage area up to code. The gift shop and market retained the high ceilings and wooden beams of the original structure, but once you passed through the swinging doors into the food-preparation area, everything was state of the art. The staff room was equipped with a sink and refrigerator, coffeemaker and a table and chairs. A small color television sat on the counter. Someone had taped an Ohio State banner to the wall.

"Hi, Allie," Libby said, smiling her gap-toothed smile.

"Hi, Libby."

"Want to color with me?"

"How about if I just watch you."

"Okay. I'm making you a picture to take back to Chicago. Are you going soon?"

Allison's throat tightened and she had to swallow hard before she could speak. "Soon, Libby."

The little girl frowned and looked down at her coloring book. "I wish you wouldn't go."

"I wish I didn't have to. Isn't Jenny here?" she asked, deliberately changing the subject. Allison still didn't know why Jenny had looked so hurt and angry after the Harvest Dance.

"She went to Aaron's house to watch the game with friends." Libby sounded disappointed. "But she painted a Buckeye on my face, see?" She turned her cheek to show Allison her embellishment. "Mike says he's too old. He didn't want one this year, but Julia and I did." Libby, too, was dressed in an Ohio State sweatshirt and pants.

"I think it looks great."

"I do, too. Here's your picture." Allison took a seat beside the little girl. Carefully, Libby tore the completed page from her coloring book. She handed it to Allison with a shy smile. "It's a picture of kids picking apples from a tree. There's three of them.

Two girls and a boy. I made them look like me and Mike and Julia.'' The little girls had golden hair. The boy's was brown like Mike's. They were in an orchard with a red barn in the distance. Libby had added big white clouds to a blue sky, and horses beside the barn. ''It's Walnut Hill. Do you recognize it?''

Allison's throat tightened with emotion. ''It looks just like Walnut Hill. I'll keep it with me always.''

''Now you won't forget us.''

She leaned forward and gave Libby a kiss on her forehead. ''I'll never forget you.''

''It's kickoff time,'' Mike called out. He was sitting right in front of the TV, his arms on the counter, his chin on his hands. ''C'mon. Where is everybody? The game's starting.''

''We're here,'' Jake said, appearing in the doorway with Julia in his arms, further proof that he was healing and that the Walthers family could go on without her. ''Did I miss the kickoff?''

''No! But hurry.''

''Don't sit so close to the TV,'' Jake said, and Mike moved his chair back six inches.

''I want Allie.'' Julia held out her arms.

''Would you mind keeping an eye on her for a few minutes? Stella's having trouble with the meat slicer in the deli.''

''I'd be happy to have her with me.''

''Thanks, Allie. And when I get a few minutes, I... We have to talk.''

Allison hesitated a moment as she reached for Julia. ''Yes, I suppose we do.'' She owed him that much.

He wasn't smiling, but neither were the ghosts of old sorrows apparent in his eyes as he gave Beth's child into her keeping. He trusted her with his most precious possessions, his children. He had come close to offering her his heart. And in return she had given him nothing but evasions and lies. She couldn't allow herself to return the love she felt growing between them, but she owed him the truth about herself. She needed to do that for her own peace of mind as well as his.

CHAPTER FOURTEEN

BY THE TIME the third quarter started, the festive atmosphere in the staff room had settled into a kind of quiet melancholy. Michigan was beating Ohio State handily. They had scored again just before the half and were up by thirteen points. So far, Ohio State's offense had committed two turnovers, and the defense just couldn't shut down Michigan's running game. It looked like the Buckeyes' dreams of another Rose Bowl season were going down to defeat. Only Tom Farley was smiling.

"C'mon, Allison," he teased. "You're the designated Wolverine fan today. My only ally. Show some team spirit." She and Tom and the children were alone in the room. Stella was busy with customers and Jake's mother had called him into the house half an hour earlier to answer a call from his insurance agent.

Allison smiled and pinched the brim of the Wolverine baseball cap he'd given her to wear. It played "Hail to the Victors" and matched the one he was wearing with his navy blue-and-gold shirt. "How's that?"

"Turn that off," Mike groused. "I'm hearing it enough from the band on the TV."

"Sorry," she said, tucking her smile away. "The game's only half over. Ohio State can still win."

"At Ann Arbor? Get real." Ohio State failed to make a first down and Michigan got the ball back again. Mike groaned loudly and threw up his hands. "This is awful. What's with these guys? They were ranked number one in the whole country, and they're blowing it. Just like last year."

"Well, it's hard to beat Michigan when they're playing at home," Allison said, turning her cap around so the gold block *M* wasn't showing.

"Hey." Tom watched her with twinkling eyes. "I'm offended. I drove all the way to Toledo to get that hat. It's against the law to sell anything blue and gold in this county, you know. I ran a terrible risk getting it past Rudy Sunderman's anti-Michigan checkpoint."

"You mean I'm wearing contraband?" Allison put her hand over her heart. "What if the Securities and Exchange Commission finds out? They might consider it unethical. I'll lose my job."

"In that case, you'd better hand it over."

Allison put her hand on top of her head so he couldn't snatch the hat away. "I'll take my chances with the SEC. Maybe Stella will wear it if you ask her very nicely," Allison said, teasing him just a little. Ever since the evening they'd gone to his place to see the wild turkeys, she'd felt as though Tom was a real friend, not just an acquaintance. She would miss him when she left Riley Creek.

"No way." Tom lifted his hands in front of him

as though to ward off an attack. "Stella wouldn't wear it. She said it offends the customers. Not because it's a Michigan hat, but because most of them are football widows in the first place."

Allison tilted her head. "And shopping with a vengeance. Maybe Stella has the wrong take on it. Maybe Jake should play up the football angle. Make them want to max out their gold cards."

"Now I see why you're a Wall Street shark in your other life," Tom said laughing. "You go straight for the jugular."

Allison felt a swift pang. *Her other life... That's what it felt like sometimes—another time, another place, another woman.* "I'm not a Wall Street shark," she said. "I—I just..."

He was grinning. "I've got money in one of the funds you manage," he said. "It's growing almost half again as fast as some of the big-name mutuals."

"How did you find out what funds I handle?"

"I may be just a hick farmer," Tom said, a sly smile lifting one salt-and-pepper eyebrow. "But I have a few connections here and there. Somebody who knows somebody who knows somebody says you're a real up-and-comer in the market."

"I've had a couple of offers," she said. "But that kind of rat race isn't for me."

"Is the Tanner, Marsh and Fairchild rat race still for you?"

"Hey! I like how you're wearing your hat. You look way cool," Libby said before Allison had to answer Tom's question. At halftime, she and Julia had given up their coloring books in favor of decorating pumpkin-shaped cookies with orange and green frosting and colored sprinkles. "Just like you were in a gang or something."

"Thank you, I think." Allison caught Tom's eye and managed a laugh. "Was that a compliment?"

"I hope not," Tom answered only half-jokingly. "Gangs are one problem we don't have to worry about in Riley Creek. At least not yet."

"Slow down!" Libby cried. "Allie, Julia's using up all the chocolate sprinkles."

"Oh, Julia. Wait a minute, sweetie. Are you sure you want to put all those chocolate sprinkles on your cookie."

"Yes," Julia said without hesitation. "All of them."

"I think I'd better do a little supervising here," Tom remarked just as Stella walked into the room and went directly to the refrigerator and pulled out a bottle of spring water.

"Supervising what?" she asked, leaning her ample hip against the counter as she opened the bottle and took a long swallow.

"Cookie decorating. I'm a whiz at cookie decorating." He leaned over the back of Julia's chair and dropped a kiss on top of her head. "How about putting fewer chocolate sprinkles on your cookie so you can see the neat orange frosting?"

"I'll make the next one pretty," Julia said, shaking chocolate sprinkles relentlessly over the cookie. "I'm making this one all brown because it's rotten, like our Halloween jack-o'-lanterns out behind the barn.''

Tom laughed and straightened up. "You win. I've met my match.''

"Do you have children, Tom?'' Allison asked.

He shook his head, then looked at Stella. "I've never been married. Never wanted to be until lately.''

"Tom.'' Stella's tone was sharp. "Don't start that again.''

"It's been on my mind.''

"I won't marry you. I've told you that over and over again.''

"Why not? I don't smoke. I don't drink to excess. I'm healthy and I've got enough money to keep us both comfortably.'' Allison couldn't tell if he was teasing or serious.

Stella evidently thought it was the latter. She screwed the top back on the bottle of water and set it on the counter with a thump. "This is not the time or place to discuss this,'' she said, indicating the children with a nod.

"Maybe it is.'' There was no mistaking Tom's attitude now. He was earnest. "I don't seem to be able to get you to answer me any more truthfully when we're alone.''

"Why in the world are you bringing this up now? I've agreed to spend Thanksgiving with you. I've sl—'' She shut her mouth with a snap on the rest of the sentence. "I have a dozen customers in the store. I don't have time for this.''

"Marry me, Stella. I love you and I want us to be together."

"I'm not marrying another farmer. End of discussion." She started to walk out of the room.

Tom moved to block her exit. Mike was engrossed in an Ohio State drive that had gotten his team to the fifteen-yard line. The girls were busy embellishing their cookies. Tom and Stella seemed to have forgotten that the children or Allison existed.

"I love you, Stella LaRue. I've loved you for a lot longer than you can guess. But I'm tired of waiting. I'm fifty years old. I don't want to spend the rest of my life alone. I own four hundred acres of some of the best farmland in the world. I farm another thousand acres for six hard-nosed old-timers who'd fire me in a minute if I didn't get them the best yields or the best price on their grain. I'm a damned good farmer and a damned good businessman or I wouldn't be where I am today."

"And you love what you do."

"Yes." He sounded genuinely puzzled. "Why should that be a problem?"

Stella shook her head. Her voice was rough with unshed tears. "Because Dick loved it, too. And when he lost our farm he couldn't get over it. Even the kids and I weren't enough. I won't go through that again. I won't lose another husband to the land."

"It won't happen."

"I can't be sure. Now please. I have to get back to the store."

Tom held her gaze, then his shoulders sagged as

though a heavy weight had dropped on him. "I won't ask you again," Tom said. "I love you. But I won't ask you again."

Her face was full of misery and resolve. "You won't have to. I've decided...I'm leaving Riley Creek after the first of the year."

THE SUN WAS A HUGE red ball, hovering just above the trees by the creek. The sky was a whole palette of colors ranging from the frosty blue of early winter, to smoke, then to pink. It had been a beautiful day, cold but still. Now the stars were beginning to appear in the eastern sky, and the moon was shining although it wasn't even six o'clock. Jake could hear a train coming from far away, and closer, the bleating of the nanny goat and the squawking of the banties as they settled for the night.

"And then Tom left," Allison said as they walked down the gentle slope of the hill toward the small pasture. "Stella went stomping out of the staff lounge right after him without saying another word. I felt like a voyeur. But they didn't seem to notice I was even there."

"Tom's waited a long time for Stella. Lately, I had hoped it was going to work out." Jake had been a little surprised that Allison had agreed to walk down to the new barn with him. She'd been avoiding him all day. He'd figured something important had happened to cause Allison to seek him out, and it had. "But after this, I'm not so sure there's much of a chance for that anymore."

"I agree," Allison said, pushing her hands into the pockets of her coat. She was wearing gloves, and he doubted she was cold, but like him, it seemed she couldn't find anything to do with her hands. Her coat was a leafy green color, long and belted, made of some silky material, completely inappropriate for a farm. The color looked great on her, though, highlighting the fiery streaks in her hair. "What will you do if Stella does leave?"

"I'll have to find someone else to manage the store. I'll hate to lose Stella, but she's not an indentured servant." He didn't want to think about Stella's going. She was a hard worker, honest, dependable and well organized, and she was his friend.

"Stella said her husband committed suicide because they lost their farm."

"Dick LaRue was a good man but a damned poor farmer. I was only about twenty when Dick died, but my dad said it was his own hurt pride that killed him as much as it was losing his family's farm. Some people are like that. Their own misery consumes them."

"He must have been in desperate straits to leave his wife to raise their children alone." Allison's voice was low and thoughtful. She always thought things through before she said them. She seldom spoke impulsively or with less than perfect honesty.

"Yes," Jake said, "I suppose you're right. I can't imagine giving in to my own pain if it meant the kids would be alone."

"No," she said, and tilted her head to smile up at him. "I'm sure you can't."

He shrugged, feeling unsettled that he'd spoken aloud like that. He had never said such things to Beth. But Allison was not Beth. With each day that passed, it was easier for him to separate the two women in his mind, and in his heart. "It's just the way I am."

"It's a good way to be," she said, scuffing the toe of her running shoe in the frozen dirt.

He changed the subject but not to the one that he really wanted to discuss. He hadn't quite worked up enough nerve for that. "I'm glad it didn't snow today. I don't think we would have gotten a lot of takers for sleigh rides. They're good for family shopping weekends, when Dad comes along and the kids get a little too rowdy in the gift shop. Nellie and Clara pay their own way those days. But—"

"Today was for football widows," she said before he could.

Jake grinned. "Yes, and they were getting their revenge. I haven't totaled the registers yet. But it was a very good day."

"I'm glad." Allison moved closer to skirt a muddy spot in the path, then stepped away as soon as she'd passed. They had avoided touching each other by unspoken agreement. All his thought processes seemed to short-circuit when they touched. He knew it was the same for her, and that she didn't like it.

He had the feeling her response to him frightened her more than a little. But he also sensed the great depth of passion and emotion she held behind that barrier of control. He saw it when she laughed and played with his children. He felt it when he held her in his arms. She was divorced, and he wondered if the physical side of her marriage had been unsatisfying for her and if perhaps she was a little afraid of making love. He'd have to take it slow, although he didn't have much time if she was determined to go back to Chicago before Thanksgiving. That's why he'd decided to ask her to go away with him tomorrow. The idea had come to him a few hours ago, and since then it had damned near taken total possession of his mind.

"Stay here," he said, indicating a place by the fence. "I'll open the door so Clara and Nellie can go into their stalls. It'll only take a minute."

"Okay." She put her hands on the top rail and rested her chin on her hands. "Nellie's not limping at all anymore," Allison observed as both horses came toward them at a walk.

"No. She'll be ready when it does snow."

"It must be wonderful—sleigh bells and lap robes and hot chocolate afterward."

"I'll take you for a ride some night when the moon is full and the fields are covered with snow. The deer come out to feed along the creek bank, and the sounds of the sleigh bells carry all the way to town." He stopped talking when he saw sadness in her eyes. She turned her face away but not before he thought he saw the sheen of tears.

"I won't be here when it snows like that," she said at last.

Nellie and Clara ambled close to the fence, reached their big heads over and blew white clouds into the air. Jake ignored them.

"Allison, give me a chance." He was suddenly short of breath. If he just had her alone, away from the kids and his family and the store, he could prove to her how much he needed her to stay with him for the rest of his life. His vow to go slow was forgotten. He would take her somewhere expensive and sophisticated. He would show her she wouldn't have to give up everything to be with him.

"I think Clara wants a treat," she said.

"I didn't bring anything with me." He spoke before he could stop himself. "Allison, we need some time to ourselves. To talk, to figure out how strong whatever this thing is between us." He couldn't say he loved her. He wanted to, but the words just weren't there. "Come with me tomorrow night. There's a place about an hour south of here. It's an old house, almost a castle, really. Some railroad tycoon built it a hundred years ago to get away from the heat and humidity in Cincinnati. It's an inn now. The food's incredible. The chef is French."

"Jake, I... There's something I have to tell you first."

Jake uncurled his fingers. He hadn't even realized he'd clenched his hand into a fist inside his coat pocket. He'd been afraid she would turn him down flat, but she hadn't. He let his thoughts flash on what might come after dinner, the two of them alone in one of the inn's bedrooms, a fire burning, Allison naked in his arms, flushed with passion. "No," he said. "Whatever it is you have to say can wait. We never have more than five minutes together here. One more day won't make any difference. I want to take you there. I want to be alone with you."

She looked out over the fields to the trees bordering the creek. "I want to go," she said softly. "But it won't change anything, Jake. I can't stay in Riley Creek. There are reasons I have to go back to Chicago. Things I haven't told you..."

"Is there another man?" The fantasy of passion and firelight exploded into cold ash.

She shook her head. "No. There's no one else. There hasn't been since my divorce."

"And are you ready to move on?"

"Are you?" she asked, meeting his eyes for the first time in several minutes.

"Yes," he said. "I've told you that. I'm ready to move on." And he was. He had come to accept Beth's death. He would cherish her memory for all his life, but she was gone and he couldn't have her back.

Allison was silent a moment, then she reached out and touched his cheek, very lightly with her gloved hand. "We've never really been alone together." She sounded slightly wistful.

"I know. That's why I want to take you away from Walnut Hill."

She seemed to make up her mind then. "It would be nice to be alone, where we can talk."

His heart started racing. At least she was admitting

there was something special between them. All he had to do now was convince her it was special enough to try to work out a future between them. But now wasn't the time. He'd wait until tomorrow when everything was as perfect as he could make it. "Just the two of us."

She smiled, but it never reached her eyes.

ALLISON TURNED AND WALKED up the hill, past the barn, past Jake's house with the soft yellow light spilling out of the windows onto the frozen ground. She stopped for a moment in the darker shadows of the bare maples and looked back at the house, and in her mind she could see the family within. A family like the one she'd wanted all her lonely life. A family that she was beginning to hope might become her own. If she could only overcome this one last barrier to intimacy.

Why had she told Jake she'd go with him? As things stood right now, she would only be hurting him if she gave in to this soul-searing need to be in his arms. She hadn't been honest with him, not about anything. She hadn't told him she was an alcoholic. She hadn't told him she was going back to Chicago not because Tanner, Marsh and Fairchild was her life, but because it was one more challenge she must pass.

She hadn't told him she had fallen in love with him.

But tomorrow she would. Tonight she would find just the right words. She would tell him about herself when they had no distractions from family and business. She would tell him everything, and if she was lucky, they could work out a future for themselves. All she had to do was tell him the truth.

It was completely dark now. The stars were coming out one by one, cold and small and far away. Allison stood watching them for a long minute. She couldn't see skies like this in Chicago, and over the past months she'd found it was important to see the stars.

She would have to start over in her life, but she had a home if she wanted it, and now friends. She could find work in Riley Creek. She didn't quite see herself as a teller at the Riley Creek State Bank, but perhaps she could start her own consulting business. She'd known one or two people who had gone that route and were now advising companies on foreign stocks and highly specialized investment strategies. She had a real talent for ferreting out small companies with growth potential, maneuvering quickly to add their stock to her fund portfolio, then sitting back to watch the other managers scramble to catch up. It was one of the skills she possessed that her superiors at Tanner, Marsh and Fairchild valued most and would pay handsomely to retain, unless she missed her guess.

She had time to work it all out, but not tonight. Not now. She was going to go home and allow herself to dream a little of what life in Riley Creek might hold in store for her, and of Jake and the lifetime of passion she would find in his arms.

"Allie?" A harsh whisper came from behind a tree

in her front yard. "Allie, it's me. I—I need to talk to you."

Allison stopped walking. She was almost at her kitchen door. She'd crossed the road and come up the driveway without noticing what she was doing. "Jenny? Is that you?"

"Yes." The word ended on what sounded like a sob. Allison moved a little closer. Jenny was sitting on the frozen ground at the base of the tree where the owl still called occasionally on quiet nights, her arms wrapped around her knees. She looked small and lost, and Allison's heart raced with apprehension.

"What's wrong?" She thought she knew. She could hear it in the slight slurring in Jenny's voice. The girl had been drinking. Jenny's next words confirmed her fears.

"I don't want to go home. I just need to sit here. I won't be any trouble. I don't want my mom and dad or Jake and the kids to see me like this. I... I've had too much to drink and I think I'm going to throw up."

CHAPTER FIFTEEN

"DO YOU WANT TO TELL ME about it?" Allison asked, dropping to her knees beside Jenny. The ground was hard, the grass crisp with frost. Jenny was shivering, her shoulders hunched against the cold. "How long have you been sitting here? Let's go inside."

Jenny shook her head. "No. I'm too dizzy. I just want to be left alone." She sniffed back a sob. Her speech was only slightly slurred. She wasn't dangerously drunk, Allison decided.

"How much have you had to drink, Jenny?"

"Two wine coolers. Or maybe three." Allison felt a flare of anger. It was so easy for teenagers to become hooked on alcohol that tasted like fruit drinks. So much easier to ignore the dangers when the alcohol tasted good. She doubted there would be nearly as many teenage alcoholics if vodka martinis or old-fashioneds were their introduction to drinking. "I just wanted to feel light and free. And I did." Her voice trailed off.

"But not for very long," Allison ventured quietly.

Jenny nodded. "Now I just want to die." She swallowed convulsively and rolled her head back and forth against the tree trunk. "This is awful."

"You'll feel better if you get the alcohol out of your stomach."

"I will not throw up in your yard." There was so much outraged misery in her voice that Allison let a brief smile curve her lips. These Waltherses were a stubborn lot, she was discovering.

"All right, just sit still and take deep breaths." They were quiet for a minute or two. It was too dark to see Jenny's face with any clarity, but her breathing slowed and grew more regular, and Allison thought she might be past the crisis. "Jen, who gave you the wine coolers?"

"Aaron. We...we drank them after the game. Aaron was really bummed out because Ohio State lost." The Buckeyes had gone down to defeat 17 to 10.

"That's not a good enough excuse for breaking the law."

Jenny lifted her hand. She was wearing gloves, Allison noted, and a warm coat. It wouldn't do her any serious harm sitting out here for a little while longer. "Spare me the sermon, Allison. I know you're a drunk."

The words were like a blow. Allison was silent as she tried to collect her thoughts. She had waited too long for just the right moment to talk about herself. Now it was too late. Jenny knew. And if Jenny knew she was an alcoholic, so did others.

"I wanted to be like you," she said bitterly. "Pretty and smart and rich, but not a drunk." She caught her breath and her next words came out in a raw whisper. "That's such an ugly word. I'm sorry. I shouldn't have called you that." She started to sob. "Listen to me. I can't hold my liquor and I'm a mean drunk, too."

"I *am* an alcoholic," Allison said. She had learned to be honest with herself about her condition, but it hadn't been easy. There was a very real stigma attached to being an alcoholic, even a recovering alcoholic. "But how did you learn about my alcoholism?"

"Aaron's uncle," Jenny said, still crying. "He drinks, too. He saw you at an AA meeting in Lima, then recognized you at the farm market one day. He told Aaron's mother where he'd seen you. I...I guess Aaron overheard them talking."

"I see. And when did you learn this about me? Was it at the dance?"

Jenny nodded again. "Aaron told me."

"Is this why you've been so cold to me?"

"I thought we were friends," Jenny said woefully. "*Real* friends. Why didn't you tell me?"

"It's not an easy thing to discuss, Jenny."

"Are you ashamed of it?" Her voice was very small and lost-sounding in the stillness of the country night.

"No. I'm sad and sorry that I lost control of my life for a while, but I'm not ashamed."

"Does my brother know about your problem?"

"No." All she had wanted was one more day. Just one day.

"I won't tell anyone your secret."

"It's not a secret," Allison said, but her heart beat slow and heavy with dread. She should have told Jake. She'd been waiting for the perfect time and now time had run out. She pushed her regret aside and tried to concentrate on Jenny. "I started drinking when I was your age. When I was older, I thought I was a social drinker who only used alcohol to relieve the stress of my job." *And alleviate the pain of a loveless marriage.* "I never missed a day's work. I never woke up in a strange room or in a strange bed, but I was lying to myself. I was an alcoholic. I've been sober now for seven months. I've worked hard to get my life back in order. I'm proud of that." She did nothing to soften the words, but in the darkness she couldn't see Jenny's reaction to her blunt confession.

"I...I never guessed— Oh, no..." Jenny leaned to the side and began vomiting. Allison moved a little closer and steadied her trembling shoulders. When Jenny stopped retching, Allison pulled a tissue out of her pocket and held it out to the sobbing girl.

"Feel better?"

"No. My head's still spinning. What a stinking mess."

"Don't mind that. And the dizziness will pass," Allison promised. "Come inside and wash your hands and face. Can you stand up?"

"I think so." Jenny's tears were dying away into little hiccuping sobs. She sounded the way Julia did when she was convinced her heart was going to break.

Allison helped Jenny stand. She was steady enough

on her feet that she didn't need any help getting into the house, but she was shivering with cold and reaction.

"How did you get here?" Allison asked.

"I walked from the highway." Jenny sank into a chair at the kitchen table and dropped her head into her hands. Allison turned on the tap and dampened a clean dish towel. "I wanted to come home and Aaron didn't want me to, so I got out at a stop sign and started walking. He didn't like it, but when I wouldn't get back in the truck, he took off. I thought I'd sober up on the way home, but it didn't work. I saw you and Jake coming up the lane from the barn and I hid behind the tree."

Allison turned away from the sink. "Is Aaron drunk, too?"

Jenny lifted her head. Her eyes were swollen from crying and she was as pale as a ghost, but she met Allison's gaze head-on. "Yes," she said. "He's drunk. He's a little drunk a lot of the time and I can deal with it. But today was bad. I never realized how scary it could be until right now."

"And he's still out driving his truck?"

"Yes." She blinked and bit her lip. "He had another six-pack of beer with him."

"You have to be twenty-one to buy alcohol in Ohio. Who got it for you?"

"His brother Nick." Allison had never met Nick Masterson, but she wished he was standing in front of her right now so she could tell him exactly what she thought of him.

"Jenny, you have to tell your parents what's happened."

"No. They won't understand." Tears welled up in her blue eyes once more.

"Then tell Jake." Jenny shook her head. Apprehension clawed at Allison's nerve endings. She had to get through to the girl. The situation was serious. "What about Aaron's parents?"

"No." She buried her face in the damp cloth. "I can't rat him out like that."

"Then I'll phone the police," Allison said. She had to act even if it cost her Jenny's friendship. "Aaron can't be allowed to drive drunk. It's too dangerous."

"They'll kick him off the basketball team. They may even expel him from school. Mr. Hartwood is really strict. This is all such a mess."

Allison came around the table and laid her hand on the younger girl's shoulder. "It always is when alcohol is involved. Come, dry your eyes. I'll walk with you to tell your parents. You know that's best, don't you?"

"I can't," Jenny whispered, but she was already doing as Allison had told her. She wiped her face with the cloth, took a sip of water from the glass Allison had set in front of her, pulled a tissue from the box beside it and blew her nose. "My head hurts," she complained, sounding like Julia again. "I'm not squealing on my friends," she repeated stubbornly. "You can rat me out if you want, but I won't tell them who gave me the booze."

"Would you rather see Aaron dead or in jail?"

"What are you talking about?"

"He's driving drunk. He might just total his truck. Or he might just hurt himself or kill himself. Or he might kill others. Is that what a true friend would do? Say nothing?"

"He'll hate me if I tell. They'll all hate me. This is awful. I only wanted to see what it was like."

"There's always a price to pay for losing control, Jenny. But could you live with yourself if Aaron or someone else died because you did what was easiest?"

Jenny opened her mouth, then shut it again. Two big tears rolled down her cheeks. "I'll do it. I'll tell Mom and Dad. But I don't want to."

"It's for the best, Jenny. I know. I've been down as low as you can go. But if you're strong enough, the only way to go is up."

Tears continued to roll down the teenager's cheeks. "Will you come with me? Mom and Dad are going to have a cow. I'm their good girl. They think I never do anything wrong."

"Your mom and dad may have a cow tonight. But they'll realize you're doing the right thing soon enough. In the end, they'll be proud of you."

"I hope so. I'll be grounded until I'm a hundred."

"I don't think it will be that bad."

"You don't know my mom and dad." She took a deep breath. "I still don't want Aaron getting in trouble with the police."

"We'll deal with that later. Ready?" Perhaps the boy's parents could handle the situation. She didn't know anything about his family. For the moment, getting him off the road was the most important thing.

"No, but we might as well get it over with."

"I'll be there beside you."

"Are you going to tell them about yourself tonight? I mean Mom and Dad and Jake..." Jenny looked so miserable and unhappy that Allison didn't have the heart to add to her burden by letting her own emotions show.

"Yes," she said, "I'll tell them tonight."

"I'm sorry," Jenny said again.

"It's okay." *But was it?* She had no idea how Jake would react. Allison swallowed against the tightness in her throat. This was not how she'd wanted Jake to find out. She could only hope he would understand.

A small cowardly part of her wanted to run, but when Jenny reached for her hand and held it in a death grip, Allison turned her back on the sanctuary of her grandmother's little house and started across the road.

"God, I'll never do anything like this again," Jenny vowed, smoothing a shaky hand down the front of her jacket. "What am I going to say? You'll stay with me, won't you, Allie?" Headlights appeared above the dip in the road a half mile away, sending their elongated shadows alongside them for a moment. "That sounds like Aaron's truck."

"Really?" Jenny's words barely registered over the pounding of blood in her ears. Jake's reaction was all that she could focus on. The feelings between them were so new, so fragile and so easily destroyed.

"Aaron's coming to look for me."

Allison stopped walking, looking over her shoulder as the headlights drew closer. "Then we'll take his keys away and call his parents to come and get him."

Jenny turned her head toward Allison. Her eyes were huge in her pale face. "You'd do that, wouldn't you?"

"In a heartbeat," Allison said. "I won't be a party to a teenager driving drunk." Then as much to herself as to Jenny, she said, "Come on. Let's get this over with."

The truck was very close now. Jenny held back, watching as its lights shone through the trees along the road, then swung over them once again as the pickup squealed into the driveway. A curtain twitched as Jake's mother looked out the kitchen window. The back door opened at almost the same time as the side door to the store. Roger Walthers stepped out onto the porch as Jake came from the barn.

"What the devil's going on out here?" Roger demanded. "Jenny, is that you?"

Jenny's mouth opened and closed. No sound came out. She gripped Allison's hand so tightly she winced.

Roger pointed at Aaron's pickup. "I thought you were with Aaron there? Now you're coming from Ms. Martin's house. What's going on?"

"Jenny! Why the hell did you jump out of my truck like that?" Aaron hollered, slamming the cab door behind him as he started toward them. "Why did you hide in the ditch so I couldn't find you?"

"I didn't hide," Jenny said, finally finding her

voice. "I walked home. You were so drunk you probably couldn't see me."

"Hey, cool it." Aaron swung around to check whether Jake and his father had heard her. He held out his hand in a warning gesture. "Calm down. I'm not drunk."

"Oh, yes, you are." Jenny gave Allison's hand another convulsive squeeze. "And so am I."

"Jennifer Nicole!" Jake's mother had appeared at Roger's side, dish towel in hand. Her face, starkly lighted by the overhead porch fixture, was white with shock. "What are you saying?"

"I'm drunk, Mom," Jenny said, bursting into tears. Roger's face was as red as Darlene's was white.

"Oh, Jenny, how could you?" Darlene started to cry.

"Go to her," Allison whispered, but Jenny was already moving toward her mother.

"I'm sorry, Mom. I...I thought it was okay." Jenny was crying again, too. "It was only wine coolers. I thought I could handle it. I'm sorry."

"She's not drunk," Aaron said too loudly, his words slurred, his voice cracking, betraying his nerves and his intoxication. "She only had a wine cooler or two like she said."

"That's two wine coolers too many." Roger hurried down the steps, his hands balled into fists. "And Jenny's right, you're drunk, too. Who got you kids the booze? I'm going to call the sheriff and have you both thrown in jail. Better yet, I ought to beat you to a pulp right here and now."

"Daddy, no!" Darlene had wrapped Jenny in her arms, but now the young girl pulled away. "Allie. You promised!"

"Wait." Allison held out her hand, moving to put herself between the teenager and Jake's angry father.

"Stay away from me, old man," Aaron warned just as Jake came up and grabbed him by the collar of his coat.

"Mind your manners, kid." His tone was conversational but laced with steel. "Dad, settle down. You can't go punching out Harley's boy. You two have to sit on the elevator board together."

"I'll resign," Roger said belligerently. "Just let me have him alone behind the barn for five minutes."

"You and who else?" Aaron blustered, but he wasn't quite as defiant as before.

"Me," Jake said, giving him a shake. It was hard to tell, but Allison thought she saw Jake wince at the unaccustomed strain on his still-healing ribs. "Now behave and tell me who the hell gave you the booze."

The fight had gone out of the boy. "Nick. It was my brother Nick."

"He's sure as hell old enough to know better," Roger growled. "Darlene, call the sheriff's department."

"No, dammit," Aaron yelled. "Just turn me loose. I'll go home. I won't see Jenny anymore. I won't drink anymore. Just don't call the cops."

"You're not getting behind the wheel of that truck again. Not in your condition."

"I'll drive him home," Allison said. She didn't

want to. She had no idea how irrationally he might behave, but she couldn't think of a better solution. Jake and his father were far too angry with the boy to be left alone with him.

"One drunk driving the other drunk home. That's a good one," Aaron said with a sneer.

"Aaron, shut up!" Jenny hissed.

"It's the truth." Aaron sounded tough but he wouldn't look Allison in the eye. "Ms. High-and-Mighty here is a drunk. My uncle Norbert saw her at AA. You all think she's so great, but she's no better'n the rest of us."

"Aaron! Stop it or I'll never, *ever,* speak to you again! Allie, I'm sorry." Jenny's voice had risen to a near hysterical pitch.

"It's the truth, dammit. She's an alcoholic. Aren't you?" he demanded, a note of desperation creeping in to undermine his bravado.

Inside, Allison died a little. It couldn't have gone more wrong. "Yes," she said quietly with all the dignity she could muster. "I'm a recovering alcoholic. I've been sober for seven months." She wanted to say more, try to explain the forces that had ruled her former life, but her pride wouldn't let her.

Silence. No one spoke for a long, long minute. The sound of a car coming down the road was loud on the cold night air.

"I'll take him home," Jake said finally. "Harley can deal with him. I've had just about enough of his mouth." Less than an hour ago, Allison had been dreaming that tomorrow Jake would tell her he loved her, and now he wouldn't even look at her.

"If I ever hear of you drinking again, I'll tell everyone in school," Jenny said, wiping her cheeks with the back of her hands. "I don't care if I get kicked out on my butt, too. Do you hear me, Aaron Masterson?"

"I hear," he said.

Allison knew she should speak up, tell them it wasn't a good idea simply to leave things to Aaron's parents. That approach would probably work for Jenny. Her support system was strong, and she was at heart an intelligent and well-grounded girl. But what of Aaron? He had a serious drinking problem; all the signs were there. A lecture from his father, losing his driving privileges, even being kicked off the basketball team, weren't going to be enough. He needed professional help. She knew. *Dear Lord, how well she knew.* She couldn't stand by and say nothing.

The car she'd heard earlier turned in the driveway just as Julia, followed by Libby and Mike, came out the back door. "What's going on? What's everyone doing out here?" Mike asked. His eyes grew round as he stared at the car in the driveway. "Hey! It's the cops!"

"Grandma, why are the police here?" Libby asked, hurrying to Darlene's side. "What's wrong with Jenny?"

"Any trouble here, Jake?" It was Rudy Sunderman, the policeman she'd seen in the emergency room the night Jake had been injured.

"We're handling it," Jake answered.

"Irv Christman called in and said he'd seen a black pickup driving fast and weaving all over the road come by his place once or twice." He jerked his thumb in the direction of Aaron's truck. "A Chevy just like the one Harley Masterson's boy drives, Irv said. Aaron, that your truck?"

"Daddy? *Daddy.* I don't like police," Julia cried as she ducked past her grandfather and made a beeline for Jake.

It all happened so fast. Allison grabbed for Julia at the precise moment Aaron slammed his elbow into Jake's stomach. Jake doubled over in pain and loosened his grip on the teenager, who vaulted into his truck. He'd left it running, so he slammed the truck into gear and jerked the wheel to drive through the yard and avoid the cruiser.

"Daddy's hurt." With surprising strength, Julia twisted out of Allison's grip and started running toward Jake.

For a second, no one seemed able to move, then Allison surged forward. Somehow she managed to get hold of Julia's wrist. She pulled the little girl into her arms so quickly that her momentum carried her almost directly into the path of Aaron's truck. She tried to protect Julia's fragile body, all the while feeling the heat from the engine behind her.

Please God, she prayed, *keep Julia safe.* She braced herself for the crushing pain of the truck's wheels, but it never came.

She landed on the ground, Julia still cradled in her

arms. Incredibly, the truck had sailed past her, skidding to a halt not two feet from the passenger door of the police cruiser.

Allison stayed where she was, fighting nausea. Julia was a dead weight on her chest. She struggled to sit up, frantic to see if the child was injured. But Julia had only been sucking in air to let out an earsplitting screech. *"You dummy!"* she cried as Aaron hurtled around the front of the truck, Jake and the cop hard on his heels. "You knocked us down."

Aaron dropped to his knees beside Allison. He was crying, crying harder than Julia, who Allison could tell was more frightened than hurt. "Are you all right? God, I'm sorry. I'm sorry," Aaron said. "I just wanted to get away. I didn't see her. Where did she come from?"

"From my house." Julia sniffed indignantly.

Aaron's mouth opened and closed. No sound came out.

Julia wrinkled her nose. "You smell funny. Are you okay?"

"No," Aaron said. "I...I need help. I want to go home."

"Julia, are you hurt?" Jake asked, dropping to his knees beside Allison and Julia.

"She's fine," Allison said, relinquishing her hold on the little girl reluctantly. "She's just fine."

"Thank God," Jake said, burying his face in her blond hair until she squeaked in protest.

"Daddy, you're squishing me."

"Allison?" Jake looked at her with a thousand questions in his eyes.

She shook her head. "I'm sorry, Jake, so sorry…"

"Julia." All the Waltherses were now gathered around them. "Oh, baby, let Grandma see if you're all right."

Julia lifted her hands to her grandmother, clearly pleased to be the focus of so much attention. "I have an owie on my elbow," she whimpered. "Kiss it and make it better."

"Allison…" Darlene began, then bit her lip. "You…you saved her life."

"Everyone okay here?" Rudy asked, standing behind Jake. His expression didn't bode well for Aaron Masterson.

"We're fine," Allison assured him.

Julia sniffed again. "I have an owie. A big one."

"We'll take care of it," Darlene said. "Come inside."

She took Julia from Jake's arms. He rose, a little stiffly, and held out his hand for Allison. She didn't want to take it, didn't want to touch him and feel his aversion, but she had no choice. Her legs were trembling from the shock and she didn't want to stumble and perhaps have them all wonder if it was alcohol and not the aftereffect of fear that caused her unsteadiness.

"Thank you," she said. Jake let go of her hand the moment she was on her feet, and she lost all hope that he would ever understand.

"I should take you in for drunk driving," Rudy said to Aaron.

"No, don't," Aaron begged.

"You have to get help," Allison said. "I know what I'm talking about. You can't fight alcoholism by yourself."

"I...I will."

"I'll take the boy home," Rudy said. "And have a long talk with his parents."

"I'll come with you," Jake said. "I'll drive his truck. I want to have a few words with Harley myself."

Allison relaxed just a little. This was the way things got done in a small town. Jake and Rudy wouldn't let it be swept under the rug. They would make sure Aaron's parents realized he needed professional help for his drinking problem.

Darlene was carrying Julia toward the house. Roger had his arm around Jenny. Libby and Mike, unusually subdued, were trailing behind their grandparents. Rudy Sunderman lifted his hand and touched his finger to his hat brim in a half salute, then gestured Aaron toward the cruiser.

"I'll be right behind you, Rudy," Jake called over his shoulder, then turned to speak to Allison. "Should I walk you home?"

Allison's heart constricted with pain again. He hadn't asked her if she wanted to go with his family to take comfort in each other and talk through what had just happened. He was sending the outsider back where she belonged.

"No, I'll be fine."

"I'll come home as soon as I can. Harley Masterson's liable to go off half-cocked. Rudy'll be there to keep him in line, but I want to make sure the old cuss understands that the boy needs help."

She managed a weak smile. "You're a good man, Jake."

"I'd want someone to do as much for me and my family." Rudy was backing the cruiser out onto the road. Jake watched for a brief moment, then looked at Allison. "We have to talk," he said.

Family, friends, community. They meant a lot to Jake. So did honest and integrity. She could see in his eyes that she had disappointed him on both counts. She nodded. "I know. I'll be waiting for you."

CHAPTER SIXTEEN

ALMOST TWO HOURS PASSED before Jake got back home. It had taken a lot of talking from both Rudy and Jake to keep Harley from doing real harm to the boy. Hard drinking and bullheadedness came naturally to the Masterson men, but not to Aaron's mother. Once she'd realized the seriousness of Aaron's problem, she'd agreed to do whatever was necessary to get him help. She'd promised to make an appointment for Aaron with a substance-abuse counselor first thing Monday morning. And by the time he and Rudy had left the Masterson farm, Harley had agreed, with much hemming and hawing, to go, too.

Jake had done what he could to ensure Nick Masterson didn't provide any more liquor for his younger brother, as well. He'd done it the only way he knew would get through to Harley, by threatening his pocketbook. Nick farmed with his father, and Jake had promised to sue them both if Nick ever bought alcohol for a minor again.

"Thanks for going along with me on this one," Rudy said as they headed back. "I know by law I should have taken the kid in for underage drinking, but there are just some times when that won't work."

"He came damned close to killing Allison Martin and my Julia," Jake said. "He could have killed my sister, too, driving drunk like that. Not to mention any number of others." The thought of how close he'd come to losing Allison and Julia made Jake's blood run cold. He wasn't quite ready to forgive Aaron, but in a small town you had to get along with your neighbors. "If Harley and Olympia hadn't agreed to get him professional help and confiscate the pickup, I might have gone over your head to the county sheriff."

"You wouldn't have had to," Rudy replied. "I would have taken him in myself if Harley hadn't agreed to get the boy help."

Jake nodded. Aaron was a good student, a good athlete, and his only chance at a college education was getting a basketball scholarship to one of the smaller schools that paid a lot more attention to a student's background than the big state-run schools did. Rudy's decision not to file charges had kept Aaron's record clean, more than likely kept him from being kicked off the basketball team, but Rudy wouldn't forget. If Aaron was smart, he'd be careful.

Rudy pulled into the driveway. "Want to come in for a cup of coffee?" Jake asked automatically. All he wanted was to cross the road to Allison's little white house, but over thirty years of his mother's teachings kicked in before he could stop himself. Darlene would be scandalized if he didn't offer Rudy the hospitality of Walnut Hill Farm.

"Thanks for the offer, but I have to be getting back

into town. I'm on duty alone tonight until eleven. Do you think Ms. Martin will want to file charges against the boy?''

''I don't think she wants to see Aaron in more trouble than he's already got. If she has any questions, I'll have her call you.'' Jake thought about asking Rudy if he'd heard Allison Martin was an alcoholic. He hadn't broached the subject of Norbert Masterson and the AA meeting, but he wondered how much the town had been gossiping about her. He knew she must be thinking about it.

''Yeah, good idea.''

''Rudy, you heard anything around town about Allison Martin having a drinking problem?''

Rudy thought a moment, then shook his head. ''Can't say that I have.'' Rudy didn't ask for more of an explanation and Jake was glad. He wished he hadn't mentioned the subject, but he couldn't forget the sight of Allison's shocked expression when Aaron had blurted out her secret. ''But then most folks in town don't know her that good at all. Not that that ever stopped 'em from talking. Too bad. She's a nice woman.''

''Too bad that she drinks?'' Jake watched his hand ball into a fist on his knee. He didn't want people gossiping about Allison behind her back. Alcoholism was a disease, he knew that much. And it could happen to anyone. His own sister was at risk.

''Nah,'' Rudy said. ''Too bad most people don't know her is what I meant. She seems like a nice woman. Might be a good thing for Riley Creek if she stayed on in town.'' He let his voice rise a little at the end of the sentence, leaving it just short of a question.

"Yeah, it sure would be.'' Jake left it at that and got out of the car, his ribs screaming in protest as he bent down to peer in the door. He should have taken one of his leftover pain pills, but he hadn't thought about it before they'd gone to the Masterson place. "Thanks again, Rudy. We'll make sure Jenny gets help if she needs it, same as Aaron.''

"I got a feeling that girl learned her lesson tonight. I don't imagine I'll be having to spend too much time keeping my eye on her.'' Rudy allowed himself a slight grin. "Too bad about them Buckeyes,'' he said. "I imagine Tom Farley's pretty full of himself tonight.''

Jake spared a thought for what Allison had told him earlier. If what she'd said was true, he didn't think Tom was in all that good a mood, not if he'd really walked out on Stella that way. But he just said, "Yeah. I imagine you're right.''

"If I don't see you again, you all have a good Thanksgiving.'' Rudy lifted his hand in a wave as Jake slammed the car door. As the policeman drove away, Jake debated going home first or heading directly across the road to Allison. He turned and looked into the kitchen window. His father was sitting at the table with Libby, Mike and Julia. The kids were in their pajamas and all of them had buttered toast and hot chocolate. His mother's panacea for anything that ailed you just before bedtime.

Darlene walked past the table with a small tray bearing another steaming mug and a napkin-covered plate. She was taking her cure-all up to Jenny's room. It was good to have his parents home. Jenny would be fine now. He knew some of the blame for her actions tonight could be placed directly at him, and the knowledge was bitter in his heart. He was ashamed his self-absorption had forced her to bear that heavy a burden these past couple of months. He'd lived in his own private world of grief for too long, but Allison had shown him the way back. She had made him believe he had a future again, not merely a lifetime of going through the motions. He was falling in love with her, her humor and her warmth and her stubborn insistence on doing what was right. But all along she'd been keeping her secret. She didn't trust him enough to tell him about her alcoholism. And if you didn't trust someone, he didn't see how you could love him.

Would she have told him tomorrow, when they were alone with each other for almost the first time? He didn't know. He would never know.

In less than twenty-four hours, he'd intended to tell her he loved her, and he'd been pretty certain she would tell him she loved him in return. Then he'd hoped that somehow, someway, they could meld their very different lives into one. Now he realized just how far from reality that dream was. Had it all been just sexual attraction? He'd begun to doubt everything that had passed between them, and his heart felt as if it might be breaking again.

ALLISON WAS STANDING at the parlor window. She'd been there a long time. The room was dark behind her; there was no way Jake could see her watching him. She didn't have to see his face to know he was torn between his promise to return to her and his obligation to his family.

She took her coat from the back of the couch and stepped outside. He must have heard the door open and slap shut behind her. He was already moving toward her by the time the echo of wood against wood had died away across the barren fields.

His footsteps were muffled by the wet leaves that had fallen since the last time she'd raked the yard. She moved to the top of the steps and pushed her hands into the pockets of her coat. Her sobriety stone was in the left and her car keys in the right. Twice in the past couple of hours she'd found herself standing with them in her hand, the craving for a drink stronger and more insistent than any she could ever remember. She understood that the trauma of the evening's events was what had sent her into this tailspin, but this did nothing to make her latest battle any easier. There was a long night yet ahead of her, and nights were always the worst.

"Jenny and the kids are okay," she said as he drew close. "I called a little while ago to make sure." That phone call had saved her the first time she'd found herself heading for the car to drive into town and get a drink. Some of her struggle must have been evident in her voice because Jake's mother had wanted her to come over and have hot chocolate with them. The temptation to go back to that house full of warmth and light and lean on their strength was seductive, but Allison had declined. She had to make it on her own.

The second time she'd felt her addiction pressing in on her she'd gone upstairs and packed.

"I saw them through the window," Jake said, stopping at the edge of the porch. His head was bare, the collar of his coat turned up against the cold. "They're all ready for bed and drinking hot chocolate in the kitchen."

"Did Aaron get safely home?"

"Yes. His old man's a jerk, but his mother's a fine woman. She gave us her word she'd get the boy professional help. I don't think you'll have to worry about his drinking and driving again."

"Good," she said, smoothing the stone between her fingers, feeling the soothing repetition begin to melt the agonizing tension that held her muscles stiff and tight. "I'm glad you went with them. I know it wasn't easy for you after what almost happened tonight."

"'Do unto others' might be a cliché where you come from, but it's the way we do things here."

His tone was as stiff and formal as though they'd never met. *He couldn't accept her alcoholism.* He didn't have to say it. She could tell. Her throat tightened with tears her pride wouldn't let fall.

"It's one of the rules I try to live my life by, too." She came down the steps. "Jake, we have to talk."

"Maybe it should wait until tomorrow. It's pretty late now, and you look tired." Physically he was so close, but emotionally he had removed himself. She had betrayed him by not revealing her secret. He would deny it if she accused him of it, but it was true. There would be no tomorrow for them, not anymore.

"No, not tomorrow. I...I won't be here tomorrow. I'm going back to Chicago. I...I have to."

To prove to herself that she was able to cope. Tonight she had nearly lost her battle to stay sober. Only realizing that Jake's parents, his children, his friends would know that she had failed kept her from going into town and getting a drink. What would it do to Jenny, to the little ones, to see her that way? She shuddered. She wasn't strong enough yet. She hadn't earned the right to stay in Riley Creek.

"Jake, I'm sorry I didn't tell you about my alcoholism earlier. You shouldn't have had to hear about it the way you did. There just never seemed to be the right time..." If only he would reach out and take her in his arms. She wanted so badly to have him hold her just once more.

"Would you have told me tomorrow night?" He was asking her so much more than that one question. His hands were shoved deep into the pockets of his coat, and the set of his shoulders was unyielding. She felt as if she were talking to an extension of the oak tree behind him, not the warm and caring man she'd fallen in love with.

"Yes," she said, lifting her chin, "I would have told you."

"But now you're leaving." It wasn't a question, but a statement.

She clenched her teeth to stifle the sob that had worked its way into her throat. "I have to go back. I have to prove—"

"What?" He whirled around and took a half-dozen steps toward the road. Allison reached out to stop him, then dropped her hand to her side when he turned back to her. "That you don't care enough about what's been growing between us to tell me the truth about yourself? That you don't trust me? That you don't need me or anyone else in Riley Creek?"

"You're wrong." She did trust him, with her life. And she did need him. That was the problem.

She needed him and wanted him so much she ached with it. And if she told him that, told him everything in her heart, he would take her in his arms, hold her, comfort her—and she would never be able to trust *herself* again. She had to know she could make it on her own, so she could return with confidence to this place she yearned to call home. So simple, really, but impossible with her emotions in such turmoil to put into words. Yet she had to try.

"I have to know I can manage when there's no one to rely on but myself." She was desperate to make him understand something she didn't fully understand herself. She couldn't come to him still afraid of who and what she was inside.

Jake looked down at the ground. If he said he loved her, she thought frantically, that would be enough. That would give her the strength she needed, that and that alone. "Allison. Let me help... I—I care for you."

She did not want his help, or his pity. She wanted his love, and he wasn't ready to offer it to her. "Please, Jake. I have to do this. Please understand. I'll be in touch."

"No, you won't," he said, then walked away.

IT WAS FIVE MINUTES before eleven that night when Allison drove past Tom Farley's house. There were lights on in an upstairs bedroom and in the kitchen at the side of the house. She turned into the driveway and stopped the car. Out by the barn a turkey gobbled a warning, then fell silent.

Allison got out of the car and walked to the door carrying a small box carefully in both hands. It was too late to wish she hadn't stopped, too late to wish she hadn't packed her bags and her grandmother's wedding dress and the gilt-framed mirror, and decided to make the five-hour drive to Chicago in the middle of the night. Too late to change anything that had happened that day.

She climbed the few steps to the small open porch and lifted her hand. Just as she was about to knock, the door opened, framing Stella LaRue in the light from the kitchen. "Stella?" She was the last person Allison had expected to see in Tom's house.

"Allison?" Stella seemed equally as surprised to see her. "I told Tom I heard a car drive up, but he only mumbled something about my hearing things and..." She gazed down at what she was wearing— a man's blue-and-green plaid flannel robe—and color rose in her cheeks. "That's neither here nor there.

What are you doing out at this time of night. Is something wrong? Is Jake sick, or one of the kids?''

Allison's heart ached at Stella's instant assumption that she was here because of Jake or his kids, as though it was only natural that she should look out for them. And Stella was right. Allison would have turned to her for help if she needed it. So why hadn't she been able to do the same with Jake?

''No. There's nothing wrong.'' She was too tired to tell Stella all that had happened since she'd closed the store. ''I...I wanted to ask Tom a favor. I want him to look after my grandmother's house until I can find a buyer for it. The pipes and the water heater need draining. I'm going back to Chicago.''

''*Now?*'' Stella asked, then held open the door for Allison to enter. ''Come inside. It's way below freezing out there.''

''I can't stay,'' Allison said automatically. ''It's a long drive.''

''I still don't know why you feel you have to leave tonight.'' Stella pulled a chair away from the table. A carved finial came loose in her hand. She replaced it and shook her head. ''I'm going to have to get rid of this junk if I move in here.''

''You're not leaving Riley Creek?''

''No, she's not,'' Tom said, walking into the room from a darkened doorway that probably led to the living room. He was fully dressed, but his hair was rumpled and he was barefoot. ''We came to an agreement tonight. I won't ever leave her as long as it's in my power to be by her side, and she's decided she can stay here with me."

Stella's face reddened a little more, but she was smiling as Tom dropped his hand on her shoulder and she covered it with her own. "I may be too damned stubborn for my own good, but I'm not a fool. The sight of Tom walking out of the store and out of my life brought me to my senses in a hurry. What's the use of seeing the world and eating in great little restaurants if you do it alone? I figure we can do quite a bit of traveling during the winter months when it's slow at the store. And...well, Tom was right. He's not my first husband. He's a damned good farmer and a damned good businessman. And I'm one of the luckiest women on earth."

"Congratulations," Allison said, finding something to smile about for the first time that day, it seemed. "I wish you both the best."

"I overheard Stella's comments about the quality of my furniture, but not what you're doing here at this hour of the night."

"I'm going back to Chicago." Tom's concern was obvious to Allison and she realized she was leaving another good friend behind in her quest to prove herself. "I was hoping you'd take care of winterizing my grandmother's house. I didn't want to ask Jake to do it."

"I see," Tom said, and she thought he did. But Stella wasn't about to be put off.

"Why not ask Jake? Did you two have some kind of fight? Pardon me for being blunt." Tom stifled a chuckle and Stella turned her head to frown up at him. "I speak my mind, Tom. I'm too old to change."

"I never asked you to change," he reminded her gently, then bent over to give her a kiss on the top of her head. "But Allison has a right to her privacy."

"No, that's okay. I've been quiet too long." Stella and Tom must have suspected that there was something more than just friendship growing between her and Jake. She owed Jake's friends, *her* friends, an explanation. *My name is Allison and I am an alcoholic.* It wasn't going to be easy this time. It was never going to be easy. Allison folded her hands over the small cardboard box of trinkets and notes of goodbye for Jenny and the kids. She'd planned to ask Tom to give it to Jake. There was a note inside for Stella, as well, since she hadn't expected to see her again. "I'll tell you everything and then I have to leave."

CHAPTER SEVENTEEN

"JENNIFER? JENNIFER Nicole."

Jenny wasn't certain how many times her mother had called her, but when Darlene started using her middle name, it usually meant she'd been at it a while.

"What?" she asked, sticking out her lower lip to blow her bangs off her forehead. The church basement must be up to eighty degrees. They kept it that way so the really old people putting together the holiday baskets would be comfortable, even if everyone else got heatstroke.

"Jenny, come here." She made her way to the table where her mother was supervising what went into the Thanksgiving boxes the others were filling. "Take this box out to the Beaversons. It's got the smallest turkey, but they'll still be eating off it for a week, I wager. Let's see…"

Her mom was talking to herself again. She'd always done it, and lately Jenny had caught herself doing it, too. She wondered if it was just a habit she'd picked up from her mom, or some kind of genetic thing like blue eyes and curly hair.

"Just one pie, that's okay. Jackson needs to watch

his sugar. Oh, and a head of lettuce and a bottle of salad dressing and half a dozen oranges and grape-fruits.'' She was clicking off items on her fingers, her eyebrows drawn together in a slight frown.

The Beaversons were an elderly couple who lived in a trailer a few miles out of town. Miranda Bea-verson had been her mother's Sunday school teacher, and her dad had baled hay for Mr. Beaverson when he was a boy. They didn't have any children of their own and Jake and her mom and dad sort of helped look after them.

''You be sure to wish them a happy Thanksgiving and tell them your dad and I are back in town and to call if they need anything, okay?''

''I will. Jake and I looked after them fine while you were gone,'' she teased. Her mom smiled and Jenny smiled back. It had been a long few days, but she'd gotten through it somehow.

Her mom and dad had moved back into their own house on Monday after the furnace was fixed, but she was still staying with Jake because Tuesday her brother Kyle and his wife, Janet, and the twins had driven in from Omaha, and they were using her bed-room. Matt and Ginger and the boys would get the guest room when they arrived tonight, leaving her on the couch in the basement, so it was better to stay at Walnut Hill a few more days.

She hadn't even told Ashley and Maria what had happened on Saturday yet. She was still mad at Aaron, but she didn't want him to get kicked off the basketball team, or worse, suspended from school.

She knew he had a chance at a scholarship and he didn't deserve to lose it because he was ill. So she'd kept her mouth shut. It was hard, but she'd done it. Besides, she wasn't proud of the way she'd acted, either, throwing up in front of Allison and all.

Aaron had stopped her in the hall after the Thanksgiving assembly that afternoon and apologized all over again. Jenny had said she was sorry, too. Sorry that she'd let him talk her into having the coolers. Sorry that he'd blurted out Allison's secret in front of everyone. Sorry that Allison had left Riley Creek without saying goodbye.

"I'm seeing a counselor in Lima," Aaron had said. "Me and my mom and dad went Monday. I have to go back and see her again after school today."

"Listen to what she has to say." Her mom and dad had asked if she wanted to see a counselor, but she'd said no. She hadn't exactly said she'd rather talk to them, that wouldn't have been cool, but that's the way it was.

"I'm not a drunk," Aaron said. "I just went over the line that night."

Jenny wasn't going to let him off that easy. She'd done a lot of thinking about it and she wasn't going to let his brown eyes and his sexy smile blind her to his faults anymore. "No. *I* went over the line. I'm not old enough to drink and I'm not going to do it again. But there's a difference. *You* have a problem with alcohol. You've been drinking since you were fifteen. You almost killed Allison and Julia. You'd better face up to it and pay attention to what the counselor tells you or I'll turn you in to Coach Rayle myself.'' Then she'd looked at him hard and walked away.

Breaking up with Aaron hadn't been as painful as she'd thought.

It hadn't hurt as much as Allison's going away in the middle of the night—even though she had left Jenny a letter explaining why she had to leave. Why she had to go back to Chicago and try to make her life work again without alcohol as a crutch.

"Jennifer, have you heard a word I've said?"

"Yes." It wasn't quite a lie. There was always a little part of her brain listening for her mother's voice.

"You'll have to knock loud. They're both hard-of-hearing and they usually keep the television volume pretty high." Her mom's cheeks were red and she'd pushed the sleeves of her sweatshirt up to her elbows to try to cool off. "Have I forgotten anything?" She looked around, spotted Mrs. Gerschutz filling another basket and pounced. "No, Bette. No potatoes for the VanWormers. They're both on low-fat diets. Give them the box of rice." Darlene lowered her voice to a whisper. "She means well, poor soul, but she's just not up to this job. I'm so glad your father and I came home for Thanksgiving."

"Me, too, Mom." Jenny smiled; she couldn't help herself. Her mom loved being in charge. Especially of the Thanksgiving baskets. Her mom thought it was a sin if anyone went without a wonderful turkey dinner since there was so much bounty in Riley Creek, and she did her best to see that that didn't happen.

Jenny was lucky and she knew it. Her mom and

dad loved her. They hadn't gone ballistic about Saturday night. Though after she'd said she didn't want to see a counselor, they must have decided to do the counseling themselves. They had talked and talked and talked. They were still talking and she had to listen because she was grounded until Christmas.

Even if she hadn't learned her lesson Saturday night, she'd be toeing the line anyway because of their ultimate threat. If she got caught drinking again, she wouldn't be allowed to go for her driver's license until she was eighteen. She couldn't think of anything worse.

"Oh, goodness." Her mom took off at a trot. "The babies, they're loose. Janet isn't paying a bit of attention to them."

Her niece and nephew, Kayla and Carson, were toddling around the basement, looking like little pink and blue penguins with their arms outstretched to keep their balance. Everyone was cooing over their antics. Her sister-in-law was watching, too, beaming with pride as she talked to the preacher and his wife.

Janet was an artist. She painted big weird paintings with lots of shapes and colors and nothing else that you could recognize. She actually even got paid for some of them. The rest of the time she worked for a cleaning service because she said it paid well and she didn't have to wear panty hose.

She loved Riley Creek with, what she called, "its Norman Rockwell ambiance." She was always bugging Kyle to try to get a job close by. She wanted to find a house in the country, open a home-and-office cleaning service—which Jenny could hardly wait for because she wanted her mom to be the first customer—and raise the twins where they could be safe and happy and the schools were good.

"Ready to go, Jen?" Jake asked, coming to stand beside her. He reached over and took the Beaversons' box from her hands.

"Yeah, all set. Are the kids coming with us to the airport?" They were going to go on to Columbus to meet Matt and Ginger's flight, which was due in three hours, but only Libby was with Jake.

"Hi, Jen," she said, her wide smile showing a new tooth. "I'm going to baby-sit Kayla and Carson." She rushed over to her grandmother and aunt, dropped to her knees and gathered up the little boy in a big hug.

"Libby's going to mind the twins so Janet and Mom can start cooking as soon as we're done here. Dad's showing Mike the finer points of pastry making, and Stella's watching Julia." Jake's answer was brief. Everything he said these days was like that.

"How did you get away without her?"

"It wasn't easy." Jake smiled, but she noticed it seemed a little forced. He looked tired with dark circles under his eyes, as if he hadn't been getting enough sleep.

Jenny shook her head. "You didn't tell her where we were going, did you?"

"No, but when we get back with Matt and Ginger and the boys, she'll forgive me. I hope."

Jenny laughed. "You wish. I'll get my coat and tell Mom we're going."

Jake nodded. "We'd better get started. We have three more boxes besides the Beaversons' to deliver before we leave town."

IT WAS SNOWING a little bit when they got to Columbus, and the roads were slippery. There was a lot of traffic on the interstate leading to the airport, rush-hour traffic and holiday traffic combined, so Jenny and Jake hadn't talked very much for the past half hour. Before that, they hadn't talked a lot, either, actually. Jake had listened to the news and weather on the radio, then Jenny had put in the sound track from *Titanic* and they'd driven along in silence.

But all the while, Jenny had been filled with questions. She wanted to ask Jake how he felt about Allison's packing her car in the middle of the night and driving away. In her letter, she'd told Jenny she was sorry she hadn't told her about her being an alcoholic. And how she hoped they could still be friends. And that someday she wanted to come back to Riley Creek.

The last part was a lie. Jenny didn't think Allison was ever coming back. If she was, she wouldn't have left the way she had.

Even though she'd been miserable on Sunday morning, when Stella and Tom had come over and told them Allison had gone back to Chicago, she'd seen what the news had done to Jake. He'd looked almost the same way the day Beth had died.

Jenny might only be fifteen and not too smart about some things, but she knew what a person looked like when they lost someone they loved. For a day or two, she'd hoped Jake would go after Allison and bring her back, the way heroes did in the movies. But he hadn't. As far as Jenny knew, he hadn't even phoned her.

She felt it was mostly her fault Allison had left before she and Jake had had a chance to fall so much in love they couldn't stand to live apart, and she wanted to tell him that. But it wasn't easy. She'd been trying to find the courage and had nearly wasted their entire drive together. They were close, real close. She could see the lights of the planes landing and taking off. She was going to have to say something to Jake, and soon.

She'd just about decided to come straight out and ask him if he loved Allison or not when Jake spoke.

"Jenny, we need to talk."

"Oh." Jenny swallowed hard. Jake hadn't said much about Saturday. She'd seen how white and scared he'd been when Aaron had almost run over Julia and Allison, but he'd never said a word in anger to her. "You know I'm sorry about that night, Jake. I've never been so afraid in my life as I was when I saw the truck heading for—"

"It's not that, Jenny. I know you learned your lesson about drinking. But you're not the only one who learned a life lesson Saturday night."

Jenny sat up a little straighter. Maybe Jake was going to talk to her about Allison.

"I want you to know I never meant to cause you any grief, Jenny. It's my fault you were under so much pressure you had to try to relieve some of it with alcohol. I should have never put that much responsibility on your shoulders.''

''Jake, I love taking care of the kids.''

''I know, but you should have told me you were getting tired of having them in your charge so often.''

''Well...'' She didn't want to lie. It had been hard to keep up her schoolwork and watch the kids and keep the house halfway clean. ''Yeah, a little. But Allison was a real help....''

Jake frowned and it wasn't because some idiot cut them off as they tried to find a place to park. ''She was a big help. She's the one who made me realize I was taking advantage of you.''

''You're my brother, Jake,'' Jenny said. He turned off the engine and it was very quiet in the van. ''I wanted to help.''

He reached over and brushed the tip of his finger along her jaw. ''You're my baby sister. And I love you, Jenny. I ought to be taking care of you, not using you as a substitute mother for my kids.''

Now, she thought, *steer the conversation toward Allison.* But her throat tightened up at the sad look on his face and she could only say, ''I love you, too, Jake.''

''Things are going to be different from now on. I'll do whatever it takes to make it up to you,'' he said, and got out of the van.

''Jake, wait.'' Jenny scrambled out her door and stepped in a puddle of half-frozen slush. ''Ugh!'' By the time she'd shaken the water off her brand-new

Nikes, Jake was already halfway down the row of parked cars. She ran after him. "Jake, there's something I want to talk to you about."

"Okay. What is it?" The automatic door opened and noise and confusion rushed out. They walked in and Jake headed for the monitors displaying the gate numbers of arriving flights. "A-6," he said after a moment of searching. "Hey, the flight's ahead of schedule. They're already here."

Jenny looked at the line of people backed up behind the metal detector. "The line's moving pretty slow."

"We'll wait for them at the baggage carousels." Jake started toward the escalator leading down to the baggage-claim area.

Jenny didn't move. She'd counted on having more time to put the plan she'd been crafting into motion. She couldn't do anything in the baggage-claim area. There weren't any flight information counters down there. This wasn't working out the way she'd hoped it would. Every other plane in the world was probably running late the day before Thanksgiving. Why did her brother's have to be ahead of schedule?

"C'mon, Jen—" Jake motioned her on to the escalator "—Matt and Ginger will be half-crazy after spending a couple of hours cooped up in a plane with Thing One and Thing Two."

Jenny managed a smile. She'd given those nicknames to her nephews when she'd been younger. *The Cat in the Hat* had been one of her favorite books when she was a little girl. "The airline probably made them put those two in doggy crates in the cargo hold.''

"Shame on you," Jake said, but he laughed at her joke, and Jenny was glad. He hadn't laughed at all since Allison had left.

She couldn't put it off any longer. "Jake, wait."

"What's wrong, Jen?"

"It's Allison." She took a deep breath, then let the words pour out. "I want to talk to you about Allison."

"Why?" He sounded wary now. They had to move away from the bottom of the busy escalator, but Jenny didn't let go of his sleeve for fear he would try to flee. There were so many people moving around them that she had to raise her voice to be heard over the noise.

"Jake, why did you let her leave in the middle of the night like that?"

"I didn't know she was gone until Sunday morning." His tone was cool, his blue eyes dark and hard as they sometimes were when he was mad about something, but Jenny didn't pay any attention.

"Have…have you talked to her?"

"No."

Jake wasn't helping her at all. If she'd forgotten how he'd been after Beth's death—the way he looked now—she would have backed off. But she remembered. And weird as it might sound, she felt as if Beth wanted her to do this, too, to make Jake realize he needed to try to get Allison to come back for all of them, but mostly for himself.

"Have you tried? I mean, have you called her or anything?"

For a moment, she thought he wouldn't answer her. He was gazing over her head—maybe looking for Matt and Ginger and the boys, maybe not looking at anything at all. "I've called the number she left with Tom half a dozen times since Sunday evening," he said finally. "All I get is an answering machine."

Jenny felt her heart start beating a little harder. "She won't even talk to you?" She curled both hands around his arm. This was worse than she'd expected. "Jake, did you say something to make her mad? To make her feel bad...that she's an alcoholic?"

He didn't look angry anymore, just sad, very, very sad. "No."

"Do you care about her?"

"Jenny, Allison left of her own free will. If she'd wanted to stay with us...with me, she could have."

"How do you know? Maybe she thought we'd treat her differently or that we'd be ashamed of her because of her problem. Maybe she's sick. Or maybe she's started drinking again because she feels so bad. I was watching you at the Harvest Dance. I know there was something special between you. I know she wouldn't just have gone like that unless she thought we didn't want her anymore."

"I can't make her come back, Jenny," he said.

"Uncle Jake! Aunt Jenny!" It was Toby and Ryan running as fast as they could through the crowds of people around the carousels. They skidded to a halt in front of Jake and Jenny. "We *told* Mom and Dad it was you. They're back there, waiting for the suitcases," Toby said excitedly.

"C'mon. We have to get our backpacks. Did Grandma and Grandpa come, too? Where's everyone?" Ryan was six and jumping around like a frog. The way he acted made Julia seem like a little china angel. Jenny shuddered at the thought of the two of them together for the next three days.

"Okay, guys," Jake said, ruffling Ryan's hair. "Ready, Jen?"

"Jake, please." She was so upset she didn't even stop talking to give her nephews a hug.

"It's over, Jenny. Allison Martin is back in Chicago where she belongs."

He looked so grim-faced that for a moment Jenny almost gave up. But she wasn't done fighting, not yet. "I…I have to go to the bathroom. I saw one at the top of the escalator. I'll meet you guys at the carousel, okay?"

Jake looked around at the crowded baggage area. "I see Matt by Carousel 3. Don't get lost."

"I'll be right back." She turned and headed for the escalator. Two sailors were blocking her way, arguing good-naturedly. The old Jenny would have stood there and fumed. The new Jenny, the Jenny with a mission, just tapped the shorter guy on the shoulder, saying, "Excuse me, you're blocking the escalator." Then she took the moving steps two at a time, never looking back.

She headed for the airline she knew had a lot of flights to Chicago. The line there was long, but one ticket clerk was standing off by herself a little and Jenny hurried up to her.

"Please, I need to know if there are any seats available to Chicago tonight."

"I don't think so," the woman said. She was middle-aged, a little overweight and she looked tired. "We're always booked solid the day before Thanksgiving."

"Please, can you check for me? It's an emergency." Inside, she was saying every prayer she could remember.

"All right." The woman began tapping away at a keyboard on the counter. Jenny held on to the edge of the counter so tightly her knuckles turned white. The woman stopped tapping, staring at her monitor.

Seconds ticked by. She couldn't stand it any longer. "Well?" she said.

"There are two seats open on the 8:10 flight." The woman sounded amazed. She tapped a few more keys. "Two seats," she said again.

An open seat. On the busiest day of the year. It was an omen. No, not an omen, but an answer to her prayers. "I'll take it," she said.

"The ticket costs $198.77."

Two hundred dollars. Jenny's heart dropped into her stomach. That was all the money she'd saved for Christmas presents and CDs and movies for the whole winter. But it was worth it. "I'll take it," she repeated.

"How old are you?"

"Fifteen."

"I'm sorry. I can't sell a ticket to a minor. Company policy."

"It's not for me," Jenny said desperately, fishing in her backpack for her billfold. "It's for my brother. He has to get to Chicago."

"Then he'll have to come and buy the ticket."

"Can you hold the seat for me?"

The woman shook her head. "I'm sorry."

Jenny felt tears come into her eyes and she blinked them away. "Please. He'll be here as soon as I can go downstairs and get him."

"Look," the clerk said sympathetically, "I have to fax these reports. It will take me about five minutes. I won't sell the seat to anybody until then, okay? That's all I can do."

"Thank you," Jenny called, already halfway back to the escalator. "I'll just be a second. I promise."

They were all waiting for her at the bottom of the escalator. Matt was carrying two duffel bags, and Jake had another suitcase. Ginger had the boys' two backpacks as well as her own. It looked as if they'd brought everything they owned, even though they were only staying three days.

"Hey, Jenny. You've grown a foot," Matt said as she stepped off the escalator.

"Hi, Matt." Her brother opened his arms for a hug, and she gave him a quick squeeze, then stepped away. She smiled in her sister-in-law's general direction before turning to her other brother. "Jake, please. Come back upstairs with me. There's something I have to tell you." Why couldn't Matt and Ginger have taken five more minutes to find their bags? Now they were going to want to know everything that was going on.

"There's no reason to go back up to that level," Jake said. "This doorway leads directly to the parking lot."

"Jake, please." She was getting desperate and knew she sounded like it when she saw Ginger's brown eyes widen a little with alarm.

"Jenny, are you okay?"

"Yes. No. Jake, there's a seat open on the next flight to Chicago. Be on it. Go see if Allison's all right. Bring her back home. It's where she belongs. With us. *With you.* I know it is." She reached down and grabbed the suitcase from Jake's hand so quickly he didn't have time to react. She thrust it toward Toby. "Watch this," she said in her best baby-sitter voice. "You guys stay here. I'll be right back."

"Jake? Jenny?" Matt threw up his hands. "What's going on?"

"Later. I'll tell you everything later." She was dragging Jake by the arm toward the escalator. "There's a seat left on the next flight," she said, looking down at him two steps below.

He was staring at her as though he'd never seen her before. As if she'd lost her mind or something.

"Please, Jake. Go to Chicago. You said you'd do everything you could to make up for what happened." She was laying it on pretty thick, but she didn't have time to be more subtle. "This is what you can do. It's my fault that Allison couldn't tell you in her own way about her drinking problem. It would have made all the difference in the world. I know it would have. I'd go myself, but they won't sell me a ticket. Jake, there's a seat left on the next flight. On the night before Thanksgiving! It's a sign.'' She lowered her voice because her throat had tightened up. ''It's a *miracle*. You're supposed to go, Jake. I know you are.''

She'd pulled him up to the counter while she talked. The ticket lady was just coming through a swinging door.

''We're back,'' Jenny said. ''Make out the ticket for Jake Walthers, please.''

''Sir?'' The woman looked at Jake.

''Jake!'' She was crying now. Her throat ached so badly with pent-up tears she could barely talk. ''I didn't get to tell her I was sorry. Not really.''

''Your credit card and driver's license, please.''

Jake lifted his hand and wiped a tear from her cheek, then reached into his back pocket and got out his billfold. ''This is crazy, Jen. What about the kids?''

''Mom and I will watch them. We'll all camp out in the living room. They'll be so busy playing with their cousins they'll hardly notice you're gone.''

Jake wasn't looking at the woman behind the counter. He was looking at her. ''She won't come back, Jenny.''

''Yes, she will.'' He was going! He wasn't even arguing with her. He wanted Allison back, too. ''I know she will.''

She held on to his coat sleeve while the woman

tapped and tapped at her keyboard. She didn't want him changing his mind. He paid for the ticket with his credit card, then stared down at his billfold. "Hell, I've only got thirty-seven dollars with me."

"Here." She rummaged in her backpack for her wallet. "I've got cash. That's how I was going to pay for the ticket. I was going to buy it. It's nonrefundable, so I knew you'd have to go." She was still crying, but laughing, too, now that she'd gotten him to do what she wanted.

"Jenny, I can't take your money."

"It's a loan," she said, pushing him toward the metal detector. "I'll charge you interest. You'll need it to get you and Allison back here for Thanksgiving."

"What the *hell* is going on?" Matt called, following them down the concourse, still lugging the duffel bags.

"Just hang on!" Jenny hollered back at him. "Here's Allison's address and her phone number. I wrote them down for you." She shoved the money and the slip of paper into Jake's coat pocket. "Give me the keys to the van. I don't want to be stuck here all night with Thing One and Thing Two." She pushed Jake toward the metal detector. "Don't come back without Allison." She gave him a wave and a smile, then turned toward a sputtering, incredulous Matt.

"Where is he going?"

"To Chicago," she said, and laughed. "I guess I have a lot of explaining to do."

CHAPTER EIGHTEEN

BENEATH HIM WAS a patchwork of light and dark. Ahead of him were even more lights, a huge carpet of them, ending abruptly in the curving sweep of the Lake Michigan shoreline. Chicago.

The cloud cover had disappeared somewhere over Indiana. Tomorrow would be clear and cold in Riley Creek, a perfect Thanksgiving day. He wondered how in hell he would get back there. A little over an hour ago he'd been greeting Matt and his family at the Columbus airport, welcoming them home for the holiday, and now he was four hundred miles away, heading for a confrontation with a woman who'd walked out on him in the middle of the night without even saying goodbye.

"I'm nuts," he muttered to his reflection in the plane window. "Just plain nuts." He had to be crazy to let Jenny involve him in this scheme.

But he couldn't blame it on his sister. There was no way she could have talked him into getting on this plane if deep down it wasn't what he wanted to do. Maybe Allison didn't want to see him again, but she'd have to say it to his face. She wasn't going to get away with walking out on what they might have had with no more than a scrawled note of apology.

He hadn't been able to do anything to save Beth.

This time, his fate was in his own hands. He was in love with Allison. He was going to stay in love with her. He would find her and hear from her own lips that she didn't want to be his wife. That was the only way he'd believe she didn't care.

With no baggage to deal with, he was off the plane and through the concourses in fifteen minutes. But then he came up against a formidable obstacle. The curbside waiting area was wall-to-wall people. He took one look at the crowd—some tired, short-tempered and travel weary, some jovial and in a holiday mood, but all determined to get into the first available transportation—and headed for a hotel shuttle van.

He figured it would be easier to get a cab from a hotel than the airport and he was right. The taxi driver had no trouble finding the address of Allison's condo. It was north of the city center, smack on the lakefront. He dropped Jake in front of Allison's building, took his money and drove away without a backward glance.

Allison lived in an old brick building that must have been a warehouse from the looks of it. The lake wasn't frozen yet, but the water was cold and inky black, and he turned up the collar of his coat against the bitter chill of the wind.

As he opened the big glass door, the doorman looked at Jake suspiciously. "Good evening, sir," he said with just enough of a pause before "sir" to let

Jake know he wasn't the kind of guest they were used to receiving at this address.

Jake nodded and stepped inside. The decor was vaguely nautical—rich, heavy fabrics, dark polished wood and shining brass lamps—understated and elegant. There was a desk just to the left of the door. Jake didn't see it until the uniformed security guard sitting behind it rose and asked him the name of the person he wished to visit.

"Allison Martin."

"Is this a delivery?" the security guard asked, not quite so pleasantly.

"No. I'm a...friend." Jake wished he was wearing something besides chinos, a chambray shirt and his old canvas jacket. He needed a shave. He probably did look like a deliveryman, and not a very reliable one at that.

"Your name?"

"Jacob Walthers."

The man glanced at his ledger. "Your name's not on Ms. Martin's list."

"She wasn't expecting me. It was a last-minute trip."

"Uh, yeah. Sure."

"Just tell her I'm here, will you?" he said curtly.

The security guard gave him the once-over again, then picked up a receiver and punched in a number on a console on the desk. A well-dressed young couple laden with packages and string shopping bags entered the lobby. They stopped talking and looked Jake over with some curiosity before continuing on to the elevators and disappearing from view. He began to wonder why the hell he'd come. He didn't belong here.

"Ms. Martin isn't answering her buzzer."

"She's not in, or she's not answering?"

"I'm not aware if Ms. Martin is at home or away. I'm just telling you she's not answering her buzzer."

"Try again," Jake said. "Maybe there's something wrong with your intercom." Jenny's words were coming back to him whether he wanted to hear them or not. *Maybe she's sick. Or maybe she's started drinking again...*

"The equipment is working fine. Look, I've only been on duty since eight. Either she left the building before then or she doesn't want to talk to anyone."

"She'll talk to me," Jake said. His hands curled into fists. He hadn't come all this way to be sent packing by some potbellied rent-a-cop. He headed for the wood-paneled elevators tucked discreetly into a corner of the lobby. They were so well hidden he wouldn't have known they were there if the yuppie couple hadn't used them.

"Hold up, buddy. You're not going anywhere." The guard came around the desk like an angry bull charging a red flag. Seeing the movement, or maybe catching the sound of their raised voices, the doorman pushed open the plate-glass door, walkie-talkie in hand.

"What's going on, Ramon?" he asked, advancing on Jake slowly but with determination.

"Don't get too close, O'Hara. This guy thinks he's going to get upstairs."

"Ms. Martin will talk to me," Jake repeated. He'd stopped with his back to the wall. There was no way he could get to the elevator before one or both of them jumped him.

"She ain't answering her buzzer," Ramon explained. "This guy don't want to take no for an answer."

"Have you seen her today?" Jake asked the doorman.

"Ms. Martin hasn't been in or out all day, and I've been here since eight this morning. I'm working a double shift so I can take Thanksgiving off."

"There's a pay phone around the corner at the marina." The guard jerked his thumb toward the lake. "You go out there and call her. If she wants to see you, she'll buzz me to let you up."

"The hell with that," Jake said. He'd had about all he could take. He wasn't used to being told he couldn't do what he knew was right. "If she's sick or hurt, she couldn't answer the phone any more than she could your damned buzzer. I'm going up to her apartment. You can either go with me and unlock the door, or I'll bust the damned thing down."

It was the wrong thing to say. They were on him immediately. He wasn't a fighting man and he'd underestimated the strength and the quickness of the big guard. The rent-a-cop slammed Jake up against the wall so hard he saw stars, then spun him around and pinned his arms behind his back. "You're going nowhere but the lockup, buddy."

Jake tried to jerk himself free of the man's restraining grip, and a searing pain sliced through his ribs. He caught his breath, kicked out his leg behind him and caught the guard just above the ankle. They both went down in a heap, rolling across the floor.

Jake could hear the doorman yelling into his walkie-talkie and realized he was calling the cops. He didn't care whether or not he spent the night in a Chicago jail. All that mattered was getting to Allison, and the only thing that stood in his way was the two hundred and twenty pounds of muscle and fat lying on his chest. Jake gave one mighty heave and rolled the man off him, then he scrambled to his feet. He was two steps from the elevator when the guard made it to his knees and drew his gun.

"Stay right where you are. This thing's loaded and I'll shoot you if you take one more step. Now get your hands in the air and turn around."

Allison. He should never have let her go. He should have come after her right away. She was so close Jake could almost hear the soft whisper of her laughter. But he wasn't crazy enough or mad enough to go up against a loaded gun. He'd lost his temper and screwed up big-time. He'd come so close only to lose her again.

THE TAXI TURNED into the parking area that fronted Allison's building. Traffic had been light on Lake Shore Drive. They'd made good time from the Loop.

"Looks like there's some trouble here," the cabbie said.

Allison had been looking out at the dark waters of the lake. She was so tired she could barely keep her eyes open. She hadn't realized that throwing herself back into the mainstream at Tanner, Marsh and Fairchild would be so draining. Or maybe she had, subconsciously hoping she'd be tired enough each night to fall asleep without dreaming of Jake. "What?" she said. "I'm sorry. I didn't hear what you said."

"I said the cops are at your building. Must be something going on."

There were two cruisers parked under the canopy, their red and blue lights dancing off the building.

"I can't imagine what it would be," Allison said, pulling bills out of her wallet.

"Maybe you ought to wait outside while I check and see what's going on." The cabdriver was elderly, with a bulbous red nose and sparse white hair—Santa Claus without the beard. He looked as if he'd put in a long day, yet he was offering his help and Allison appreciated the gesture.

"Thank you," she said, summoning a smile. "That's not necessary. There's a policeman over there. I'll check with him before I go into the building. It's probably just someone arguing or maybe playing his stereo too loudly." Things like that almost never happened at Marina Pier Place, but neither did robberies or violence. That's what she paid such a hefty security fee to prevent.

"Okay, ma'am," the cabbie said. "Have a good Thanksgiving. Don't eat too much."

She stretched her smile a little wider. "The same to you."

"No problem there. I'm gonna be alone. Just going to have a TV dinner, I guess. One day's the same as the next to me since my missus passed on."

"I'm sorry," Allison said. A little shiver went down her spine. She was going to be doing much the same thing. Her "TV dinner" was a gourmet turkey dinner from a wonderful little diner down the street— oyster stuffing, candied yams, cranberry sauce and a heavenly pumpkin flan—but the loneliness she heard in the old man's voice echoed her own.

"Don't mind," the old man said, resetting his meter. "On Friday, I'm driving down to Champaign. Spend the rest of the weekend with my son and daughter-in-law and grandkids. I'll get more than my share of the real thing then. G'night."

She watched him drive away, the emptiness she felt refusing to be banished. Jake and the children, his brothers and their families, all of them gathered in the dining room at Walnut Hill, a family sharing a meal of bounty and of love. She wanted to be there with them, to be part of that celebration, those traditions. She missed them all with an intensity she hadn't known she was capable of.

She had made her choice. She was back in Chicago, back at Tanner, Marsh and Fairchild, although she no longer seemed to belong there. She'd been welcomed back with open arms, but the duo of young executives who'd taken her place were savvy and efficient and she found herself reluctant to take back control of her portfolio. She didn't care enough anymore to put in the fourteen-hour days, the six-day weeks. She'd have to make some kind of decision about her future at Tanner, Marsh and Fairchild, and soon. But for the moment she was concentrating on staying sober—one day at a time, sometimes one hour at a time, but she was making it. And she would make it through tomorrow, alone, on a day made for families and togetherness.

"Ma'am. It's best you wait outside," the police officer said as she approached.

"What's the problem, Officer?" she asked, moving away from the glass door.

"There's a guy tearing up the place, trying to get to some woman in one of the condos. A girlfriend maybe, I don't know. Do you live here, ma'am?"

"Yes." A little frisson of alarm ran along her nerve endings. She'd lived at Marina Pier for three years. Nothing like this had ever happened before. "Is he dangerous?"

"He tried to take on the security guard and the doorman, but he wasn't armed. He seems to have settled down now. Could be it was just a lovers' quarrel. We'll have him out of the way in a few minutes. Just as soon as we locate the woman he claims he's been looking for and make sure she's okay. Her name's Martin. Allison Martin. Do you know her?"

"I'm Allison Martin." Without another glance, she hurried past him into the building.

Jake was sitting on a bench against the wall, hand-cuffs pinning his hands behind his back. There was a button torn off his shirt, a scrape on his cheek and a frown between his eyebrows that drew them together in a straight, dark line as he argued with a second policeman, the doorman and a security guard she'd never seen before.

"Jake," she said, her breath coming quick and shallow. He was here, in Chicago. He had come for her.

He broke off his argument and looked at her. The frown didn't disappear. If anything, it grew darker for a moment, then he smiled just a little and the emptiness she'd been feeling dissolved in a rush of heat and hope. "Allison. Are you okay?"

"I'm fine. I... Officer, what's going on?"

"Are you Allison Martin?"

She nodded.

"Do you know this man?"

"Yes," she said. "He's...he's a friend. His name is Jake Walthers. What has he done?"

"Trespassing and resisting arrest. Maybe more, depending on what you have to say."

"Jake?" She'd never seen him resort to violence. He seemed to be staring at a point just past her left ear. "Why are you here?"

"You didn't answer any of my calls. You didn't answer your buzzer. These yahoos wouldn't let me upstairs to check to see if you were all right."

"I'm fine. I...I was working late. Please, O'Hara—" she turned to appeal to the doorman she'd known as long as she'd lived in the building ''—it's all just a mistake. He's a friend, truly.''

"Well," O'Hara said, "if you say so."

The policeman she'd talked to outside came into the lobby. "This guy checks out," he said, handing what looked like Jake's driver's license to the other officer. "Clean as a whistle."

"He threw a punch at me," the security guard grumbled.

"Officer, please. It's almost Thanksgiving." Jake's mouth was a hard line. A muscle jumped in his cheek, but he said nothing, leaving her to plead his case. "There's been no harm done. And he *is* a friend." She didn't bother to smile or cajole. "I have been out of touch. My work... It's true I haven't been returning calls. It's understandable that my friend thought I might be ill. It's all my fault, really. I'm very sorry."

Silence filled the lobby. The security guard shuffled from one foot to the other. O'Hara looked down at his shoes. "It's getting late," the cop said at last. "I'm ready to go off duty, and I've got a twenty-two-pound turkey to stuff when I get home, so I'd rather not spend the next two hours doing paperwork on this." He motioned Jake to stand up and unfastened the cuffs.

"Thank you." Automatically, Jake began rubbing the circulation back into his hands. "I won't be any more trouble."

"You sure as hell better not be." The cop handed Jake back his driver's license. "Let's break it up here.'' He waved Ramon and O'Hara away. ''Hensen, you want to radio in and tell them we're clear?''

''Sure.'' O'Hara followed the policemen out into the November night, and the guard gave Jake one more sour look before returning to his desk.

''I think we should go upstairs,'' Allison said.

Jake nodded curtly. ''Whatever you say.''

The ride up to her fourth-floor condo was the longest she'd ever taken. The rush of pleasure and longing that had washed over her when she'd first seen Jake ebbed away. Whatever impulse had brought him to Chicago had now given way to anger and embarrassment.

Jake waited while she dealt with the locks and switched on the light in the small foyer that led directly into her living room. It was cold. She fiddled with the thermostat before turning to Jake. ''Let me take your coat.''

He hesitated as though he hadn't made up his mind to stay, then handed her the heavy canvas coat. His hand grazed her fingertips and she moved away before he could see how shaken she was by the chance touch.

''That'll teach me. Never come to the big city looking like a hick farmer. It'll only get you in trouble.''

After hanging his coat in the closet, she gestured toward the living room. She closed her hands tightly in front of her. ''Jake, I'm more sorry than I can say. The security in this building is strict. It's what the residents want and expect. I had no idea you'd come here or I would have added you to my list of approved visitors." She was rambling and they both knew it. She stopped talking.

"I understand."

She wanted so badly to cross the room and put her arms around him, but her feet felt as though they were rooted to the floor. She had been wrong to leave Riley Creek as she had, as if she was ashamed of herself, or worse, as if she didn't care enough for all the Waltherses to explain to them why she had to leave.

She'd returned to Chicago, to her job and this cold and sterile condo, and found it all felt alien to her. Leaving was one of the biggest mistakes she'd ever made, but she hadn't figured out how to put it right. Now Jake was standing in front of her and she still didn't know what she should say or do. She felt panic constricting her throat, threatening to silence her.

She spoke hurriedly. "Why are you here, Jake?"

"I've been asking myself that same question."

"I'm sorry I left without telling you I was going," she said, knowing those words sounded like mere platitudes and not a plea from her heart.

"Why did you leave?"

As Allison searched in vain to find the right words, she noticed the angry red welts around Jake's wrists where he'd fought against the handcuffs. He'd been willing to go to jail to make sure she was all right. She would never forget that.

"I shouldn't have come," Jake finally said. "I shouldn't have let Jenny talk me into this harebrained trip."

"Jenny sent you? Why should she do that? Is she in some kind of trouble?"

"She's worried sick about you. She thinks it's her fault you were forced into revealing your drinking problem to all of us because of what happened with her and Aaron. She thinks that's what drove you away. Was it? Or was it something else, something between you and me?"

"I was going to tell you everything, Jake. Sunday… I thought by Sunday I could find the right way."

"Instead you ran away."

"Yes." To a life she no longer wanted or needed.

"You didn't have to hide your alcoholism, Allison." His face betrayed no emotion. His eyes were lost in shadow.

She moved past him and began turning on lights. She didn't want any more secrets between them. It might already be too late to salvage a relationship, but she wasn't about to live with the knowledge that she could have done more.

"It's not easy for me to talk about."

"Is that why you never answered my calls?"

Tears stung her eyes. She blinked them back. Tears meant weakness. She couldn't be weak, not now, not ever. Ignoring Jake's voice on her answering machine had been hardest of all to bear. "I didn't know what to say. I still don't."

He looked around the room. The walls were off-white, the furniture a montage of pastels and neutrals that had been deliberately arranged so that nothing interfered with the magnificent view of Lake Michigan.

"This is where you belong." His voice was as impassive as his face.

"I thought it was."

He took a step toward her. "What do you mean by that?"

Allison felt her pulse accelerate. "I thought I needed to come back here. To see if I was strong enough to make it in the world that almost destroyed me. I'm an alcoholic. I needed to know that I can resist it on my own, with only God's help, no one else's."

"Even mine?"

"I couldn't stay, Jake. What if I started drinking again?" Her voice was straining against tears. She felt them on her cheeks, tasted them on her lips. "What would that do to the children? To Jenny? To us...?"

His face was no longer a stone mask. It was full of misery and pain. "Is that what you think of me, Allison? That I'm such a poor excuse for a man that I could only love you if you were without flaws?"

"There are times I can't even love myself."

"So you ran away."

"No." She stood a little straighter. "I...came here to prove to myself I could do this." She couldn't call this place home, not anymore. Riley Creek was home.

Jake spread his hands in an encompassing gesture. "Is this worth the fight?"

"My sobriety is worth the fight. But this? No," she said quietly. "This is not what I'm fighting for."

"Then come home with me, Allie."

Fear roiled inside her. She would fight with all her might to stay sober, but there could be a next time. She shook her head. "I can't—"

"You can't love me?" he asked, coming nearer.

She lifted her hands, wiped the tears from her eyes. "I love you," she whispered. "I love you too much. I love your children. I love your home. I want to be part of your life. But I'm afraid."

"Afraid of what, Allie?" He was very close now, but still he didn't move to hold her.

She swayed toward him, aching to be enfolded in his embrace. "I'm afraid I'll come to rely on you too much. Come to rely on all of you too much. It was already happening before I left. Whenever I felt as though I needed a drink, there was Stella or your children to distract me. Or you..." She took a small step backward. "I was beginning to feel as if I could let my guard down a little."

"I'm glad." He reached out, and before she could back away again, he took her in his arms. "I'm glad you realize we're all there for you." He bracketed her face with his hands. "I'll always be there for you. Always."

"It's too risky. One day...one day I might give in."

"Life is risky, Allie. Love is even riskier. I know. I learned the hard way, but if I'm willing to take the risk a second time, can't you?"

"What if I start drinking again?" She put her hands

on his chest and felt his slow, steady heartbeat beneath her palms.

"You won't. I think I know you better than you know yourself. You're a strong woman, Allie, stronger than you give yourself credit for. And I love you with all my heart."

"You've never said you loved me before."

"I was a fool not to, but I'm saying it now. I'll shout it from the rooftops if you want me to. And I'll say it every day for the rest of my life." He laid his cheek against hers. His breath was warm against her hair. "Loving someone and relying on them doesn't mean you're weak. It takes a hell of a lot of strength and faith to love someone and to keep on loving them through good times and bad. Say you love me, too. Say it again so I know you mean it." He lowered his head, touched his mouth to hers. She could feel him smile against her lips. "Make this whole damned day worthwhile. Say you'll marry me and come back to Walnut Hill."

"You don't know how much I want that, but—"

"Shhh, no more buts. Say it." His lips were only a heartbeat away, much too far.

"I love you."

He brushed his mouth across hers. "That's what I needed to hear. It's been one hell of a day. Make love to me. Fall asleep beside me. Wake up beside me. Tonight and every night for the rest of our lives."

"Yes," she said as his mouth began to cover hers. "Yes to all those things." And then she didn't say anything else for a long, long time.

Hours later, she woke to moonlight streaming through her bedroom window. She looked at the clock. It was almost five. Thanksgiving Day.

Jake's arms tightened around her. He was awake, smiling at her. "Good morning, love," he said with a kiss that took her breath away.

"It's the middle of the night."

"It's six. I always wake up at six."

"It's five."

"In Riley Creek, it's six."

"You have a point." She kissed him back.

"If we leave right now, we can be home by noon," Jake said when the kiss ended. She smiled a little to hear the breathlessness in his voice matching her own. "Will you come home with me?"

Home. To her it was the most beautiful word in the English language.

"Yes. I'd like that more than anything in the world."

"Good," he mumbled, nuzzling her ear. There was a hint of laughter underscored with passion in his low, rough voice. "We'll have to drive your car. I flew out here on a wing and a prayer, ya know."

"The gas tank's full. We can leave whenever you want." She swung her legs over the edge of the bed.

"Not so fast." He pulled her back, settling himself between her legs. "There's plenty of time." Jake kissed her again. "If my calculations are correct— and I think they are—we can make love and still be home in time to call dibs on the wishbone."

CHAPTER NINETEEN

One year later...

"ISN'T THE TURKEY done *yet?*" Mike bent down to look through the oven window. "It's three o'clock. I'm *starved.*"

"Go watch the football game," Libby said.

"How about a celery stick?" Allison motioned to the veggie platter on the counter. The kitchen in Roger and Darlene's house wasn't as big as hers at Walnut Hill, and this Thanksgiving afternoon it was filled to overflowing with family and good smells. "That will hold you over until the turkey's done."

"I want people food, not rabbit food."

"It's good for you," Ginger told him. She was standing at the counter, preparing to take the cranberry salad out of the mold.

Janet waved a celery stalk under Mike's nose. "Take it or leave it." She was in the early stages of pregnancy and a little short-tempered. Mike's lower lip crept out a fraction of an inch. Janet relented and handed him a purple-and-red frosted pumpkin cookie, one of Julia's and her cousin's more exotic efforts. "Here, don't tell Grandma."

"I heard that. That cookie will ruin your appetite, Michael Jacob."

"No, it won't. It'll save my life. I'm *starved*," Mike reiterated, and scooted into the dining room before Darlene could confiscate his cookie and hasten his decline. He was wearing a brand-new Ohio State jersey he'd purchased with his own money just before the Michigan game the weekend before. "For luck," he'd said, and it must have worked. Ohio State had beaten Michigan for the first time in four years to win a Rose Bowl berth.

"Mike's grown like a weed this past year," Ginger said, lifting the copper mold very carefully, then smiling with satisfaction as she surveyed the shimmering salad resting on Allison's grandmother's antique Blue Willow plate.

"Two inches since spring," Allison confirmed. She was sitting at the breakfast-nook table folding napkins while Libby slipped them into the napkin rings. Mike was definitely growing; all three of the children were. She laid her hand on her stomach, feeling the bulge of a tiny foot or elbow beneath her palm. All *four* of them were.

"What's that?" Julia demanded, trying to poke her finger into the cranberry salad. Ginger caught her hand just in time.

"Red gelatin with cranberries and nuts," Ginger explained. "You can have a taste at dinner."

"Just one bite," Julia decreed, inspecting the cranberry salad with a discriminating eye. "I might not like it."

"Julia! Your turn!" Toby's voice echoed up from the basement. "Hurry up! Jenny's getting loose. We have to tie her up tighter."

"Goodness, what are you doing to Aunt Jenny down there?" Ginger wanted to know.

"Nothing. We're just playing bank robber and she's the bank guard." Jenny was sixteen and growing into a lovely young woman. There had been no more problems with alcohol. She was dating Sam Watchman, the boy who'd been her escort to the Harvest Dance the year before. The romance had blossomed while they were both taking driving lessons.

Aaron Masterson, too, seemed to have gotten his life under control. He'd graduated from Riley Creek High in the spring and was now attending college in Indiana, playing basketball and football and attending AA meetings on a regular basis. He had stopped by the farm market a couple of weeks earlier to say hello to Jenny. Allison thought he still had a crush on her sister-in-law, but Jenny had moved on and she thought that Aaron would, too.

"Julia! She's loose. Help me! She's going to set off the alarm and the cops will come."

"I gotta go. I gotta help capture Jenny." Julia gave Allison a blinding smile before sticking out her tongue at Libby and dashing down the stairs.

"Brat," Libby muttered, carefully arranging the napkins on a tray to be carried into the dining room. While she worked, she was admiring her lime green nail polish. Allison had helped her with the manicure the night before, but she wouldn't take responsibility for Libby's choice of colors. "I don't think she'll ever grow up."

"She'll have to grow up when the new baby gets here." Janet pointed toward Allison's distended middle. "Honestly, Allie. You look ready to pop."

"I feel ready to pop," Allison admitted. She wasn't due for another two weeks, but she felt as if the baby might come at any time, and Margaret Bostleman had confirmed that suspicion two days earlier.

"Bite your tongue, Janet," Darlene ordered. "No babies are going to make an appearance until after we eat, do you hear? I have been slaving over this stove since six o'clock this morning. And no one is going to go anywhere, even the hospital, until after we eat." She was laughing as she said it and Allison laughed, too.

"Yes, Mother Walthers. I hear and obey." Darlene made a face. She hated to be called Mother Walthers, and Janet and Ginger and Allie all knew it.

"You do just that, Daughter."

"Even if she has to sit there with her legs crossed all day," Ginger teased.

"You have a mean streak, you know that?" Janet said. She and Kyle hadn't planned on adding to their family so soon after the twins, and she hadn't quite adjusted to the idea of being pregnant again, so Ginger's comment wasn't appreciated.

Ginger winked at Allison. Allison bit her lip to keep from smiling and went back to folding napkins. It was fun to have women friends, family, to laugh and talk with this way. Janet and Kyle had moved back to Ohio in the summer. Janet had planned to open her cleaning service in time for the holidays but had put her plans on hold until after the new baby was born. Ginger and Matt were also considering a move in the not-too-distant future. Matt had been offered a job with an Indianapolis firm. That meant they would be living only a three-hour drive away. Darlene and Roger were lobbying strongly for their son to take the position, and Allison hoped that he would. She understood more each day what it meant to Jake's parents to have their children and grandchildren near at hand.

The year had gone so fast. She and Jake had been married in a quiet ceremony at the United Methodist church just before Christmas. Ever since she'd been doing some consulting work for Tanner, Marsh and Fairchild. Then she'd assumed most of the responsibilities of the farm market in the spring when Jake had taken on an additional eighty acres to farm.

Stella had stayed, too, marrying Tom at the end of July. With her help, Allison had initiated an aggressive advertising campaign, marketing Walnut Hill as an all-day destination for visitors from Ohio, Indiana and Michigan.

"Jake. Come help me with the turkey," Darlene called into the living room. "Roger won't budge from in front of the TV when the Lions are playing," she lamented, shaking her head. "I'll have to pull the plug to get him to come to the table."

Allison smiled at her husband as he came into the

kitchen. He moved close behind her and dropped his hands on her shoulders. "Everything okay?"

"I'm fine," she said, lifting her hand to cover one of his. She loved him more every day. "Hungry, though."

"It doesn't look like you have much room for food left in there," Libby said. She was impatient for the new baby to arrive. Allison and Jake had chosen not to learn the baby's sex from the ultrasound test, and as a result, conversation was dominated by a lot of guessing games.

"I always have room for your grandma's turkey and stuffing."

"Flattery will get you everywhere," Darlene answered from the depths of the refrigerator.

"You're eating for two." Libby grinned, showing straight new permanent teeth that the dentist said wouldn't require braces. One more blessing to be thankful for.

"Why don't you take these into the dining room and put them at each of our places?" Allison suggested. Libby picked up the tray and left the kitchen.

"What else can I do for you besides get the turkey on the table?" Jake asked his mother.

"Start rounding up the children and haul your father in from the TV to help get the food on the table. He thinks if he bakes the pumpkin pies and carves the bird, he's done his share."

"Yes, ma'am," Jake said. He was kneading the tight muscles at the back of Allison's neck and didn't stop what he was doing. He always seemed to know just what to do if her back ached or if she couldn't sleep because the baby had decided to get energetic at three in the morning.

She knew he'd been anxious at times about the birth, no doubt remembering how Beth had died. But Allison was healthy and both she and Dr. Bostleman had tried to assure him of that so many times she thought he'd finally begun to believe them. And because Jake believed, the children believed and so there were no old fears dimming their anticipation of the new baby's arrival.

Allison thought about Beth Walthers often, wondering if Beth could see how happy she was and hoping that she knew Allison had grown to love her children as fiercely and completely as she loved the baby growing inside her.

Jake bowed his head and kissed the nape of her neck. "How are you feeling now?"

"I've never been better."

"I love you," he whispered, keeping his promise, the promise he'd made to her one year ago.

She turned her head and smiled into his eyes. "I love you, too," she whispered back.

She really had never been better. She had a family now, a husband she loved and who loved her back. She was making friends and forging a place for herself in the community. She couldn't imagine living anywhere else.

It wasn't a fairy-tale life. There were bad days when the demon of her addiction raised its ugly head, but she'd fought it each and every time. With God's help and Jake's staunch support, she would go on resisting for the rest of her life. She believed in herself. And she had the whole Walthers clan to back her up. Her husband, her children, her *family,* would always be there for her, with her, to help her hold back the darkness and walk in the light.

HARLEQUIN SUPERROMANCE®

GUARANTEED PAGE-TURNER!

Every now and then comes a book guaranteed
to enthrall the reader from start to finish.
Harlequin Superromance—the series known for its
innovation and variety—is proud to add these
books to their already outstanding lineup.

IT HAPPENED IN TEXAS
by Darlene Graham

Marie Manning wakes up to discover that there's a body on her
property. And Marie's world goes from safe to scary. It doesn't
help that Sheriff Jim Whittington thinks she knows more than
she's telling. And it certainly doesn't help that Marie's heart
beats a little faster every time the officer comes around....

Be sure to watch for it in November 1998
wherever Harlequin books are sold.

HARLEQUIN®
Makes any time special ™

HSRPT812

They're ranchers, cowboys, men of the West!

O LITTLE TOWN OF GLORY

by Judith Bowen

**Visit the town of Glory in December 1998!
A good place to go for Christmas...**

Calgary lawyer Honor Templeman makes a shocking dis-
covery after her husband's death. Parker Templeman had
another wife—and two children—in the small town of
Glory. Two children left to the care of their uncle, Joe
Gallant, who has no intention of giving them up—to
Honor *or* her powerful father-in-law.

Available wherever Harlequin books are sold.